The Shattered Tree

The Shattered Tree

A Bess Crawford Mystery

C H A R L E S   T O D D

WM WILLIAM MORROW *An Imprint of* HarperCollins*Publishers*

This is a work of fiction. Names, characters, places, and incidents are products of the author's imagination or are used fictitiously and are not to be construed as real. Any resemblance to actual events, locales, organizations, or persons, living or dead, is entirely coincidental.

FIRST EDITION

Library of Congress Cataloging-in-Publication Data has been applied for.

ISBN 978-0-06-238627-4

16 17 18 19 20   RRD   10 9 8 7 6 5 4 3 2 1

For Jane Chelius

For being the most extraordinary agent any author could have
For the books
For the birds
For the travel
And above all for the friendship.

With much love from both of us.

The Shattered Tree

CHAPTER ONE
Where It Began

October 1918

HE CRAWLED AS far as the shattered tree and lay there, faint from the effort. But he knew he had to keep moving. When he stopped, when the sweat dried on his skin, he'd begin to shiver again, wracking his body until his teeth chattered. There wasn't enough left of his uniform to keep him warm, and his captors, God help them, had taken his boots. Good English leather. He'd stolen them himself from a corpse.

He grimaced, afraid to look at his torn feet. He'd lost too much blood from his other wounds. The one in his leg had mercifully stopped bleeding, and the cut in his hairline had clotted over, but the damage had been done. He was light-headed from lack of food, finding it hard to concentrate. A crow couldn't find enough to eat in this countryside after four years of war. He'd be dead soon if he didn't reach his own lines.

To his left the firing was heavy. Rifles and machine guns. An assault under way. *But in which direction?* He could see the flashes, but they told him nothing. *Which way?*

He forced himself to sit up against the torn bark of the trunk.

Think! For God's sake, collect your wits or you're done for.

But the firing was fading, and he knew in some corner of his mind that the battle hadn't stopped. He was losing consciousness.

Fighting it, clenching his teeth with determination, he dragged himself upright, holding hard to the shattered trunk. The ground moved under his feet, heaving and shifting, and he thought he would fall down again, unable to hold on. Wet earth pummeled him. And then the shifting stopped, and he realized a sapper's tunnel must have gone up somewhere in the sector to his left. Shaking his head to clear it, he nearly fell down.

Voices. Hands. He blinked, trying to see. *Pray God, no. Not now—*

They had to force his fingers from the bark of the tree before they could lower him to the stretcher, and then they were doing something else.

A blanket. Something between him and that wretchedly cold wind. The warmth betrayed him, and he lay there, unable to put up any defense at all.

He didn't care any longer. He couldn't fight any more. Let them take him back, it didn't matter.

The ground was rough; the men handling the stretcher stumbled across it, jarring his body from side to side. He remembered some of it, in and out of awareness. Listening to the soft grunts of the men carrying him, watching the stars pass in and out of light clouds overhead, struggling to keep his bearings. He was still shivering, vaguely aware of being warmer but not yet warm enough. They had put a strap across the blanket, across his chest, holding him and it in place as they tramped in the darkness.

Lamplight turned low. Voices. A face peering down at him. Blurred. The straps taken off, the blanket lifted. He almost cried out as the cold swept in. And then the blanket was lowered again and he clutched at it desperately.

"And what have ye brought me this time?" a Scottish voice demanded. A woman's voice. "He's deid. A waste. Ye ken I'd hoped for a live one."

"Shall I put him with the corpses, then?" Another voice, nearly as unintelligible.

"That's shivering, no' death throes," the stretcher bearer at his head said impatiently.

"No, bring him forward. We'll give it a try. Anyone else out there?"

"He's the last."

"Good. Deliver him, then get yourselves something to warm your insides."

He could hardly decipher the exchange. He tried to groan, to make some sign that he was still clinging to life, however tenuous his hold on it. But what issued from his mouth wasn't a groan, it was a croaking laugh, rising from his parched throat.

The face peered down at him again. He could make out straggling sandy hair beneath a once-white cap. Pale blue eyes, kinder than the voice. Freckles, a sea of them, running together as his vision failed him.

"God save us," the voice said. "I think we've caught ourselves a frog."

CHAPTER TWO

Somewhere in France, October 1918

I WASHED MY hands, then dried them quickly, nodding to the orderly to bring the next patient into the tent.

Dr. Winters turned from scrubbing his instruments to peer at the man being lifted onto the table.

"Shock," he said. "Loss of blood and shock. I see he's French. Odd, in this sector. Do we have a name?"

The orderly said, "No, sir." He shrugged. "There's hardly enough of his uniform left to find a pocket."

"Then let Base Hospital sort him out." Dr. Winters lifted the blanket, did a cursory examination, and lowered it again. "All right, get him to bed, a hot water bottle or two, and tea, as much sugar as you can find. He's no longer bleeding, there's nothing here that can't wait." He raised one of the wounded man's eyelids. "Possibly concussed from that head injury, but the eye is responding normally to light. Where are the ambulances?"

"They're just coming in, sir," the orderly reported.

"Then he's for them. Sister Crawford, is this your run?"

"Yes, sir," I told the doctor. "Nothing was said about sending anyone else up to replace me. Sister MacRae is on duty until dawn, and Sister Marshall is sleeping." I cocked my head to listen. The firing had stopped, and the shelling hadn't begun. Respite. "You'll be all right. It should be quiet enough."

"I doubt it," Dr. Winters replied wearily. "I could use a dozen of you. See that they don't keep you."

"I'll do my best," I said with a smile. "And I'll bring back as many nurses as I can find."

"Half a hundred will do. All right, off with you." He turned to the orderly as they heard the ambulances pulling in. "Get him stabilized as best you can, then put him aboard. And afterward if you can find a cup of tea for me as well, I'd be grateful."

The orderly summoned the stretcher bearers, who had been squatting just outside the tent, enjoying a cigarette.

As they began to lift the stretcher, one said, "Good thing he's out, poor sod."

The orderly followed them. "Easy, lads. Let's warm him up as best we can, and straight on to the line."

Dr. Winters and I watched them go, then I went to fetch the hot water bottles and another blanket against the cold night air. There was hardly any sugar in the emergency tin, but I did what I could.

Sister MacRae was supervising the loading of the other patients as I came back.

Dr. Winters was waiting for me. "Bess?"

He was the same height as I was, a sturdy man with prematurely graying hair and sharp blue eyes. He'd worked himself to near exhaustion, and the fighting hadn't let up, despite the promise of an end to it. I was worried about him.

"Sir?" I paused at the tent flap, looking back at him.

"Nothing. Go on. Just—tell them we need more hands. And supplies are low. Ask them to resupply us as soon as they can. The next run, if possible."

"I'll speak to Matron myself," I said, and he smiled.

"Yes, do that."

Our latest patient was hunched into a knot, still shivering in spite of the blankets covering him. With the help of the orderly I put one hot water bottle at his feet and the other close by his hands, then added another blanket from our precious store. He wasn't awake enough to swallow the tea, and so I sent it on to Dr. Winters, who needed that bit of sugar too.

The light was a little better where he lay now, and I gently searched again for a name. Officers generally wrote them in a pocket or on the underside of a lapel, sometimes even at the neck, so that their body could be identified if they were dead or too badly wounded to speak. As the first to treat a patient, we made every effort to identify him, because whoever brought him in was likely to know who he was, or the sector where the stretcher bearers found him might well connect him to a man later reported missing or thought to have been taken prisoner. With casualties running high, the task of keeping up with the living, the wounded, and the dead was enormous.

As I pulled at the remnants of the pocket, it came away in my hand. I could just see where a strip of something had been ripped out of the uniform's fabric. As if the owner had sewn in a piece of cloth with his name written in permanent ink. Then why rip it out again?

The only reason I could think of was to keep the Germans from knowing who he was if he was taken prisoner. A general's son—or that of someone in the French cabinet—someone important enough to become a hostage?

It didn't matter. When he was awake, he would be able to tell the base hospital what his name was.

That done, I hurried to my quarters and picked up my kit, stuffing a half-dry uniform in the top and a sack with a pair of muddy boots on top of that. I hadn't had time to clean them. Closing the flap, I went out to make certain I had all the paperwork I needed for each patient being transported. We were halfway through the process when a star shell burst almost overhead, and one of the men swore. It was always a forerunner of an attack.

"Don't they ever stop?" he growled. "We'll hardly be able to keep up with what's coming."

In the strange glare of the shell, slowly descending, we looked drained of color, our faces deeply shadowed and almost frighteningly unfamiliar. It had faded by the time we had the last patient safely strapped down, and I was turning to find my seat in the ambulance carrying the severely wounded.

Sister MacRae appeared out of the darkness, holding a letter.

"Will ye post it for me?" she asked, and before I could answer, she was making her way back to the surgical tent.

I tucked the envelope into my pocket and waved to the lead driver. He was already rolling as I took my seat in the second vehicle from the rear.

I'd ridden with our driver before, a man named Robinson, square face, sandy hair, tired eyes. We were all tired, I thought, as he greeted me.

"Sister," he said, starting the motor. "How bad is our cargo tonight?"

"Two bleeding still, one of them worrying. One with broken ribs, haven't punctured the lung yet, but I think he's wound tight enough to keep them in place for now. A head wound, and a man delirious from fever. He's the greatest risk. A case of appendicitis. And one weak from loss of blood."

"They'll be starting the shelling shortly. I'd as soon not stop unless we have to."

"Then fingers crossed."

I'd been at this aid station for a week now, and we'd moved up twice, to stay within reach of the worst cases. Sister Nelson had worried that the Germans might push back and we'd be overrun, but I didn't think it would happen. This sector had made fairly even progress for days, and it seemed likely that we could keep up the pressure on the German lines. But, I thought as we bounced over a rut deeper than most, war didn't follow rules. Still, losses had been fairly heavy on both sides, and I rather thought it was HQ that pushed so hard, not the men in the field. A respite in the worst of the fighting would be welcomed if only for a chance to sleep. One of the artillery officers had already warned me, though.

"We'll use up our stock of shells. A mad barrage. Wait and see. No one wants to transport the damn—the blasted things back to England."

We rattled and bounced and slid through the dark, following the ambulance ahead of us, lights dimmed almost to the point of vanishing from sight if we fell too far behind. Robinson did what he could to prevent the worst of the jolting, but there was no way to avoid much of it.

Robinson said, in the darkness, "Your father's Colonel Crawford, is that right?"

"Yes." My father had retired from active service a few years before the war had begun, and he had made up for that by doing his duty wherever he could. London had often found a use for him, much of it too secret to discuss with my mother or me, which sometimes meant that he disappeared for days or even weeks at a time. We had grown used to that over four years of war, but it had not got any easier. He had been in France more than a few times, although he never spoke of it. Nor did Simon Brandon, my father's Regimental Sergeant-Major. London had not wanted him to return to active service for reasons that were obscure but took him into danger more often than not. As my mother had said dryly on one occasion, "The Army seems to prefer to kill him their own way, rather than allow the Germans to try their hand at it."

But of course the Germans had tried. More than once. And almost succeeded.

Robinson threw a quick glance my way. "I'm not supposed to talk about what I see, but the Colonel was in Calais this week. Spy hunting, gossip had it."

Surprised, I looked at him. "Was he indeed?"

"Aye, I took wounded down to the port for loading, and there he was, coming off the *Sea Maid*. Arthur pointed him out to me."

Arthur was another orderly I'd got to know fairly well. His cousin had been in my father's regiment, and if Arthur claimed he'd seen my father, then I believed he had.

There had been no word from home for a fortnight. That was not unusual, given the volume of mail the censors were required to deal with, but I couldn't stop a niggling worm of worry from creeping in when the post was slow in arriving. It was one reason I wrote home as often as I could, so that they wouldn't worry about *me*. Careful letters, light ones that wouldn't trouble the censors. But my mother knew how to read between the lines.

Robinson swore, then apologized as we hit a particularly deep rut and the ambulance struggled to bridge it and stay on track. I clutched at the handle of my door and braced myself. Behind me I heard one of the wounded cry out.

But we made it safely to the base hospital after all, and I was relieved to turn my cargo, the worst of the wounded first, over to one of the Sisters there. It was her task to assign them to wards.

"I don't like the look of the appendix case," she said quietly, for my ears only. "I'd best send him straight to surgery."

I nodded, and after instructing the stretcher bearers, she moved on to the next man.

Soon afterward, I presented our list of much-needed supplies to Matron, and then she and I went through the list of incoming patients before walking to each bedside, assessing their condition after the arduous journey.

The ribs case was breathing well enough, the bleeding patients were still stable, and a doctor was already bending over one of them.

The delirious patient was being strapped down, and a Sister was preparing to give him something to bring down his fever. His wound didn't appear to be gangrenous. Yet.

The appendix case was already being prepped for surgery.

We came to the last bed, and I thought at first that this patient was asleep. A sister was just bringing in a fresh hot water bottle wrapped in a towel to put at his feet, and another had warmed the blankets that had been spread across him. The shivering had stopped, and it was likely he'd dropped into an exhausted state. We still had no name for this one. *Lieutenant X* was on his chart. The orderly at the forward aid station had just been able to make out his rank.

The ward was quiet, it was an ordinary transfer, and someone was already packing an ambulance with our precious supplies, thanks to Matron's efficiency. I'd even managed to persuade her to send us another Sister. Dr. Winters had wanted two, but he'd be grateful for one.

And then without any warning, the night was torn apart by a scream.

The delirious man, an officer with one of the Highland regiments, had flung the Sister buckling his straps halfway across the ward, glass breaking and the tray she had set on his table falling to the floor with a ringing *clang*. Matron and I turned quickly, but the Scot was across the empty cot where the appendix case would have been, and before we could stop him, he had clamped his hands around the throat of the French officer.

Blankets went flying off the bed; the Sister with the hot water bottle backed away in surprise. The patient under attack had come alive with such an astonishing burst of strength and energy that Matron, reaching for the Scot's right arm even as I caught at the left, was thrown back into me.

I could hear someone shouting for help as Matron and I went down on our knees. In the same instant, the Scot's flailing foot grazed my forehead and struck Matron squarely on the chin. Dazed, she sank to the floor even as I fought to get to my feet. By this time, the doctor who'd been examining the ribs case was there, and I shoved Matron into his arms. As he was dragging her to one side, out of the fray, I turned back to the two men, who had been struggling on the cot and were now fighting on the floor on the far side.

I went after them, trying to break the grip the Scot had on the other man's throat, but he was large, and I was making very little progress when the doctor caught the Scot's hair in one hand and pulled his head back. And then two burly orderlies were dashing down the aisle between the rows of cots. One of them set me aside, and I left them to it, scrambling out of their way as the Scot flung the doctor off. I heard him swear as his head hit the side of the cot.

Either the Scot was tiring, or the two orderlies were more than he could deal with. He was still fighting them, but they'd pulled him off the Frenchman, who was still doing his bit, landing a blow himself. I turned to check on Matron and the Sister who had been attending the Scot before all this began.

Matron was still dazed, but I managed to get her to a chair. The doctor, his face flushed and angry, was bending over the Sister who had been thrown to one side. He seemed to be working with her left shoulder.

As the battle surged back and forth, it moved out into the aisle, leaving the Frenchman half sitting up against the cot, wild-eyed and breathing hard. I wasn't sure he even knew where he was or what had just happened to him. I turned my attention to him, bending over him, intending to help him back into his own bed. But he held me off, his hands shoving me away as he shouted something that was nearly lost in the uproar the orderlies and the Scot were still making just behind me.

"It's all right, it's over. He's very ill—the Scot. He had no idea he was attacking you—sometimes that happens," I said, trying to calm this man down as well.

He shut up in midsentence, staring at me, then turning his gaze toward the Scot, whom the orderlies and the doctor were finally dragging back to his bed. Someone else had come in and taken the doctor's place, attending to the Sister with the shoulder injury. Every other patient in the ward was wide awake and staring toward the commotion.

"It's all right," I said again, but he shoved himself to his feet and started for the door of the ward. I had all I could do to stop him, catching his arm, reminding him of his wounds, of his exhaustion, anything I could think of to turn him about.

But it was his own weakness that betrayed him. Faltering, all at once he leaned heavily on me, and in the next instant, he passed out, nearly taking me down with him.

I lowered him to the wooden floor of the ward, and there were others coming in now, another Sister and two more orderlies. We got my patient back into his bed, covered him again, found the hot water bottle—which had rolled under a neighboring bed—rewrapped it in the towels, and put it at his feet.

At the forward aid station, Dr. Winters had been too concerned by the wounds on the man's head and leg to pay any attention to his feet. And in the dark, shoving the hot water bottle under the blankets as he lay waiting to be loaded into the ambulance, I hadn't seen them either.

Now I realized how badly cut and bruised they were, as if he'd walked a long way without shoes. How he'd managed to hold me off just now, on his way to the door, was a mystery. Saying nothing, I tucked him in and asked one of the other orderlies to sit with him for a bit.

"He was badly frightened by that attack," I said quietly. "Coming up out of a deep sleep to find someone trying to throttle him. He may still be unsettled when he wakes up again. Keep an eye on him for a while."

"Yes, Sister. You've got a scrape on your forehead. It's starting to bleed."

I put up my hand and realized he was right. I remembered the toe grazing my head as Matron and I tried to pull the two men apart. "Thank you. I'll attend to it."

Matron had come up to me. "Are you all right, Sister Crawford? Have someone look at that scrape."

"Yes, thank you, Matron. And you?" By this time the Scot had run out of whatever mad strength he'd found in his delirium, and his shouts had become agitated mumbling dwindling into muttering. I thought they must have managed to sedate him somehow, and that it was slowly taking effect. The orderlies were replacing the straps across his chest and legs; the doctor was watching grim-faced and still out of breath, to make certain the man was not feigning. In the other cot, the Frenchman was lying there with closed eyes, but I could see the tightness around his mouth.

"I'm fine," Matron lied, for I could see that she was still shaken by the suddenness of the attack. We all were, and the other Sisters were trying to settle other patients back into their cots. "I expect your ambulance is ready to return to the aid station. I'll leave you to meet it. Thank you, Sister Crawford." She cast a glance at the now subdued Scot, breathing heavily and only partly conscious, then turned to the ward at large.

"All right, then, as you were, gentlemen. Lights out in five minutes."

They subsided, and I took a last look at my patient before walking on to the ward door. There I stopped at the ward Sister's table and asked for something to clean my forehead.

She had stepped out to accompany the appendix case to the surgical theater and so had missed the start of the commotion. As she reached for a pad and poured a little alcohol over it, she said, "I was shocked. According to the report you brought with you, Lieutenant MacGregor has been quiet until now. Did he know the other patient? Was that the problem?"

I took the pad and pressed it to the scrape, feeling the sting as it touched the raw skin. "His fever must have spiked. We had no trouble with him at all at the aid station. And as far as I know, he's never seen the Frenchman before."

"What's wrong with the Frenchman?" She pointed to a set of charts on her table. "I haven't had a chance to look."

"Exhaustion. Possible concussion. Loss of blood," I said. "Keep an eye on him if you can. And have a look at his feet, will you? As for Lieutenant MacGregor, he may reach a crisis tonight, unless you can keep that fever down. I'd watch his breathing as well. Pneumonia. There's a possibility of gangrene. That wound doesn't look very good."

"Yes, of course." There was little we could do for the pneumonia cases but try to lower the fever and give them something to help clear their lungs. "But he's a big man. He could well be strong enough to overcome the infection."

"I hope so," I said, and thanking her for her assistance, I tossed the pad into the bucket for waste that was to be burned, and walked out to meet Robinson and my ambulance. The new Sister was already in the back, and I could smell the strong soap that had been used to clean there. She wrinkled her nose at me and settled herself. Dr. Winters would be happy to see me returning to the aid station, and I could just make out the boxes piled high in the rear all around her. Badly needed supplies that he would welcome even more.

I was already in my seat, my door closed, and Robinson, looking over his shoulder, was busy reversing, to head back toward the Front. And in that instant I realized something.

The shivering man, the one too weak with exhaustion to be treated by Dr. Winters, wore the uniform of a French officer. But when he was shouting at me back in the ward, he'd spoken German. Fluent German.

"Wait," I said, quickly reaching out to touch Robinson's arm before he could drive on. "There's something I must do."

"Too late, Sister." He gestured forward. "The shelling's started. We'll be needed."

I could see the horizon bright with flashes from the German guns, and hear the rolling sound of a barrage. The respite I'd counted on had been all too brief.

"It's urgent," I said. "I must speak to Matron." Something in my pocket rustled as I turned toward the door, already opening it. "And there's Sister MacRae's letter. I promised to post it."

He grumbled, but I was already out, nearly slipping in the mud, heading back the way I'd come. I reached the ward, and handed Sister MacRae's letter to the ward Sister, then asked where Matron was.

"She's in her office, I believe. She's just ordered tea. Can I help you?"

"Thank you. I had a question to put to her, nothing urgent."

But it was, and I tapped on her door.

"Come," she said, and I stepped inside.

She was an older woman, well into her thirties, but she looked even older tonight. I could see a bruise starting on her chin, where she had been caught by the flailing foot. It would be painful tomorrow.

"Sister Crawford?" she asked. "I thought I'd heard the ambulances leaving."

"I felt I should tell you. The patient. The one who was attacked. Did you hear what language he was shouting in?"

"French, I expect," she said wearily, and at that moment one of the Sisters brought in a tray with her tea. I waited until she had set it on the table and closed the door behind her.

"It was German," I said.

She forced a smile for my sake.

"Perhaps he's a Frenchman from Alsace-Lorraine. It's not unusual."

Perhaps he was. I felt a little foolish. Even after nearly fifty years of German rule, many people from that area were bilingual, using their French secretly.

The French provinces of Alsace and Lorraine along the Rhine frontier were given to Germany by the Treaty of Frankfurt after the 1870 war with Prussia. The excuse was that parts of the area spoke German, although the real reason—according to my father— was military. Memories were long, and much of Europe hadn't forgot Napoleon's victorious campaigns. Territory on the far side of the river—the eastern side—was considered a necessity to protect Germany from any future French dreams of a European empire.

"I thought I ought to mention it," I said, suddenly uncertain.

"And very rightly so," she told me, but her eyes were on the steaming pot of tea.

I thanked her and left her to it.

CHAPTER THREE

Two weeks later

COMING BACK FROM leave in England, I discovered that I'd been reassigned to Dr. Winters. At his request.

He grinned when he saw me stepping out of the lead ambulance.

"Sorry," he said, and I could see he didn't mean a word of it. "But I like having you about."

I returned the smile. "Has it been that bad?"

"God, yes. And Sister Weeks is all fingers and thumbs. A good nurse, I grant you, but not very able in my surgery." He took my kit bag from me and carried it toward the quarters tents. "I hear you've been home. How was London?"

"I saw very little of it," I confessed.

Disappointed, he said, "I was hoping you might have managed a concert or a play. Something rather normal and interesting to talk about."

"I was in Canterbury mostly," I told him after a moment's hesitation, hoping he wouldn't ask me any more. "With friends."

"Then talk to me about Canterbury."

He hadn't been home in three years.

I couldn't tell him the truth, that the shops were nearly empty and the shortage of food was worse. That everyone seemed tired, weary of war and death and doing without.

"The cathedral is still there," I said brightly. "I went to see it. One could get lost in the blues of the windows."

"Ah. A little island of peace."

"Yes."

He set my kit inside my tent, then looked at his watch.

"There's time for tea before you come on duty. Sister Weeks can see to the patients waiting to go back with the ambulances." He paused. "We've had a good many jaw wounds."

They were always the worst, men with half their faces blown away. They survived, but so little could be done for them. We fed them, kept the wound clean, and tried to cheer them up. We lost some to infection, and others went home to England, their war over, their future uncertain. But I'd heard that work was being done on reconstruction that would at least make it less unbearable for them to see themselves in a looking glass or shop window.

Dr. Winters was staring up into the sky. Stars twinkled in the cold night air. "It's quiet at the moment, but until this morning the shelling has been intense. On both sides."

I remembered what the artillery officer had said. That every shell would be fired before the war ended.

Thanking the doctor, I went into my quarters and changed into a fresh uniform. Then I sat down on my cot and pressed my hands over my eyes. I was tired, not refreshed, after my brief leave. I longed for a week at home in Somerset, far away from the sound of the guns and the endless lines of wounded. But that was not to be.

I wrote a short note to my parents, to let them know I had arrived safely, although I couldn't tell them where. One of the drivers could mail it for me. I wondered sometimes if my father had friends and fellow officers who kept him apprised of my whereabouts, and I wouldn't have put it past my mother to have made friends with some of the women in charge of the Queen Alexandra's Imperial Military

Nursing Service who could tell her how I fared. My parents seldom interfered in my life, but having a daughter in harm's way had been worrying. I'd had some close calls. And so they must have tried to stay in touch. I smiled at the thought. Sometimes being loved was amazingly comforting.

That done, I reported for duty and made myself acquainted with the cases that hadn't gone back by the ambulance convoy that had brought me forward. There had been a cold rain for several days, and a number of patients had come in with chills. I could hear them coughing as I approached one of the tents we used for temporary cases. If they didn't go into bronchitis or pneumonia, they'd be all right. However, we never saw them in the line of wounded until they were in a bad state. They'd argue with their sergeants to stay in the trenches as long as possible, rheumy eyed and coughing and already starting to feel feverish.

It was late that night when a corporal came running from the communication trenches several hundred yards ahead of us. He was in a Lancashire regiment, I could tell from his insignia as he got near enough to call softly.

"Sister?" he said breathlessly. "There's a man in bad shape. We daren't move him. Our sergeant. Can you send someone?"

I'd been sorting the incoming wounded, and I turned to call to Dr. Winters. He came at once, thinking I had someone bleeding heavily. I told him what the corporal had reported.

He scanned the line of wounded waiting to be processed. Twenty patients, none of them life threatening, as far as I could tell.

Dr. Winters must have come to the same conclusion, because he asked, "Anything here that Sister Weeks can't handle?"

I shook my head.

He called to her, asked her to take over, then gestured to me. "Let's go."

We followed the corporal back to the communications trench as Dr. Winters questioned him about the sergeant's condition.

It didn't sound good.

We hurried down the trench, ignoring the smells and the thick mud underfoot that sucked at our boots with every step, and very quickly came upon the patient lying on a stretcher.

He was bleeding from a gash in the neck, and I heard Dr. Winters swear under his breath as I knelt beside him to examine the patient.

"The shot has nicked the artery," he said quietly to me, and began to do what he could to stop the bleeding.

Necks were so much harder than a bleeding limb, where we could apply a tourniquet until a doctor could take over. The only choice was to bandage the wound well and hope that we could carry the sergeant back to the aid station without losing him. There, with better light, we could tell just how serious the damage was and whether there was still something in the wound—a bit of his uniform, perhaps—that was preventing the bleeding from becoming a hemorrhage.

The sergeant was watching us with pain-dulled eyes, reading our faces, gauging his chances. I tried to smile for him, to assure him that he would be all right. But it was not going to be a certainty.

"Let's move him now. Carefully. Slowly." Dr. Winters was on his feet, intent on his patient and the fresh bandaging.

The corporal said, "I'll inform the Lieutenant. He'll want to know." And he also stood, starting back the way he'd come.

We never saw the sniper. The corporal was trotting along head down, almost at his trench, when a shot rang out, and he dropped like a stone.

I ran forward, keeping low as I'd been trained to do by my father, and bent over the wounded man. But there was nothing to be done for him. The shot had caught him in the throat and severed his spine. He must have been dead before he hit the ground. I closed his eyes just as two men from his company came running, and I rose to try to warn them before they came into range and were shot as well.

"*Stop*—don't come any farther," I cried.

Then everything seemed to happen at once.

As the two men came to a halt just short of the communications trench, another shot rang out, and I heard an officer shouting.

"Someone find me that bloody *sniper!*"

I felt something spin me around, and in the same instant I saw the ground coming up fast to meet me. I only had time to throw up an arm to protect my face from the mud as I fell across the dead corporal's body.

Dazed by the suddenness of what had happened, I lay there for an instant.

A round of firing came from the trench behind me, and after a moment I heard another voice exclaim, "Got him this time, the bloody bastard."

Someone was bending over me. "Sister? Are you all right?" he asked anxiously.

It was an officer, possibly the one I'd just heard shouting.

"Yes, of course," I said, smiling. "How silly of me, I tripped." As he reached down to offer me a hand, I added, "I'm afraid your corporal is dead."

I stood up just as a searing pain shot through my side. Looking down, I saw a red stain spreading across my already bloody apron, only this time it was fresh, it was warm against my side, and it was mine.

I registered that just before the officer saw it.

"You're hurt."

"It's nothing. I need to get back to the aid station. They need me." My fingers were probing my side, and they quickly found the wound.

"You're bleeding. I'll have one of my men escort you."

"No, I'm fine, it's not very deep—"

The shock hit me, and I staggered.

The officer shouted a name, and someone was there to take my free arm as my rescuer held on to the other.

They half led, half carried me part of the way, and then my head cleared, and I found my feet.

"I'm fine, truly I am. I can walk the rest of the way." To prove it, I straightened up, gasping at the fire in my side, and then I summoned a smile. "I'll never ignore a patient again when he tells me it hurts," I added lightly.

Just then Dr. Winters came back to see what was keeping me, and he ran forward as he realized I was wounded.

"How bad is it?" he asked me. After all, I'd been evaluating wounded for years, I thought; I ought to know what had happened to me.

"My side. A deep graze, I think. Bleeding but nothing seriously hit. The sergeant?"

"I think he's going to make it." He took my arm from the officer and called for an orderly who must have been hovering nearby, because he was there almost at once. He relieved the other soldier, but they seemed to linger, uncertain if I was all right.

To Dr. Winters, the officer said with some satisfaction, "We dealt with him. The sniper."

Dr. Winters nodded, then he led me away, back toward the line of wounded still waiting. It looked longer now.

I tried to shake off their hands, but the two men held me in a tight grip.

"I'm going to be all right," I said. "See to them first."

"It's being taken care of. Let's have a look at that wound." Instead of taking me to the surgical tent, he insisted on putting me in my own quarters. Dismissing the orderly, he went on, "This is no time for modesty, Sister. Let me clean that wound."

I hesitated. "I can see to it myself." I was standing without his support now, and although the tent seemed to have a tendency to move erratically, I knew I could manage. "Bring me what I need, then go back to work. I promise, if it's worse than I think, I'll come at once."

He left me, finally, after more persuasion, and then quickly returned with something to clean the wound and a roll of bandages as well as a pot of salve. He set them out carefully on my cot. "Can you undress with one arm?"

"I can try."

"I'll send Sister Weeks to you."

"No, truly. I can manage."

I wasn't as certain as I sounded, but after searching my face to be sure I wasn't about to pass out, he finally left.

I sat down weakly, grateful to be off my feet. My side burned as if I'd struck a match to it, and every movement only made it worse. But somehow I got out of my apron and my uniform, then my undergarments, and, shivering with the cold, looked down at the tear in my side.

It had missed anything vital, I thought, examining it with the aid of the mirror I used to pin up my hair. A long crease, deep into the skin, but not far enough to touch anything beyond it. Still, infection could be more deadly than the wound itself, and I set about cleaning it as best I could, putting salve on it to prevent infection, and then I was struggling to bandage it myself when Sister Martin stuck her head through the flap and said quickly, "Oh. I can manage that for you."

I was grateful to her. "What's happening out there?"

"Nothing Sister Weeks can't deal with. The sergeant clotted; I think he is going to be all right, if the wound is clean enough." Her hands were busy with my side, gently checking the wound, then carefully bandaging it. "Not bad enough for a Blighty ticket, but you'll have to go to hospital."

A Blighty ticket was passage home to England for treatment. Some of the wounded hated it, feeling they were deserting comrades left to face danger and possible death alone. Others hailed it as a relief, a respite from horror.

I knew she was right about hospital too. I sighed. In my mind I'd already gone over what had happened. "I think he pulled his shot as soon as he realized it was a Sister. He'd struck the corporal squarely in the throat. It was dark, he caught movement, took aim, and just at the last minute he saw his target clearly. Too late to stop the shot, but by jerking the rifle he still nearly missed me."

"You give him too much credit," Sister Martin snapped. Although we had very good snipers on our side, feelings ran strongly against the enemy firing from a hide, where he couldn't be seen. It wasn't quite the thing, in the view of a good many people.

But war wasn't always played by cricket rules.

"There," she said. "That should keep it from bleeding. I'll help you dress again, and then you can lie here until the ambulance run. Do you need anything for the pain? You must, surely?"

I didn't want morphine to put me out.

"I'm all right, I can do my bit," I argued again, hating this, hating having to leave my post. I realized suddenly how many soldiers had said the same thing to me, and I'd firmly assured them that I was a better judge of their wounds than they were.

As Sister Martin was firmly assuring me now.

She handed me a mug of water and some aspirin, and told me to lie down, let the bleeding stop, and not make a nuisance of myself.

I grinned up at her as she cleared away the basin and the cloths and bandages.

"Yes, Sister," I said meekly, and she shook her head.

"Cheeky," she declared and started for the tent flap. "Now be good. Don't get in the way."

I lay back on the cot and tried to find a comfortable position. But whatever I tried, it hurt, and the fire seemed to be spreading. It was only the nerve endings in the area around the wound making themselves felt, I told myself, and put my good arm over my eyes to shut out the lamp's light.

And I lay there gritting my teeth, stubbornly refusing to call for anything more than aspirin because I could hear the sounds of a barrage now, and I knew how many patients coming in would have shrapnel wounds, most of them very serious indeed. I could wait.

It seemed like an eternity before the rumble of the ambulances arriving brought me wide awake just as Sister Martin returned. "I'll pack your kit for you. You never know. They might not send you back to us."

I could hear her moving about but I didn't turn my head. "I heal quickly," I said. "I'll be well again before you know it." Even as I spoke the words I remembered the trouble I'd had with the arm I'd broken when *Britannic* went down under me.

"Of course you will," she agreed, but I didn't think she believed it.

Ten minutes later, I was seated next to the driver in the lead ambulance because the back was full. Dr. Winters came to speak to me, assuring me that Sister Martin had given him a good report, and that I'd be fit very soon.

"As for the wounded with you, they're stable. There won't be any call for you to attend them." He handed me a pillow to cushion my side and stepped back, offering me a worried smile.

I settled myself, nodded to the driver, and we set out.

It was torture.

I think I passed out shortly before we reached the hospital.

It was sheer luck that I went to the hospital where we'd taken the wounded Frenchman. On the last two ambulance runs before I was a patient myself, the convoy had been sent on to another hospital because there were no beds here.

Of course, I wouldn't be put in a cot in one of the wards. They were all male. I'd be given a room in the quarters set aside for nurses.

And so I had a fair idea of where I was when I opened my eyes.

Matron, peering at me over the rim of her glasses, said, "Well, hello. We wondered if you'd be awake in time for tea. I've had that wound looked at. You'll be fine. It should heal cleanly."

I'd said as much to patients, then watched their fever rise without warning and infection carry them off by the next morning, in spite of all we could do.

I smiled. "A comfort," I said, and she smiled wryly in return.

"Yes, well, we try to keep spirits up. It's good medicine to do so."

They brought me tea on a tray, and with it a bowl of soup. I drank the soup and then the tea, and felt myself feeling increasingly drowsy.

Had they put a sedative in my tea?

There was no time to give to a wounded Sister. With the best will in the world, the staff would still have to care for those far more seriously injured. I'd been fed, a fresh bandage had been put on, and I could safely sleep for a few hours. Rest, the best healer.

That was the last coherent thought I had before the darkness came down.

The next morning I awoke with a very dry mouth from the sedative and a slight headache. By afternoon, I didn't need anyone to tell me my fever had spiked. I lay there as the doctor looked at my wound, sniffed it, and shook his head.

"No infection. I don't think it's anything more than the wound trying to heal," he said as he straightened up and gave orders to the Sister who had accompanied him.

I was to have tea and soups, nothing solid, and aspirin for the fever, and as much rest as possible.

I'd watched his face as he bent down to sniff, and I didn't see the telltale expression of someone finding suppurating of the wound that would indicate something worse.

One of the troubles of being a trained nurse—I knew what could happen. I grimaced at the thought.

Dr. Webb caught the grimace. "Are you in that much pain?" he asked quickly. Another bad sign that there was more damage than superficial examination could see.

"It hurts," I admitted. "But the pain hasn't spread."

"Hmmm. Yes." Rubbing his chin, he considered me. "What would you say to being sent to Rouen?"

There was a base hospital there with the new X-ray machines, brought over early on by the Americans from St. Louis. I could tell he was considering looking for bits of my uniform or other fragments in the wound.

"Not yet," I said, remembering the condition of the roads. Another ambulance ride would be decidedly the wrong thing for me just now.

He nodded. "Then we'll go with the treatment I've described. Good day, Sister Crawford."

Sister Melville came in during the afternoon to change my bandages and inspect the wound once more. It hurt to move, but I clenched my teeth and said nothing as she worked. She offered to give me something for the pain, but I was still groggy from the last sedative. I smiled and shook my head.

And, part of me demanded, *have your own patients done exactly the same thing?*

By the dinner hour, I was regretting my bravado. One of the VADs came in with my tray and stayed to gossip. The Voluntary Aid Detachment had been started by the Red Cross and the Order of St. John, providing a range of care in Britain and finally in other theaters of the war.

Millie—as she asked me to call her—had been a laundress, an ambulance driver, and a cook, and presently was a ward maid. "But I've learned enough to become a nurse next month, if the war doesn't end before that."

Her enthusiasm kept me entertained as I ate. She even asked how I came to be wounded—she had never been sent to one of the forward aid stations—and how badly it had hurt.

I told her a little, then as I finished my soup and the bread that had accompanied it, she seemed to run out of questions of her own, and I asked in my turn, "I hear there was a French Lieutenant being treated here."

Her face lit up. "There was, and he was as handsome as I'd heard Frenchmen would be."

"What was his name?"

"He couldn't tell us for two days. He was just 'the Frenchman.' It's Moreau. Philippe Moreau. His mother was born in Alsace-Lorraine. She married a cousin, he said, to keep what money there was in the family."

"A love match? How romantic," I responded, to encourage her.

"He didn't say. But I expect the French like arranged marriages. I'd want a love match, myself. But I'm told that Frenchmen take mistresses anyway. So perhaps it doesn't matter."

"Who told you that?" I asked, surprised.

"One of the orderlies. He'd been to Paris. He said."

"Is this French officer married?"

"I don't believe so. He never asked us to write any letters for him. You'd think his wife would want to know he was safe. We took that as a sign."

"And where is he now?"

"We sent him on to Rouen. We needed the bed, and his diagnosis was exposure, loss of blood, and exhaustion. His wounds were serious, but not life threatening; he needed food and rest more than he needed urgent care, and Dr. MacDonald decided he could be safely moved. Although I must say, his feet were in a terrible state. I expect they will take longer to heal than his other injuries. Except of course for his forehead. That will leave a scar, I'm sure of it, but his hair will cover most of it. Still, he won't be walking for a while to come."

As a rule, patients were sent to where they had the best chance of surviving. And after that, to wherever they needed to go to heal. We took convoys full of the worst cases home to England, where they could take the time necessary to recover. Broken bones, lost limbs, head wounds, internal injuries, surgical patients—anything that couldn't be dealt with quickly and the man sent back to his company. We handled the emergencies. There weren't enough beds or doctors and nurses to do more than that.

It was natural to send the Frenchman on to Rouen.

And then my gossiping friend told me something more.

"Matron was eager to see the last of him. I can't imagine why. He was such a lovely man."

"Did you speak to him?"

"We were ordered not to. He had the most charming accent. I was helping Sister Evans change his bed, and he was awake, asking us where he was. He couldn't seem to take in the fact that he was in a British hospital. I expect he didn't remember how he got here."

Or the night he'd been angry enough to speak German?

"He spoke English, then?"

"Yes, he'd spent some time in London before the war, I believe."

"Did he speak German?" I could have bitten my tongue as soon as I realized it would seem to be a strange question.

"Good heavens, why should he?" She looked quite shocked.

"The French have fought the Germans often enough. It wouldn't be surprising for their officers to study the language. And I believe many families had German governesses or nannies."

"We had an officer, a German prisoner, brought in a few days after the Frenchman had arrived, and Matron asked the Lieutenant if he could translate for the nurses, but he said he couldn't. That his mother wasn't allowed to speak German at home. The family didn't want to forget that they were French, you see. And he was sent to France for schooling."

I could think of nothing else to say, except "How interesting."

Millie grinned, taking the tray and setting it to one side before bringing me a basin of water to wash my face and hands. "I can tell you, the Lieutenant had all of us atwitter. He'd been moved in with the other ranks his first night—it was the only bed available—but he was returned in the morning, just when I'd been assigned to that ward. The other staff made any excuse they could think of to pop in and see him for themselves. I had to restock sterile bandaging a number of times."

Sent to the other ranks to keep him and the Scot apart?

"Was he friendly?"

"Not very, no. But then he lay there with his eyes closed most of the time, and Sister Darrow told me he must have had a ferocious headache."

Or didn't want to speak to anyone?

I listened to her chatter for a moment or two, then asked, "I can't help but wonder why he was so far from his own lines." We seldom had French wounded here.

Her eyebrows flew up. "But didn't you know? He'd been a prisoner of the Germans. Somehow he got away. That's why he was in such a state. He'd walked, trying to reach his own lines. No food, hiding during the day. It must have been quite terrible. I saw his feet for myself."

So had I. That made sense. I finished my bath, feeling quite exhausted. Millie plumped my pillows, lowered the lamp by my bed, and wished me a good night.

On the brink of sleep, I found myself thinking about Lieutenant Moreau and his denial that he could speak German. Had he thought himself back in that prison camp when he was attacked?

And yet . . .

His outburst hadn't sounded like the handful of words a man might pick up in a camp dealing with his captors. There had been fluency, not a halting attempt.

I'd lived in India, where there were any number of local languages. Indeed, of necessity, many people spoke several. From my Hindu nurse I'd learned Hindi, one of the two umbrella languages of the north, and from our Muslim gatekeeper, I'd learned Urdu. But my ear had become accustomed to some of the local tongues, even when I couldn't speak them.

I would have been willing to wager that the French Lieutenant's German had had no French accent.

I slept much of the next day, and then on the following morning, I awoke to find Matron leaning over my cot, calling my name.

It seemed I had a visitor.

I blinked at her.

My next thought was, *Oh good heavens, Sergeant Lassiter has heard and has come to learn how best to find the sniper who shot me.* He was Australian, and just audacious enough to think he could talk his way in to see me. And then it occurred to me that Matron would never countenance a sergeant's visit to my quarters, avenging angel or not.

Who then? Not my father, the Colonel Sahib, as my mother and I called him after our years in India. Although word might have been passed to him that I was in hospital. Simon? But even Simon wouldn't be allowed in my quarters.

"Who is it?" I asked, running out of possibilities. If it had been one of my flatmates, who had studied nursing in London at the same time I had—Diana or Mary, or even Elspeth—there would have been no need for Matron to accompany her.

"You'll see. Now, let me attend to you." And she helped me wash my face, brush my hair, and make myself presentable.

Satisfied, she left me, and moments later, my mother walked into the little room, followed by Simon, who seemed too large for my quarters as he closed the door behind him.

"Mother!" I exclaimed, trying to raise myself a little in the bed and instantly regretting it.

"No, stay where you are," she ordered quickly. "I don't want you to hurt yourself."

Turning, she took the chair that Simon had brought forward for her and drew it up close by my cot. Putting a hand on my brow, she said, "You still feel a little feverish. Are you in any pain?"

"A little," I admitted. Looking beyond her to Simon, I said, "However did you manage this?"

He grinned. "I am merely her escort. Your father's orders. Apparently he was prepared to speak to the King, if need be."

It was my turn to smile.

Simon had been a part of my world for nearly as long as I could remember, my father's batman and then his Regimental Sergeant-Major, and always a friend close to the family. He had got me out of many a scrape when I was small, and I would have trusted him with my life. If my mother had insisted on coming to France, my father would have moved heaven and earth to get her there, and if he himself couldn't accompany her, Simon would have been expected to see her safely here and home again.

"I can only stay for a bit," my mother was saying. "I promised to be out of the way as soon as I was assured you were all right."

"I'm so glad you've come," I told her, and I meant it. I hadn't seen much of my parents on my last few leaves, and I'd missed them. A few days at home in the midst of this war had always been my anchor, keeping the nightmares of what I had seen and done at bay, putting my world back into perspective. I knew how lucky I was to have that sanctuary. I had chosen nursing on my own, had persuaded my parents to allow me to join the Queen Alexandra's Imperial Military Nursing Service, and however worried they might have been about my decision, they had allowed me to make what I felt was my contribution to this war.

If I'd been a son, I'd have been expected to serve in the regiment in which generations of Crawfords had served, and no one would have thought twice about it. I couldn't, of course, but I could try to keep the sons of other families alive to fight again another day.

They knew the risks, my parents. My own father had served as a soldier most of his adult life, my mother had followed him from post to post, and they had both survived dangerous times. But I expect it took quite a different courage to send a child—in their case an only daughter—into harm's way when they had no illusions about war. It was only at times like these when their worry showed.

I lay there and listened to my mother telling me about Mrs. Hennessey, who owned the house where I had a flat for my infrequent leaves, in one breath and our cook's ginger cat, Thomasina, who ruled the back garden, in another. She had brought me two small pots of honey for my tea, and an even tinier pot of plum jam from our own tree.

"Not my best effort," she said ruefully, "with nothing to thicken it, but it will have to do." And she moved on to news of my father, who was away again, this time—she thought—for the Foreign Office. "But who knows," she added lightly, concealing her own worry, "it could be for the Bey of Tunis for all I know."

"He was in Calais not very long ago," I told her—much to her surprise, for she hadn't known he'd crossed the Channel. Nor had Simon, I could see from his expression. "One of our ambulance drivers spotted him on the quay and recognized him."

She asked again if I was all right, if I needed anything, if the wound was serious enough that she might carry me home with her. But I reassured her that all was well, and no one would wish me to take up the space a wounded man might need.

They spent an hour with me, and then it was time for her to leave. I said a very reluctant good-bye, and as she rose to seek out Matron and thank her for her kindness, I said, "Could Simon stay for a moment? I have a question I'd like to put to him."

"Yes, of course." She smiled. "It will give me an excuse to come back."

When the door had closed behind her, I said quickly, "I don't look too pale, do I? Mother seemed worried, although she tried to hide it."

"You are pale. I've been shot, Bess, remember? I can see how tired you are from enduring the pain. Let them give you something."

In fact, he'd fought against morphine too, until there had been no alternative.

"The pot calling the kettle black? I try not to be any trouble, and I do hate to feel my head swim with the sedatives. But, Simon, there's something else. I'm probably wrong, it all happened so quickly. Still." And I told him what I knew about Lieutenant Moreau. "It's a rather common name," I added, "and yet if he did escape from the Germans, he'd have been in a French prisoner column, wouldn't he? Then how did he manage to reach our lines instead of his own?"

Simon was frowning. "There haven't been any more spy rumors than usual. Although the French were fairly certain the Germans had a spotter in Paris during the shelling earlier in the year."

The Germans' so-called Paris Gun had been the talk of the Army. Anyone returning from leave in Paris from April to August had seen the damage.

The frightening thing was that the shells didn't come screaming over. They were fired so high that they came in silently, and at first there had been fears that the city was being bombed from high-flying zeppelins. But no one had actually seen one, and it was soon realized that the Germans were using a new and very efficient weapon. It had raised the possibility of a last attempt to take Paris and change the course of the war. The shelling had kept the city on edge for weeks.

The new weapon had turned out to be a gun that was so large it had to be fixed on railway cars, and fired from them. With the Allied advances as the Americans engaged the enemy, it had been withdrawn to prevent its capture, and either hidden or dismantled, depending on which rumor one heard. We would have given much to get our hands on it, and failing that, on the engineering plans for it.

"Was he ever found? This spotter?"

Simon shook his head. "If he ever existed. But it would have made sense to have someone there to advise and report. Especially if the gun had been a prelude to an attack."

"I don't imagine Lieutenant Moreau could be that man. At the same time, I felt I ought to say something."

"And quite right. Stranger things have happened. But I'll report it to the Colonel, and he can make the necessary inquiries."

My mother was back, coming forward to give me a last kiss, and Simon gave up his chair for her. I hadn't had a chance to ask him to keep me informed somehow.

And then they were gone, and my room seemed too quiet and too empty. I was reminded of the time I'd had measles, and I'd been kept in a dark room, to spare my eyes. Only my mother had been allowed in, for fear the contagion would spread through the cantonment. It was she who fed me and bathed me in something to soothe the rash.

I was smiling at the memory when a new VAD ward maid brought me my breakfast.

CHAPTER FOUR

DURING THE EVENING my fever spiked again, and when a convoy of wounded was collected to be sent on to Rouen, I was among them.

Dr. Webb said, "We've been worried from the start that there might be something in the wound. Or that it might have run deeper than we knew. It's that X-ray machine for you, Sister. I'm told it's completely painless."

"I'm sure it is." I looked him in the eye. "How likely is it that the machine will find the problem? Or am I already seeing the beginning of a serious infection?"

"I needn't tell you that infection is our greatest fear. I also don't need to tell you that infection kills more patients than we care to admit. Once it's established, there's too little we can do. I'm erring on the side of caution, Sister Crawford."

"Then it's more than just being in the way."

Smiling, he said, "Much as I would like to say that you're a nuisance, you are not. No, Matron and I have discussed the matter. Rouen it is. If it weren't for this worry, it would have been England instead."

And so, bundled onto a stretcher like the other wounded, I was carried out to one of the ambulances and put inside.

There were three other cases traveling with me: one with a bandage that covered most of his head and a good part of his face, another with shrapnel deep in his shoulder, and the last with trench foot so putrid I could smell it.

We made good time to Rouen, despite rain that began some twenty minutes out of the base hospital. The jolting was bad, although this road had never been shelled. It was rutted from hundreds of vehicles and thousands of marching feet, and I tried to cling to the sides of my stretcher to prevent the worst of the shaking. Above me I could hear the shoulder case swearing under his breath at every bump. The foot case and the head wound lay quietly—too quietly, I thought, for a head injury.

Reaching the once-fashionable racecourse where the Rouen Base Hospital had been set up, we passed through the gates and then stopped for the Sister—in this case, an American nurse—handling the reception of incoming patients.

Her cheerful American voice reached us from the ambulance just ahead of us, and then an orderly was opening the door to ours.

"Good morning. Ah, the wounded Sister. We'll have you out in just a moment."

I said, "I'm worried about the man in the upper berth there."

She climbed in with a flourish of skirts and reached for his hand to take his pulse. "Oh, dear."

Clambering out again she had a quiet word with the orderly, and then stretcher bearers came on the double. The sergeant was whisked away as gently as possible in the circumstances, and I could hear the footsteps of the bearers receding into the distance.

Soon enough we were all where we ought to be. I found myself once more in the staff quarters, and twenty minutes later an harassed doctor came in to look me over.

"Hmmm," he said, examining the wound. "Yes, I can see the problem. Ever been X-rayed before?"

"No, sir."

"Well, it's painless. Nothing to fear. We'll send you over in the next hour. It's been busy here all morning. Urgent care first. Now, according to this, your fever has risen to high levels twice. The first time, quite understandable, fresh wound and all that. But this second time? Well, we'll see, won't we?"

With a brief smile he was off, and I closed my eyes, grateful not to be bouncing about. I must have drifted off to sleep, for the next thing I knew two burly stretcher bearers had come in to shift me from my cot. We moved along the outer ring of the hospital for some distance, then turned toward the building housing the X-ray equipment.

The machine was noisy and cumbersome, but far from terrorizing. While she worked, the young woman who operated it so efficiently talked about finding bullets, shrapnel, bits of debris, broken bones, even kidney stones with the X-rays. What she found in my side was nothing so dramatic—a particle of button that had been missed when I was first examined.

"You'd be amazed how frightened some of the men are, when they come in here. They're certain we'll find something that will keep them from returning to the Front. And then there was the French Lieutenant who refused to let us look at his head wound. We managed to do it, and there was no fracture. But he was quite upset."

I was dressing again, and I turned my head to look at her. How to broach the question I wanted to ask? I fell back on Millie, the VAD ward maid.

"Don't tell me this was the handsome Lieutenant Moreau who left broken hearts behind when he was sent from Base Hospital Three to Rouen?"

She laughed again. "It must have been. Lieutenant Moreau? He could think of nothing but being released to convalesce in Paris. I wondered if he had a wife or sweetheart there. We were sad to lose him."

For an instant I thought she meant he'd died. And then I realized that he had been released. But how, with his wounds?

"To Paris?" I asked, to be sure.

"Oh, yes, one of the orderlies put him on the train for the city. His uniform was in shreds, and so we gave him an American one to wear until he could replace his own. A nurse in the surgical ward has one of those lovely Brownie cameras, and she took his photograph. That seemed to upset him no end. He told us he was afraid his mother might see it and worry. He did look quite pale, that scar where your lot had shaved his head a little. And he was still wearing his sling. His feet were too heavily bandaged to put on shoes. We had to cover them with sacking."

Worried about his mother? I wondered. *Or about being identified?*

"I'd like to have a copy of that photograph to take back with me. We could pin it up in our quarters where Matron wouldn't see it."

Cameras had been forbidden in the early days of the war, a directive handed down by the Army, for fear captured film might be useful to the enemy. But my father had said he believed the Army had not wanted photos of what was happening in France sent back to worry the home front.

"Speak to Wilma Johnson. She might be able to make a copy for you." She gestured to her machine. "I can manage this, but photography is a mystery to me."

The stretcher bearers were outside waiting for me, and they carried me back to my quarters.

My search for Nurse Johnson was put off by surgery early that evening to remove my bit of button. The doctor even showed it to me.

"Keep it for a souvenir, if you like. The good news is, we got it. The worrying news is that there was a tiny pocket of infection around it, but I think we cleaned it out well. You'll be sore for a day or two, but we'll soon have you on the road to recovery."

And so another day passed before I could ask the nurses who attended me about Wilma Johnson. The ether had made me slightly nauseated, and Dr. Meadows had been right about the soreness. It was as if the bullet had creased me a second time. I could only pray that neither Sergeant Lassiter nor Simon got wind of this and came to find me.

When at last I could ask for Miss Johnson, she was on duty and I had to wait until she was free.

She was a large-framed woman with bright red hair and very pretty blue eyes.

"Hullo, my dear," she said briskly, coming into my room. "And how are we feeling this evening?"

"Better," I told her truthfully. "I understand you have a camera?"

"Yes, my father gave it to me as a gift just before I left for France. I've enjoyed using it. Would you like me to take your photograph, to show your family back in England that you're recovering nicely?"

"Actually," I said wryly, "I wanted to ask for a copy of the photograph of Lieutenant Moreau, the French officer we sent over to you here. He left a trail of broken hearts behind him and I thought it might be quite lovely to show the others how well he looks fully recovered."

"He wasn't fully recovered. He won't be doing much in the way of walking for a bit, and his arm is still mending. I took my photograph with him standing there, pretty as you please, and as soon as I'd snapped the shutter, he was back in his wheeled chair, pale as my apron."

"Still. Standing there in his American uniform, he'll look a hundred times better than he did when he came in to us. He couldn't even tell us his name."

"I see what you mean." She hesitated. "Did you work with him while he was there?"

"I did," I answered, though it wasn't quite true. I could tell something was on her mind, and I wanted to know what it was.

"One night when I was on ward duty, he was having a nightmare. And he spoke German in his sleep. I couldn't tell you what it was he was saying, but there are quite a few Germans living in St. Louis, families who have been there for several generations. I've heard the older people conversing in German among themselves, and I'd swear that's what I heard Lieutenant Moreau speaking as well."

"Did you report it?" I asked.

"It was just that one time, and so I didn't. I thought there might have been a good reason for him knowing it."

"It's possible his family is from Alsace-Lorraine. They were forced to learn German there after the Franco-Prussian War. Many of them still count themselves as French."

Her frown eased. "That'll be it, then. I'm glad I said nothing." She smiled, and dimples appeared in her cheeks. "I've been amazed here in Europe at the number of strange languages I've heard. There was a Sikh in my ward one day, and on another occasion, a French Colonial from Africa. Tanganyika, or some such place. I met a Russian in a coffee shop in Rouen. He'd escaped the revolution, he said, and he was selling pretty little enameled boxes. Snuffboxes, he said. His family didn't have time to collect very much before they fled. And there have been Belgians, of course. Refugees, many of them, and soldiers as well. One of the Belgian soldiers spoke Flemish. Everyone thought it was German, but I knew better."

We chatted for a quarter of an hour, and then she said, "You must be tired, my dear. I'll see if I can make a copy of that photograph for you. I have the negative in one of my boxes."

I thanked her, and hoped she would remember.

The next day, Dr. Meadows pronounced me on the road to recovery, and he asked if I would like to finish my convalescence in Paris. "It doesn't make sense to send you all the way to London. But you aren't ready to take up your duties. Can you manage on your own in Paris? There's a house, calls itself the Hôtel de Belle-Île, where I've sent a number of wounded. They should be able to find a room for you. It was turned into a convalescent clinic in 1915, and it's well managed. I'd recommend it."

I could have asked for London, but I'd seen my mother only a matter of days earlier, and I didn't expect to be more than a few days longer recovering. I'd reach London just in time to turn about and leave for France. I wanted more than anything to return to Dr. Winters and the forward aid station.

"Yes, I'm sure I can manage."

"I'll see to it that you are given the address. There's a doctor in residence, but I doubt you'll have much need of his services. With that button out, you'll be right as rain before very long. But don't overdo it," he cautioned.

And so it was settled. To my surprise and delight, Wilma Johnson did remember, and the next afternoon, before an orderly took me to meet my train, she brought me an envelope, saying, "I wouldn't open this until you are on the train. It might not be a good idea."

As I thanked her, she handed me a cane as well. "You'll find this will come in handy. I'm not sure there will be anyone to meet you in Paris. Is it the right height?"

It was, I discovered, and I told her how grateful I was. Ten minutes later I was being taken through the streets of Rouen to the railway station, and the orderly found a seat for me on the train, settling my kit at my feet. Then he was gone, and I was alone.

Except, of course, for several carriages filled with British and American soldiers and officers on their way to Paris to recover, like me, or on leave for a precious few days. As I pretended to doze I could hear them making their plans. The museums, I'd been told, were closed for the duration, but there was the theater, the burlesque, or the private gambling clubs another officer had given them cards for. A few were looking for Mademoiselles, and others for that strange arrangement of *les marraines de guerre,* or wartime godmothers. I wasn't precisely certain how this translated, but a godmother in Paris could care for and oversee the needs of men at the Front or even convalescing in the capital. Men whose only leave might be five or ten days a year. If that. No one seemed to think this arrangement an oddity, and the men in the carriage and the corridor outside where I was sitting spoke of these women with fondness and pride.

When I finally felt rested enough to open my eyes, the conversation moved on with speed. I pretended I hadn't heard a word.

* * *

A corporal from Somerset helped me take my kit down and he carried it off the train as well. Cane in hand, I thanked him for his help, and then I turned to walk out of the Gare Saint-Lazare to find a taxi to take me to the small British clinic. By the entrance were clusters of women in black with patriotic sashes selling little flags and other mementos, each of them representing some charity—for the refugees, the wounded, the men at the Front, Belgian women and children—but I had no francs as yet to give to them.

The first person I saw as I stepped into the watery sunlight on the busy street was Captain Barkley, the American who had gone to fight with the Canadians long before the United States had come into the war. He was just saying good-bye to another officer who appeared to be taking a train back to Normandy.

The Captain had once had rather a rough time helping me avoid getting killed, and I wasn't quite sure whether to speak to him or pass him by.

He looked up just at that moment, surprise and recognition on his face, followed by a smile. "Bess? Good Lord, what brings you to Paris? And a cane—Bess, are you hurt?"

He came over and took my hand. "You're pale. Are you all right?"

"I got in the way of a sniper's bullet," I said cheerily, although I was quite tired from the journey to Paris, short as it was. "I think he realized his mistake at the last possible moment, and so I got off very lightly. Hardly more than a graze. It's healing. And that's what has brought me to Paris."

He had a taxi waiting at the curb. He lifted my kit bag and started toward it. "First tell me where you're staying. And then I'm taking you to dinner. Such as it is. There's a food shortage here as severe as any in England. But I've managed well enough."

He put the bag in the front with the driver, and then gave me his arm to the rear door. Settling me inside, he walked round the taxi and took the seat on the far side of me. I wasn't really in the mood for company, but I was grateful not to have to make my own way to the Hôtel de Belle-Île.

"How are your parents?" the Captain inquired as we drove away from the station.

"Well, by all accounts," I said. "My mother visited me only recently, and I'm to write as soon as I am settled." It wasn't completely the truth, but I was trying to forestall any gallant decision on the Captain's part to let my parents know he'd seen me and that I was well. I hadn't even had an opportunity to tell them I was in Rouen, much less Paris. "And how is your knee?"

"Quite itself again," he said, a note of relief in his voice. "I hardly notice it these days. Even in wet weather."

"What brings you to Paris?"

"I've had a few days of leave. Not enough to travel to England—we're in rotation. But I was glad of the change."

Paris was still a haven for the war-weary, French and British alike. But knowing Captain Barkley as well as I did, I had to wonder if he was telling me the truth. He had fought tooth and nail to return to the Front as soon as possible after he was wounded, and he had even tried to trick the clinic staff into believing his recovery had gone faster than medically possible. And here, at the very end, he wasn't likely to choose a pleasant week in Paris over standing with his men in these final days, seeing them through safely.

But the last thing I wanted to do was to ask questions—and be asked them in return.

We soon found my hotel, which as it turned out wasn't far from where he was staying.

Despite the name, the clinic had taken over not a public hotel but a once-grand private mansion from the fin de siècle, boasting a large, walled forecourt with tall gates, elaborate stonework more suited to a public building, a pedimented doorway with a pair of what appeared to be polished oak doors sporting enormous brass knobs and knocker, and multiple chimneys. If anyone less than a duke or an ambassador had lived here, I missed my guess. But in size alone, it would be well suited to a convalescent clinic. What's more, I'd expected to find it well out of the city, but it turned out to be quite centrally located.

It was one of many houses, I later discovered, that had been turned into accommodations for the hundreds of wounded and convalescents coming and going in the city every day. Many of the former owners, having fled to the south, were grateful to the Allied armies for seeing to their upkeep, such as it was. I didn't think the owners would be pleasantly surprised at the state of their homes when they returned to Paris after the war. Wounded men—the Australians in particular—were often inclined to whatever indoor sports their imaginations might create.

Captain Barkley carried my kit into Reception, made certain that I was properly settled, and then promised to call for me after I'd rested.

The orderly behind the desk had not known what to do with me. I'd seen his expression of alarm as he scurried off to consult with Matron.

She, on the other hand, was not at all fazed by the arrival of a wounded nursing Sister.

"We are a house of men," she told me. "Wounded officers for the most part, who share rooms on the first and second floors. Ranks, the few who are sent to us, are on this floor. Staff in the attics. There is a lounge and a dining room on this floor as well. I don't know what Rouen was thinking, sending you to us, but there's the Nursery, of course. It hasn't been converted for use because it's rather distant from the wards. It will do. This way, Sister Crawford."

And so I followed her up the stairs to the second floor and to a pair of rooms at the far end of the passage, with windows on the front and the side of the house.

She frowned as she walked into the first room. It would have been where Nanny or a governess slept, with an adjoining door to the nursery itself.

The suite didn't appear to have been cleaned since war was

declared. Dust and cobwebs gave it a distinctly abandoned look, but the mattresses had been rolled up and covered with a sheet. Matron opened a cupboard in the nursery, and we saw an array of toys stored there. Mostly for a little boy, I thought, for there was a ship for sailing on a pond, a sailor's cap beside it; a miniature train that could be pulled along the floor by a string; a few little stuffed animals, ears and tails and toes frayed from much loving attention; a chessboard; and a variety of balls. She shut the door. "I shall ask Madame Ezay to see to this. Meanwhile, you may rest in my quarters. Shall I send up a cup of tea? I'm afraid there are no biscuits."

"That would be lovely," I told her gratefully. By this time I was longing for a chance to sit down. My side was throbbing from climbing all the stairs, but I said nothing about that.

Matron's room, as it happened, was a small sitting room on the first floor, where once a maid must have waited for a summons from her mistress, because the furnishings were spare and the wallpaper was plain. The bed was a cot, and there were a washstand and a desk and chiffonier as well. Mercifully there was a more comfortable chair by the hearth than the one at the small desk. I took it and tried not to wince as I eased myself into it.

"I must leave you now," Matron said briskly. "But someone will come for you when your own quarters are ready."

"Thank you, Matron. Sorry to be such trouble for your staff."

"The blame lies with Rouen, not you, Sister." And she was gone.

I leaned back in the chair, absorbed the warmth from the small fire on the hearth, and thought of Mrs. Hennessey's house in London and the flat I shared with other Sisters whenever I was in town. But I had chosen Paris, and there would be no complaints. All the same, I wondered how I had thought I'd have the energy to pursue the matter of Lieutenant Moreau.

By the time my room was ready, I was quite drowsy and comfortable.

When Captain Barkley called for me at six, the sun had already set, and Paris, the City of Light, was dark and quite dreary on this wet autumn evening. I had been tempted to beg off and doze by the fireside instead. Of course, he was in the best of spirits, and I knew that he would have swept me off to dinner over my objections. I really did like him, but he was quite *managing,* and that could be tiresome.

We were just driving down one of the long, elegant boulevards—not far from the Ritz Hôtel—when I saw a face in the taxi coming toward us. I glimpsed it only for the briefest of moments, and then we had passed in the crowded street. But I would have sworn it was Lieutenant Moreau in that other Renault.

So much for putting aside my search.

The food shortage was no laughing matter. What passed for coffee would have made Paris ashamed in any other situation, there was no tea at all, and the wine had been watered. Even the bread, always such a wonder compared to anything England could offer, no long had that crisp crust surrounding such lightness. Instead it was heavy and the crust darker than the usual golden color.

I'd been here a number of times with my parents, for we sometimes sailed to Toulouse and took the trains north rather than travel around Spain and the stormy Bay of Biscay. My father liked trains.

In spite of the food, it was a lively meal. Captain Barkley and I got on well together, now that he appeared to have forgiven me for once having dragged him over half of France.

Under the glittering chandeliers in the larger room where we had our table, diamonds glinted and the silverware was perfectly polished. Although the fashionable ladies of Paris were denied the usual accoutrements of fashion because of the war, they managed to look as elegant as ever, their dressmakers making up in ingenuity what they lacked in silk fabrics and feathers. Quite different from the more depressing look of London. I felt rather dowdy in my best uniform, although it seemed that the military style was popular even in velvets.

During a lull in the conversation, I asked the Captain if he knew anyone in French Army HQ.

He started to answer me, then stopped short, staring at me.

For an instant I thought he was afraid I'd stumbled on the truth about what had brought him to Paris. I should have known better.

After a moment he said, "Don't tell me. Bess? Are you in any trouble? Is that why you're in Paris?"

"No, truly, I'm convalescent. It's just—there was a French officer in Rouen." I didn't think this was the time to add anything about where I'd first encountered him or what had happened at Base Hospital Three. "I thought I'd see how he was progressing. It was his feet, you see. His boots had been taken while he was a prisoner. He was released from hospital, but I doubt he'll see any more fighting, if the war does end soon. Rumors are flying that it will." There. I had neatly changed the subject.

Or so I thought.

Only partly reassured, Captain Barkley put down his knife and fork. "How well do you know this French officer?"

"Not well at all," I told him. I reached into my purse and took out the photograph Wilma Johnson had given me. "He's wearing an American uniform here, of course—his own was in shreds and had to be replaced."

"You have his photograph?" He took it from me, staring at the uniform and then at the man's face. What seemed to disturb him most was the uniform. "He seems to be standing on his injured feet well enough."

"The photographer told me he nearly fell into his chair as soon as he heard the camera's click."

"Are you certain he's French?"

It was my turn to stare at him. "What else could he be? Really, Captain—?"

"No, I'm serious, Bess."

"He was wearing a French officer's uniform," I said.

"I don't like the sound of this. Are you sure he's not still wearing his American uniform?"

"I have no idea." It was true. In the taxi earlier, I'd only seen his face briefly. Although I tried, I couldn't bring back anything that might tell me what uniform he was wearing. "It was given him by the staff in Rouen. I don't see that it's anything to worry about. I'm sure he must have replaced it by now."

"Yes, well, one of the reasons I came to Paris was to look for any Allied deserters who'd decided the war was about to end and wanted to be alive to see it."

I found that interesting. At the Gare he'd told me only that he'd been given a few days' leave. I couldn't help but think that neither of us had been quite honest with the other. But then he wasn't Simon Brandon or the Colonel Sahib, who knew I could be trusted.

"I can assure you that anyone who stops him and questions him will be in no doubt that he's French. Not American."

"There are French-speaking people in Louisiana. It was once a French possession, if you remember."

I smiled. "I do recall my history lessons."

"I know you, Bess," he said after a long moment, passing the photograph back to me. "You aren't likely to be looking for a former patient—or a handsome Frenchman—unless there's a very good reason behind it. Not when you've been wounded yourself."

Captain Barkley was right; he knew me too well.

"Curiosity," I said lightly, although it took some effort. "He was found clinging to a shattered tree on the edge of No Man's Land. It was one of the coldest nights we'd had, and his uniform was in tatters. He had quite a few wounds, most of them not life threatening, but they'd bled enough to weaken him, and he was exhausted as well, dehydrated, and barely coherent. I learned later he'd escaped from the Germans and made his way back to the nearest lines. An extraordinary story. And extraordinary courage."

"I see." He wanted to ask more questions but was already thinking better of it.

I waited.

"You're an officer's daughter. A trained nurse." His tone was accusing, as if I had no business concerning myself with this Frenchman. As if he had already guessed that I was looking at trouble.

"I know."

"You must remember that, Bess. It wouldn't do to call attention to yourself. This isn't London." The lecture delivered, he changed the subject. But I was wishing I'd never mentioned Lieutenant Moreau.

We finished the meal, and the Captain took me back to my hotel.

"It wasn't too much for you, was it? Going out to dinner? You look tired."

"It was lovely," I said. "Good for my spirits if not my wound."

"Bess." He paused. "Perhaps I can help you find this Lieutenant Moreau. It might be best."

I had been afraid of that, that he might decide it was better to join the enemy than to lecture her. "I'm not actively *hunting* for him," I said.

"I think you are. And you aren't up to the task."

Oh dear.

"Can we talk about it tomorrow? I'm quite tired. It's been a long day."

"Yes, of course," he said quickly, worried about me.

The truth was, my side was hurting. I'd taken aspirin before going out to dinner with the Captain, but it was wearing off, and I was counting the minutes before I could go to bed.

Perhaps I should have begged to go to England after all, I thought, slowly mounting the stairs to my rooms. And come back to Paris when I was well again.

But the French officer was still in Paris, and he might not be when I returned.

I shook myself, figuratively speaking. Tomorrow I'd feel better. And everything would seem possible.

And it was true, I did feel rested, having slept well enough, for the governess's bed was comfortable and there was a small fire on the hearth to take the chill off the room. I had looked at the sedatives I'd been given, if the pain grew unbearable, thinking they might at least make rest possible, but I'd seen too many patients become dependent on that relief. Instead I took another aspirin, went to bed, and surprised myself by drifting off almost at once. A measure of my fatigue.

Madame Ezay brought me a cup of tea and then suggested that I take my breakfast in my room. It was difficult to be sure of her age. She was possibly thirty-five, possibly forty. Dressed in black, her dark hair in a severe bun at the back of her neck, she appeared to be nothing more than a charwoman, but there was intelligence in her face, and a lively curiosity.

I asked if she had lived in Paris before the war. If she had worked for the family who had owned the Hôtel de Belle-Île.

She told me she had come from Lille, that she was a war widow, and that her only son was now at the Front.

"Eighteen, Mademoiselle. Only eighteen. When he joined his regiment, his uniform was too large at the neck and too short in the sleeves, a boy merely. The next time I saw him he was a man. Strong and a good inch taller. Filled out too, and very like his father. It broke my heart, but what is a mother to do when her son wishes to fight for his country? I blame the Boche. The Germans. If they had stayed at home and minded their own business, I would not be a widow and fearful for my only child."

"You came to Paris to be closer to him?"

"*Bien sûr.* Of course. Lille is too far, he would never have enough leave to come to me. And so I came here instead."

She took my tray and walked toward the door. "Do you have brothers in the war?"

I told her that I was an only child, like her son.

"Then your mother must worry for you, as I do for him. Write to her. Letters are a mother's comfort."

With that she was gone.

I'd hardly finished my breakfast when Captain Barkley was downstairs asking to see me.

"Good morning," I said brightly when I joined him in the small parlor.

"You look better today," he said. "I was anxious last night."

"The journey . . ." I let it go at that. "But what of your work?"

He grinned sheepishly. "I must say, it's hardly been arduous. My men and I have been combing the usual places we might find a deserter. Because I'm an officer, I can find my way into the more elite salons. These people keep the most outrageous hours. Artists, writers, musicians—they often see the sun up."

Surprised, I said, "Do you generally find deserters in such places?"

"Not often, but often enough. After the war, we're going to see a rash of writers and artists who learned their trade in Paris. I can understand why, it must be exhilarating for them. The small towns of America haven't prepared them for what they find here."

I couldn't imagine deserters from the trenches attending the famous salons of Paris. So what was the Captain really doing attending them? Was this just a cover for something else? "You sound as if you admire them."

"My future is taking over my father's business. And the nearest I've come to painting was on one of our locomotives when I was working my way through the company, learning the various trades. As for writing, I couldn't create a poem if I tried a lifetime."

"Don't you miss the fighting?" I asked, curious.

The Captain grimaced. "I was due for leave, I didn't want it, and so they assigned me to Paris. I've just replaced the officer you saw leaving as you arrived. I've been here three days."

"Then I mustn't keep you from your work." I had my own to do, and I had already learned that Captain Barkley wasn't going to be helpful. And then his next words stunned me.

"Bess. I sent a message to your father, telling him I'd been at the Gare when you arrived and offering to keep an eye on you."

I had to bite my tongue.

My father had once assigned Captain Barkley to be my bodyguard. It had not been the happiest of times. Not that I didn't like and admire my protector, but he had a rather old-fashioned notion that women would melt in the rain if there was no man about to hand them an umbrella. And to tell the truth, I must have tried his patience more than I should have done, because my duty took me into danger, and that was something I'd accepted along with my commission in the Queen Alexandra's. I wasn't foolish—there was no excuse for that, it put others at risk—but I did my duty where I was needed, just as my fellow Sisters did.

"Has he replied?" I asked, with some trepidation.

"Not yet," Captain Barkley admitted. "But while artistic Paris sleeps through the morning, I'm at your service," he added, in an attempt to seem lighthearted about it. Even though I had done my very best to hide it, he must have sensed my disapproval.

"I'm afraid I'm not up to much in the way of sightseeing."

"If you're quite serious about this Frenchman, I am willing to do what I can. If only to relieve your mind of that worry."

Indeed?

"I really don't know where to begin," I said, hoping to put him off. "I've only just settled in. And for all I know, he's been sent to Chartres or somewhere equally distant, and is recovering there."

"If his feet are still in bad shape, your Frenchman will most likely be staying indoors. That's going to make it more difficult for us," he replied, taking me literally. "But I went around to French HQ before I came for you this morning, and I have a list of such hotels and rooms catering to the needs of wounded officers."

Oh, dear.

"Did they know Lieutenant Moreau? The French Army?" I asked, unable to stop myself.

"Yes, of course. In fact, there are a number of officers by the name of Moreau. At least one of them is missing. That very likely means he was separated from his men in a retreat or fell in a charge. He hasn't been posted as captured."

"Oh. Well, I shouldn't think this Lieutenant Moreau has reported to his regiment yet. Or word hasn't come down to the proper authorities that he's still recovering. And he'll need to find a tailor, if he doesn't have a spare uniform."

"That's possible, if walking is as difficult as you say."

"Perhaps he lives in Paris—has a flat here. Perhaps he hasn't needed to go to one of these convalescent homes."

"That's possible too." And then he added reluctantly, as if he hadn't meant to tell me, "But so far the Army hasn't—the thing is, Bess, Philippe Moreau *hasn't* reported. So they don't know precisely *where* he's staying. In fact, they don't have a *Philippe* on the rolls. Not as a first name."

"His family might not call him by his first name. Especially if he was named after his father. Too confusing."

"All right, I grant you that," he said grudgingly.

And yet the Lieutenant had come to Paris well before me. Surely he'd want the Army to know as soon as possible—for his family to stop worrying about him? What's more, I'd seen him just last evening in a taxi, so he was out and about.

Captain Barkley was assigned to hunting for deserters. The last thing I wanted him to guess was the chance that Lieutenant Moreau might just be one of them.

Nor was I best pleased that the Captain had been so busy about my affairs. But to be practical about it, he had saved me some time, and perhaps even found out information that I had no access to. Not as a nurse or even as a woman. I certainly couldn't ask the Colonel Sahib to approach the French on my behalf. I'd been considering how best to find out where Lieutenant Moreau might be staying, and Captain Barkley had done just that without giving my search away. Perhaps Captain Barkley had done me a service after all. Swallowing my annoyance, I said, "Very well. What do you suggest?"

"Breakfast," he said, clearly relieved.

And so we had breakfast in a little café down a side street from the Place Vendôme, the beautiful square where Napoleon had put up his great column to match those of the Caesars of ancient Rome. The omelet was surprisingly good. I expect the fresh eggs and onion had come from the black market. The sausages were another matter, limp and tasteless, but I said nothing to the Captain about that. The coffee was even worse—the French had been going without anything that might have passed for real coffee for some time now. I was almost on the point of ordering wine, it was so bad, but I thought it might embarrass Captain Barkley.

He grimaced as he took his first sip, then said, "I know an officer in the Hussars. He was wounded at Verdun and now works in an annex of Army Headquarters. I think you'll find him helpful."

"How do you know him?"

Captain Barkley hesitated. "He deals with the dead. His department keeps the records of wounded and dead, and where the fallen have been buried."

"Difficult but necessary," I agreed. "Then we're going to where he works?"

"He's meeting us here in an hour. I didn't think you'd care to have this search of yours become official just yet."

"That's very thoughtful," I said, beginning to wonder if it was thoughtfulness or if the Captain considered my search for Lieutenant Moreau to be frivolous and not worthy of official time.

We were just finishing our meal when the door of the café opened and a tall, prematurely graying man of perhaps thirty-five stepped in, looked around for a moment, and then spotted the

Captain. He wore the uniform of a Captain too, but one sleeve was pinned up where he'd lost his left arm.

Captain Barkley rose as he approached, and introduced us. I was amused at the surprise in the Frenchman's eyes as he bowed slightly in a well-bred way.

"You didn't tell me your nursing Sister was young and quite pretty," Captain Broussard said to Captain Barkley in French. And then to me in quite good English, he added, "Have you been to Paris before, Mademoiselle?"

"Several times, with my family," I told him. "It's a lovely city, I'm happy that it hasn't suffered too much at the hands of the Germans."

"The Paris Gun?" he asked. "It was rather terrifying for everyone, I can tell you. I was here last spring when it began to rain shells down on us without any warning. That was bad enough. The worry was, it was a prelude to invasion. Paris had been in danger at the start of the war, and we were prepared to believe the Germans intended to take it in a final effort."

The last three and a half months had seen some of the fiercest fighting of the war as the Americans joined in the fray. I knew that all too well from the casualties we were coping with. It wouldn't have been surprising if the Germans had decided to shell the city into submission. An ultimate coup to turn defeat into victory.

"But it stopped, the Paris Gun. I can't tell you how glad HQ was. They were debating whether to bring troops down from the Front to defend the city. It could have been quite a disaster. But Barkley here tells me you're looking for someone, a Lieutenant who was recently wounded and in your care?"

I gave him the same information I'd given my companion, and Captain Broussard nodded.

"Yes, I can see that you'd be worried for him. Lacerated feet, you say? And other serious wounds, loss of blood. I looked through my records this morning. He hasn't come in to notify us he's here. But it hasn't been long, has it? You've only been here a day, I believe?"

"Yes, that's right." I didn't tell him the Lieutenant had been released almost a week earlier. Or that I had seen him recently.

"But if he's not able to walk—well, that would explain the delay. He may have a flat in Paris, with no family in residence to support him. Most of us sent them away in the early days of the war, as the Germans came down the Marne. And then again last spring when the Paris Gun began firing." He reached into his pocket. "Moreau is not an uncommon name. There are five Lieutenants on the rolls by that name. Seven more are dead. Philippe, you say?"

"Do you know if any of them came from the Alsace-Lorraine region?" I asked.

"Moreau isn't an Alsatian name. But there is his mother. We don't know her maiden name, do we?"

"No, sadly," I admitted. "It was just a wild guess."

"I see."

He took out a square of paper and unfolded it. I could see notations on the sheet. "Here is Paul Moreau, Lieutenant, reported missing in action in the summer—eleven August, in fact. That could be your man. And another—Pierre Moreau. Suspected to have been captured in January of this year, although we don't have verification that he's a prisoner." He shrugged. "It happens. If he was captured by the Germans, and notification hasn't reached us, he might have died en route to Germany. Or he might have been too seriously wounded when he was taken, unable to give them answers to their questions."

"Do either of these men live in Paris?"

Even though Captain Barkley had told me there was no Philippe Moreau on the Army rolls, I wasn't prepared to rule out the idea that Philippe wasn't one of the man's given names. It was in the records at the base hospital, but he might have used his family's name for him, just as I might have told someone that I was called Bess, rather than Elizabeth. I could think of no good reason for him to lie.

Unless—unless he hadn't wanted anyone to know his real identity. That niggling thought kept running through my head, refusing to be silenced.

"Paul is from a village just north of Paris. It's called Petite-Beauvais—after the cathedral town. Pierre is from a hamlet near Fontainebleau." Captain Broussard looked at his watch. "I'm so sorry, I have a meeting at ten. I wish I could have been more helpful. If you learn anything more—or if you locate this wounded man—please let us know."

"You've been very kind," I told him. "Thank you."

"My pleasure, Mademoiselle. I hope we meet again in happier circumstances."

And then he was gone.

Captain Barkley watched him walk out into the street and hail a taxi.

"I hope he was helpful," he said to me.

"I was certain the name was Philippe." I folded my napkin. "Do you think it would be possible to find a taxi that would take us to this village? On the off chance we might find the man there? Or to Fontainebleau?"

"Bess, you're convalescent. You shouldn't be taking a taxi anywhere."

"I'm convalescent—but not precisely an invalid. I'm not strong enough to return to my duties. Nor am I bedridden."

"Yes, I understand that. But you should be resting. Reading. Sitting in the sun for an hour or so each day. There must be a small back garden at the hotel. You're still quite pale."

"I can't believe that a short journey by taxi will harm me."

I think he was afraid I might try the journey on my own as soon as his back was turned, for after a moment he said, trying to keep the worry and irritation out of his voice, "If I organize one of these journeys for you, will you promise me you'll take the advice your doctors must have given you and be quiet?"

"Captain—" I began.

"Bess, you must stop and consider your family. How they'd worry if your wound became infected or, God forbid, opened up again."

He was right, there *had* been surgery. But it was not likely to open again, if I was careful. And a taxi to either village was not beyond my own reach, even if the Captain refused to accompany me. In a day or two, I would surely be stronger.

CHAPTER FIVE

As it turned out, at three o'clock that afternoon, Captain Barkley arrived not in a taxi but in a private motorcar he'd commandeered from somewhere. I thanked him but didn't ask how he'd managed such a coup. I did wonder if perhaps the motorcar had belonged to Captain Broussard.

I also wondered if Captain Barkley had told him why it was wanted.

All but embraced by pillows to protect my side from the buffeting, we drove sedately through Paris, and I had a moment to admire the Arc du Carrousel as we swung around it. In the distance, with heavy clouds as a backdrop, was the great Eiffel Tower, now closed off for military use. It had been such a sunny morning that I hadn't anticipated rain later in the day.

We turned south, threading our way over roads almost as bad as those going in and out of Rouen, toward the great forest where French Kings once hunted.

But our destination was a hamlet nearly surrounded by the famous Forest of Fontainebleau. It took us a quarter of an hour to find it.

There were no more than a dozen or so houses in a clearing, a single muddy lane connecting them, and a church that was hardly larger than a pilgrim's chapel.

The owner of the tiny greengrocer's shop, an elderly dyspeptic man, stared at us suspiciously as I asked if he could direct me to the house of Madame Moreau.

Instead he gestured for us to follow him, and then he led us to the bakery. As we stepped through the door I could hear the *thump! thump!* of dough being kneaded for the next day's bread. The pleasant smell of this morning's bread still lingered in the air. The baker, a heavyset man of middle age, looked up, unhappy with the interruption. But he nodded to the greengrocer, who explained, in the local dialect that I found difficult to follow, that we were looking for Madame Moreau. I did catch that the greengrocer had mentioned that as the baker was *le maire* of the village, he was the proper person to answer us.

The baker stared at us in his turn.

"Is it bad news that you bring?" he asked the Captain in French.

I replied for him.

"*Mais non,* Monsieur. We are searching for a cousin of the family. We hoped that she might help us find him. He—" I hesitated, uncertain just how much I should tell him. Instead I fell back on a more general reason. "He was wounded last month and sent home to his family. I nursed him, and while I am visiting Fontainebleau, I wish to inquire how he fared."

There were British and American and even Belgian nurses in French hospitals. It wouldn't seem strange for me to be attending a wounded Frenchman.

"Ah." He considered the matter for a moment and then spoke to the greengrocer before saying, "Alas, I cannot stop what I am doing. But Armand will show you."

I thanked him, and we followed the greengrocer out of the bakery. The Captain, at my heels, said, "Where to now, the priest?"

The greengrocer must have understood the word. He turned to me and replied, "*Je regrette,* but the priest comes only every other Sunday. We share him with another village. There is no money to support him full-time." He pointed to a house close by the chapel, where a woman was sitting in the doorway, taking advantage of the last light of the setting sun to do her knitting. "Madame Moreau," he said, and left us to it.

"Are there no young people here?" Captain Barkley asked as we passed a stooped, white-haired woman with a long willow stick herding six or seven geese toward a pen.

But the men were at war, I thought, and the women, those without young children to care for, had gone to Paris or to work in the factories.

We came to the small cottage where Pierre Moreau must have grown up. His mother, her hair streaked with gray, her face lined with worry, looked up as we stopped before her. A basket at her feet held several pairs of stockings and at least five or six carefully folded scarves. The yarn of the one she was currently knitting, like the others, had been dyed a dull gray-blue. An old dog lay in the cottage doorway at her feet. He roused up to stare at us, decided we posed no threat, and lowered his head to his paws once more.

But Madame's eyes widened in alarm. A nurse and an officer could only mean bad news.

I said quickly in my best French that we were visitors seeking information.

She frowned at that, her dark eyes showing suspicion now, the sort of thing one saw often in out-of-the-way hamlets and villages, where interlopers could mean trouble: tax men, long-lost relatives, someone wanting something from the people and having no scruples about how they got it, traveling merchants with shoddy goods to sell . . . the list went on.

I spoke to the old dog, but he simply snored on.

"Why have you come to my house?"

I reached into my pocket, pulling out the photograph of Philippe Moreau that I'd been given in Rouen.

"I wondered, Madame, if this is a member of your family? A

cousin perhaps? I nursed him when he came to us badly wounded. I would like to know that he recovered and is well."

"You're not a French nurse," she said, taking the photograph but not looking at it.

"No, Madame. I am British. But we treat the wounded brought to us, without questioning how they came to be in our sector. This man—his name is Philippe Moreau—was bleeding from a number of wounds when our orderlies found him. And his feet were badly cut up from walking so far. His boots had probably been stolen while he lay unconscious. There's a possibility that he'd escaped from a column of prisoners and tried to find his way back to Allied lines. He was very courageous."

"And what are you to him?"

"I have already told you. One of his nurses."

"And this man?" She thrust her chin toward Captain Barkley.

"He is my escort today, Madame. It would not be fitting for me to travel about the countryside alone. And it is his motorcar that has brought us here."

She looked the Captain up and down. I don't think he was following her *poilu* French any more than he had that of the men. I was having more than a little trouble myself. She must have liked what she saw because she set down her knitting, thrusting the needles into the scarf, and turned to look at the photograph.

She held it close to her eyes, peering at it for a very long moment.

"I don't know this man. Philippe Moreau, you say?" She shook her head. "There's no Philippe in my husband's family. It isn't a name they carried down."

"Do you recognize him at all?" I persisted. We'd driven nearly forty miles to find this woman. "Perhaps he's a relative your son discovered in the war and spoke of to you in a letter."

She rose, careful of her knitting, and stepped over the dog in her doorway to disappear into the front room of the cottage. I could barely glimpse the furnishings, dark and of an older generation.

But there was a photograph on the wall of a man whose face it was hard to see clearly in the dimness. He was wearing the uniform of another time.

After a moment Madame Moreau returned with a photograph of her own, this one in a small tin frame. "This is my son. See for yourself, there is no likeness."

The photograph was of a young man in French uniform standing stiffly by the cottage door, looking straight into the camera. He was shorter than the man in my photograph by a good four or five inches, his hair was very dark, and he had a hook of a nose that dominated his thin face.

"Sadly, no," I said, passing the photograph to the Captain.

"My son is a prisoner. They try to tell me he must be dead, because the Boche have not notified the Army that he is taken. But I know better. I know Pierre. He is not dead. Perhaps he's hiding in Belgium. They speak French, he could have been mistaken for Belgian." She took the photograph as Captain Barkley held it out to her, and looked down at the face. "The image of his father," she said fondly. "He would not desert me."

I thought it was sad, her certainty.

"Have you no other children?" I asked.

"Two daughters, but they are wed and live elsewhere. Jeanne Marie is in Chartres, and Henriette is in Nancy. She married a man from Alsace."

"What is his name?" I asked quickly.

She told me, and added, "A great lumbering man, he is, and she a head shorter than you. But he's good to her. And to me. I have no objection to him. Which is more than I can say for that fool married to Jeanne Marie. He went haring off to war, leaving her with three little ones and a mother-in-law no better than she ought to be. She is housekeeper to a priest, you understand, and yet she writes letters to a dozen officers, yes, and sends them little packets of food or books or the latest music. Frivolous. That's what she is. She should attend to her own grandchildren, helping my daughter care for them. Jeanne Marie would have liked to work in a factory and make more money than her allowance as a sergeant's wife. But there is no one to help her with the children." She went on cataloging the sins of Jeanne Marie's mother-in-law.

Captain Barkley glanced in my direction, but there was no stemming the tide. The old dog yawned and rolled over. And Madame Moreau finally came to an end of her tally.

"Tell me about your son," I said.

It seemed that she was a widow. Her husband had died of a stomach cancer in the early days of 1910, and an uncle living in Toulon had paid for Madame Moreau's orphaned son to be educated in the town of Fontainebleau. He had wanted to be a lawyer, an *avocat*.

"But the war put a stop to that," she said with a grimace. "I would have liked for him to become an *avocat*. He would have made more money than living here, farming."

"Is he married? Are there grandchildren?" I asked.

"Alas, no. There was a girl he'd met in Fontainebleau, but she was too young to marry. So her father said. But I think he believed she could do better than my son."

Captain Barkley cleared his throat, letting me know that he was losing patience, now that we'd learned what we could from Pierre Moreau's mother.

We thanked her for her time and walked on, reaching the end of the hamlet before turning around. I could see curtains twitching in windows as people watched us, but no one came out to speak to us.

"Do you believe her?" I asked.

"Her son looks nothing like the man you treated. I daresay he's not a relation either."

I took a deep breath. "Yes. I think this was a dead end. I'm sorry. I shouldn't have taken up so much of your time."

But I had seen the larger photograph in the cottage, on the far wall. And the man in it hadn't looked a bit like his son. Of course it might have been Madame's father. That was possible. I couldn't see his face well enough to judge if he resembled Philippe Moreau.

"No harm done," he said cheerfully as we turned to walk back to the motorcar.

I was suddenly alert. Had he somehow known all along that this was a wild goose chase? He'd been so agreeable about driving this far—even though he hadn't seemed very enthusiastic when I'd first suggested such an outing. And he was just as cheerful at the prospect of driving back so late, even though we'd drawn a blank in that hamlet in Fontainebleau Forest.

How could he have known?

We reached the motorcar and got in. November's early darkness was failing, and we were running with our headlamps lit by the time we'd reached the main road to Paris. I could feel rain in the air, a heavy dampness that was beginning to overlay the evening chill. We stopped at a village on the road for our dinner, although it wasn't much better than the one we'd had in Paris. But there were fresh cabbage and carrots and a dish of boiled onions, and they were very good.

"From our own garden," the proprietress told us as we complimented her on the meal.

It was late when we finally reached Paris, and my side was aching despite the pillows. There were troop encampments outside the city, and the roads had suffered from the lorries and boots, just as they had near Rouen. I could see the lamps lit in the tents, gleaming in the darkness, and somewhere nearby a man was singing to the accompaniment of an accordion. It was a sad song, judging by the music, although I couldn't hear the words.

The Captain and I had been silent for some time as he concentrated on the state of the roads.

"Penny for your thoughts," I said, turning to look at his face in the light from the headlamps.

"I was thinking of my men," he said grimly. We were close enough now to hear the guns in the far distance, and in the dark night the reflection in the clouds of exploding shells flickered like summer lightning. "I'd keep them safe until the end of the war, if I could. We've lost too many. But of course that's not possible. I keep praying that my task here will be finished in time to get back to them when they're sent up the line again."

It was a feeling I understood very well. My father's men had been all-important to him throughout his career in the regiment, and even now my mother visited the widows of those who had been lost over the past four years, offering consolation, advice, and the knowledge that these families were not alone.

After a time, I said, "Do you think it would be possible to borrow the motorcar for one day more? To drive to Petite-Beauvais?" We were well into the outskirts of the city now.

"Not possible," he said.

I didn't argue. I'd proved to myself that I could manage, given pillows and a large dose of determination. I could find my own way.

And it would be better than sitting alone in the Nursery at Belle-Île, listening to the laughter and movement below, a book on my lap and no interest in reading it.

Sometimes instinct and experience set alarm bells ringing when one really has no idea why. And certainly the more I learned about this man who called himself Philippe Moreau, the more I wondered.

Why bother at this stage of the war? It would all be over soon, if the rumors were right. Why worry about one man's odd behavior?

It was just that with men still dying out there at the Front, I felt a responsibility to them, just as Captain Barkley or my father or Simon Brandon would have done.

If there was nothing amiss with Philippe Moreau, if he was everything he ought to be, so much the better. I could finish healing and return to the Front with an easy mind. If something was wrong, the sooner someone in authority knew about it the better. All I had done was ask questions.

But so far there had been no real answers.

As I climbed the stairs to the Nursery, I bit my lip against the discomfort in my side, and my back was aching from trying to ease the jolting over the miles. I did what I had to do to ready myself for bed and was asleep before I remembered to turn out the light.

The next morning, I was just finishing my bath, with the help of Sister Fielding, when Madame Ezay came to tell me the handsome Captain was waiting for me in Reception. And I was to bring my coat and those pillows, *s'il vous plaît*.

Sister Fielding grinned at me.

"He's very attentive, Bess. He positively haunts the door. How many times is it that he's come to call?"

"I'd asked a favor of him. It appears he's granted it."

"How could he not?" she asked dryly. "Here, let me button that. You mustn't twist around to reach it."

Captain Barkley and I set out in a companionable silence.

Petite-Beauvais was north of Paris, perilously close to where the German advance down the Marne River valley had been stopped by the French Army—while the British Expeditionary Force was sent to Mons to protect the coast roads and offer a flanking attack. Even so, some of the villages we passed through had boarded-up shops and cottages where fleeing refugees had thought it best not to return. The devastation of clashing forces had laid to waste much of the country-side farther north. In fact, I was beginning to wonder if we'd find anyone at all at our destination.

All morning there had been a lull in the artillery barrage we had seen and heard last night. I was grateful for it.

I didn't ask why the Captain had changed his mind. I thought it best not to. At least not at the moment. But it had occurred to me in the middle of the night that perhaps my father had asked him to keep an eye on me and see to it that I didn't find myself in the midst of something I wasn't well enough to handle.

It was something the Colonel Sahib might well consider the better part of wisdom. Indeed, I was surprised that I hadn't found Simon Brandon on the doorstep of the Hôtel de Belle-Île, carrying out my mother's orders.

It was exasperating—and comforting—to know that there were people who cared and who tried not to meddle in my life even when they were worried enough to try to shield me from the worst of my tendencies to want to help others.

The weather hadn't improved. The feeling that it was about to rain hung over us in the lowering clouds that had obscured the top of the Eiffel Tower as we left Paris and even now rested on church spires and the tops of the taller trees. Drawing a deep breath was difficult, the air was so humid.

Finally we turned off the main road we'd been following for the past half hour and wound our way down a rutted lane that led us through two other villages before we came to the outskirts of the one we sought.

The German advance had not reached this far, of course, but the village had that tired look that comes of privation and worry. There were several dozen houses clustered along the road and down the lanes that crossed it. Other lanes led directly into those square muddy farmyards that are so typically French, the outbuilding serving as part of the protecting wall. We explored a little at my request, so that I could get my bearings.

At the far end of the village was a stone church, square and sturdy, with a short tower. I thought perhaps it had been higher at one time, the rest of it lost in an earlier war. Shops lined the street in the center of the village, and women were busy going about their marketing. They were wearing black, most of them, a rusty black that spoke of long use. The only bit of color was a dark red coat belonging to a little girl of perhaps five or six. She turned to look at the motorcar, her thumb in her mouth, her eyes wide.

Several of the women paused to look toward the motorcar as well. An English nurse and a Canadian officer appearing out of nowhere must have seemed quite strange, because I didn't see any smiles. Instead there was apprehension, as if we brought bad news with us.

In the distance I could hear the guns again, first the ranging shots and then full salvos. Relentlessly pounding the lines on both sides of No Man's Land. I could picture the aid stations preparing for the first casualties. Shrapnel wounds were always difficult to cope with, tearing flesh with hot metal fragments without regard to uniform or rank.

"Where should we start?" Captain Barkley asked quietly. "My French is not as good as yours."

"Right. The church, then. Or that house standing just by the churchyard. It could be the rectory?"

We drove back to the church, leaving the motorcar in the road and walking up the footpath toward the house. I could feel a misting drizzle on my face as we reached the door.

A middle-aged woman opened it almost before the knocker had struck the plate, and I thought perhaps she'd seen us coming, watching our approach from a window.

"*Bonjour,*" she said, in the almost singsong manner the French use when coming into a shop or greeting a friend on the street. "How may I help you? Monsieur le Curé is in the church, if you are seeking him." She considered us, a knowing look that took in the tall man in uniform and the young nursing Sister at his side, calling at the rectory. I smiled at the thought that I was eloping with Captain Barkley, and she returned the smile.

But just then the door to the church porch opened, squeaking loudly on its rusting hinges, and a man in the long skirted black cassock of a French priest came hurrying toward us. He was wearing the typical flat-crowned, broad-brimmed hat as well, half hiding his face.

"*Alors.* He is coming now. Will you step in, please?"

She led us to a large room dimly lit by a pair of windows. There was heavy dark furniture and darker upholstery. The walls were papered with a striped pattern from another era, and the carpet was nearly as old. Not a prosperous rectory today, but then this was a small and very likely poor village, made poorer by war.

As she moved to light two lamps, I sat down on the hard horsehair seat of one of a pair of rosewood chairs, and Captain Barkley stood just behind me, waiting for the priest.

The woman—the Curé's housekeeper, surely—stood waiting too as we heard his footsteps outside and then moving swiftly across the uncarpeted floor of the entry.

He greeted us formally, politely, but there was an expression of worry in his face that told me he too expected bad news. He was an older man, his black hair heavily streaked with gray and his dark eyes still black lashed, giving him an oddly youthful face despite its lines. I thought perhaps he was nearer forty than fifty, but that the war had aged him.

"We are so sorry to take you from your duties," I began in French with a smile after the introductions were over. "We are here looking for a former patient, to see how he is recovering."

The Curé and his housekeeper exchanged glances.

"There is no recently wounded man here. But I know there are three from Petite-Beauvais in clinics. Paris, Lyon, and I believe in Nantes," the priest said after a moment. "Perhaps you have the wrong village?"

"Ah," I said, recovering quickly. "Perhaps he hasn't yet come back to Petite-Beauvais. We are too soon. Lieutenant Moreau is his name." I purposely didn't use his given name.

Judging from their response, I might just as well have asked if the Devil lived in the village. I tried not to appear surprised. Behind me, Captain Barkley started to speak, then, thinking better of it, cleared his throat.

"Before the war, the Moreau family lived in the house just beyond the church," Monsieur le Curé told me after a moment. "But there is no one living there at present."

I hadn't seen a house, only a stand of parkland woods.

"Oh. I *am* sorry," I said, in a such-a-long-journey-for-nothing tone of voice. "Is his family in Paris?"

Captain Barkley spoke in English. "Sister Crawford here nursed him when he was found wounded by a stretcher party. She was told he's now at home, completing his convalescence." He neglected to add that it was a British stretcher party and a British hospital.

"Indeed," the priest said, nodding, clearly understanding him. "I am glad to hear he is recovering." He had not taken a chair, and I thought he must be wishing we would go.

"I should like very much to have news of him. I know the staff would welcome it," I prompted.

The priest moved to stand by the small fire in the grate, his hands behind him. I noticed that the hem of his soutane was muddy, like his shoes, but his cuffs and collar were a snowy white. I wondered where he had been walking before we had discovered him at the church.

"Lieutenant Moreau hasn't lived here for a number of years. The house is closed. It was not a happy family—I expect there were too many memories. His father died when he was quite young, and then he lost his brother as well. I expect he would prefer to convalesce in Paris, if possible."

"Is his mother still alive?" I asked, curious. I'd have settled for an interview with her.

"Sadly, no. She died in the first year of the war. A bitter woman. She hated all things German, and the invasion was more than she could support."

Not surprising, if she had come from Alsace.

The Captain asked, as if he'd heard that thought, "I understand she was born in Alsace."

"Madame Moreau? Certainly not. Hers was an old family in Lyon. Her father had been *le maire* there."

"Are you sure?" I asked, taken aback by this news.

"But of course I am," he replied, more than a little affronted.

"Do you by any chance have Lieutenant Moreau's direction in Paris?"

"Alas, no. He took a flat there when he attended the Sorbonne."

Then who would let the Lieutenant know if something happened to the house or the estate? But I had already annoyed the priest once, and I didn't care to do it again. We really had no right to be here asking questions.

"Is Philippe one of Paul Moreau's given names? He seemed to prefer being called Philippe by the nursing staff."

He turned away, poking at the fire for a moment. "No, it is not," he answered with finality when he turned back to me. But his gaze was on the housekeeper.

I could hear something scraping at the windows, rather like fingernails. I turned to look, but there was only a bare lilac outside. The wind had risen, pushing a branch against the old glass. The clouds I'd seen in Paris must have become a storm.

The housekeeper noticed it too and hurried to light a third lamp on the table next to me. The large, high-ceilinged room seemed to absorb what light there was as the sky darkened outside, making the old rectory positively gloomy. As the match flared, I saw her glance at me speculatively, then quickly look away.

Did she think I was looking for a man I'd treated and fallen in love with? There was something in her glance that told me it might be likely.

I said, "I was just one of the Sisters who treated Lieutenant Moreau after he was brought in quite seriously wounded. He made no complaint. But his feet were nearly raw. He couldn't walk."

It was true, but under the sharp eyes of the housekeeper, it sounded hollow, as if I were making excuses for searching for Lieutenant Moreau.

Just then it sounded as if a handful of pebbles had been thrown at the window as the first heavy drops of rain were flung at it by the wind.

The Curé went swiftly to the glass, pulling the lace curtain aside to look out.

"The children will be coming out of school. I must go." He all but ran from the room, and I could hear the rasp of an umbrella as he pulled it out of a stand. The door opened and closed, and he was gone.

Captain Barkley and I stared at the door to the room, then turned to the housekeeper.

"He'll walk the little ones home," she informed us. "You won't wish to wait for him to see to all of them."

I rose, unable to think of anything more to say. Then it occurred to me to ask, "Is the Moreau house truly empty? There's no family there? No staff?"

"What staff? There's the war. If they aren't in the Army, they're in the factories. This village has done its duty."

Captain Barkley said, "You must have been afraid, when the Germans came down the Marne Valley."

She looked at him. "Most everyone left. The Curé and I stayed. Someone had to take care of our homes. We buried the church silver. They're Protestants, the Germans. They have no right to our silver."

"Not all of them are Protestants," he said.

"No? What they did to Belgium. Unspeakable. Godless men."

She was encouraging us to leave, edging us toward the door. We had no choice but to go.

In the passage by the main door, I said, "Why did Lieutenant Moreau choose to be called Philippe, rather than Paul? We thought it rather odd at the time."

She stared at me as if I'd struck her. Then she said, "I know nothing of this. His family called him Paul. Georges Paul Armand Étienne Moreau, after his grandfather. That was his name."

I remembered the photograph in my apron pocket. Taking it out, I showed it to her. "This is the only photograph I have."

She barely glanced at it. "I have known Paul Moreau, man and boy, and this is not a likeness of him."

So much for that. I returned it to my pocket and thanked the woman as I buttoned up my coat. The rain was coming down now in blowing sheets. The priest would be having difficulties with his umbrella. It was useless to ask the Captain to fetch his. It would be inside out as soon as we opened it. With a wry glance at the Captain, I nodded to the housekeeper, then ran down to the motorcar, feeling the raindrops pelt my cap and hair, hitting my shoulders and making me blink as they struck my face and eyes. Pushing my pillows aside, I slid into my seat and shut the door as quickly as I could.

Captain Barkley, having to turn the crank, was very wet by the time he could join me. I used my apron to dry my face and found a handkerchief to pass to him.

It had been chilly when we left Paris, but now with this autumn rain, the temperature had dropped dramatically. Even in my regulation winter coat I was shivering. Captain Barkley reached into the back and found a rug that he handed to me. Grateful, I spread it over my lap and my legs, drawing it snugly around me.

"She never gave us her name," I said, looking back. The door to the rectory was firmly shut. "Neither did he."

"Well. We were strangers."

"Yes, I expect that was it."

We reversed and drove slowly back through the village. I saw what must be the small schoolhouse. It appeared to be closed, empty. Where was the priest with his umbrella? Or the children's parents, coming to fetch them? There was no one in sight.

"I expect the schoolmaster kept them in until the worst had passed," Captain Barkley said, leaning forward to look beyond me. "It would be the sensible thing to do."

The street was empty, no one out in the rain, not even a dog sheltering under the cart standing outside what appeared to be the ironmonger's shop, the traces resting on the ground.

"A strange place," I commented.

"Unwelcoming," my companion agreed. "Are you all right? Running like that? There's surely an umbrella in the boot. I could have fetched it for you."

It was true, running had been a bit much. My side had been angry with me by the time I pulled myself into my seat and swung the door shut. But I shook my head.

"I'm all right."

His gaze scanned my face. "I think you're not telling me the truth."

I was saved from answering when a woman dashed out of the doorway of one of the last cottages in the village. She was waving to us and trying to stay under her tattered umbrella at the same time, her face a picture of concern, as if she expected us to ignore her.

Captain Barkley saw her at the same time I did and slowed to a stop, veering closer to her without splashing her. I wondered if he'd often handled this motorcar before.

I put down my window, and she said breathlessly in French, "Are you returning to Paris? Please, may I ride there with you?"

She was dressed in black, with a black cloche hat covering her dark hair and framing a plain face that still possessed that *something* that said a Frenchwoman. The way she wore her ordinary coat and hat, the way she held herself, all spoke of breeding and style.

Captain Barkley leaned across me to answer, "Yes, of course. Get in."

She quickly furled her umbrella and opened the door behind me, almost leaping in.

"Ah," she said as she leaned back against the seat. "*Merci.* Thank you so much. I am saved from borrowing a bicycle to ride to the next village. There is no train here—not that they come very often to the next village."

"Do you live here in Petite-Beauvais?" I asked, after we'd very briefly introduced ourselves, in the way of strangers.

"No, I don't. I came to see my governess. She died two days ago, and I have stayed on to arrange the service with Father Robert.

Thank God, we didn't have to bury her in this. Yesterday was lovely. She would have liked such a beautiful day."

"I'm so sorry," I said.

"You are a nursing Sister? The Queen Alexandra's?"

"Yes. I'm in Paris on a brief leave."

"Ah. Where have you been posted?"

I told her a few of the places I'd been sent.

"Then you've seen much of the worst of it. I too am a nurse. A nun," she added with a faint echo of hostility in her voice, almost as if she expected me to put her out of the motorcar at once.

Nursing orders of nuns had served in French hospitals for centuries, until some years ago when the French government had decided their hospitals should be staffed by nonreligious personnel.

"Are you indeed?" I asked with interest. "How did you manage to serve?"

"Ah. You know our history then. *Bon.* When Belgium was invaded, I removed my habit, put on civilian clothing, and went to offer my services as plain Marie-Luc Daucourt. You should have seen the office of the military commander in charge. You would have thought the French Revolution had never occurred."

I knew what she meant. Even when I went to volunteer, women with no training at all were eager to offer their services as nurses or hospital organizers. Diana, one of my flatmates, told me that a duchess had been standing in the line just ahead of her. Some of the early volunteers were even Suffragettes, seeing this as an opportunity to prove that women could serve their country just as faithfully as the men rushing to enlist. Many of the earlier titled enlistees chose instead to use their resources and contacts to establish hospitals in private homes, and even great hotels closed for the duration. What's more, these women were very efficient at it. Others set up or joined VAD groups or went to France and Belgium to do what they could on their own. Levels of training varied, too. I'd been very surprised and pleased when another of my flatmates, Lady

Elspeth, had completed her course and gone to France to serve in the QAIMNS hospitals and aid stations.

"I saw much the same thing myself. A romantic adventure. Or a misplaced desire to serve without understanding what it entailed. That was often the Army's view in the beginning," I said.

"Yes, it's true." She took off her hat and found a handkerchief to wipe the worst of the rain off the felt. "And so I volunteered at Panne, where the Belgians had set up an excellent hospital. After that, I stood in railway stations with other nurses and nuns, caring for the wounded in trains sent back from the Front. It was terrible—no bandages to speak of, except field dressings. No cots, men lying in their own filth in bloody straw, no food, no medicines. Not even water. This was true well into 1915. It was the most terrible experience, to see the need and be so helpless to fill it. But then the Army began to realize that they were losing men who shouldn't have died. And still they resisted using nurses. I have met doctors I could gladly have killed. Me. A nun," she went on bitterly. And then to Captain Barkley, "I beg your pardon if you're a doctor."

"I'm not. But I've seen the conditions you are talking about."

"Where are you posted now?" I asked. I thought she must feel safe talking about such things to someone else in the field. Or perhaps after the emotional upheaval of the past few days, the death of someone close to her and all the memories that must have brought back, she found it hard not to talk to someone, even strangers, and it was unlikely that we would ever cross paths again.

"In Boulogne. There are very fine hospitals there now. I came to Paris intending to move forward again, when my governess wrote that she was ill. The last stages of cancer. And so I did what I could for her, God rest her soul, and was with her at the end. She was a good, caring woman. She gave me more love than my parents—" She broke off as if fearing she'd said too much. After a moment she changed the subject.

"What brings you to such a village as that one? I saw you earlier, driving up and down as if you were looking for someone." She gestured with one hand, a very French action. "It didn't occur to me then that you might be returning to Paris. And then the rain came, and I was rather desperate."

"We went to the rectory, to speak to the priest there. Father Robert, I think you called him?"

"Yes. A very good man, very kind." She leaned forward, as if it had suddenly occurred to her why a young couple might wish to find a priest. "Are you married? Oh, I'm so sorry! You can let me out at the railway station. I didn't mean to— This is your wedding journey."

I saw Captain Barkley smile in the reflected light of the headlamps. It was very uncomfortable for me to turn sideways to speak to our unexpected companion, and so I faced the front again.

"Actually, Captain Barkley here very kindly volunteered to drive me to Petite-Beauvais. I was looking for a Lieutenant Moreau. A patient I was concerned about."

I couldn't see her face. But I sensed the sudden movement in the rear seat, a change in her position.

"I know the family. A casual acquaintance. The house is empty, I think."

"So I was told."

After a moment she asked, "Is it usual for an English nurse to look out for a patient in this way?"

"I wasn't sure how he was managing. It was his feet, you see. He could hardly put one foot before the other. He should have stayed in hospital, but there was a need for beds, there always is. And he was French, not British. We couldn't just send him on to England while he recovered."

There was surprise in her voice as she said, "I thought perhaps you were with a French hospital. There are many British women who have worked in them."

Then, as we left the villages behind and turned down the main road—which seemed to be even worse now in the rain, slick and wet and hardly more than a wide muddy track—she changed the subject again.

"We will have much to do, rebuilding our country, when the war is finished," she said thoughtfully. "I hope there will be the money to do that. And all the farms. What will become of them? There is so much blood in the soil. I have seen such devastation in Belgium as well. Liège and Bruges and Brussels. They are shocking. Worse even than what has happened in the north of France."

Belgium had managed somehow—miraculously, with hardly any army and no artillery—to hold the German advance for nine bloody days. A small country that, by its courage and suffering, had become a byword in a war where courage and suffering were daily events. I'd heard the Colonel Sahib and Simon speculate over what would have happened in this war if the Belgians had not been able to stop the advance. France would have had no time to mobilize, to protect the Marne Valley, much less the coast. Paris could very well have fallen, the government retreating to Lyons or even farther south. It was unthinkable.

Captain Barkley, who had been concentrating on his driving, relaxed a little as we came nearer to Paris and the roads marginally improved. He said, glancing over his shoulder at our passenger, "Where does the Moreau family stay when they're in Paris. Do you know?"

"I have no idea," she said. "No doubt there is a residence here. Petite-Beauvais is their seat. The family has lived there for many generations. They are not rich, you understand. But they have many interests, and these have made a comfortable life for them."

I wished now that I'd taken a moment despite the downpour to look at the manor house. But it was empty, and at the time there had seemed to be no point in going there.

"There's a family connection with Alsace, I'm told?"

"A cadet branch of the family lived in Nancy and Strasbourg.

They handled many of the family interests there. Sadly they were not able to leave before the German invasion in the War of 1870. It was thought from the start that we would surely win."

That war, which we called the Franco-Prussian War, had also unified Germany. And made Germany strong enough to use events in Sarajevo to launch its attack on Belgium and France.

Sister Marie-Luc was saying, "They were reduced to poverty when the Germans came. Their business was confiscated because they'd fought against the Germans. They were forced to live outside the city in a small dowager house. My governess refused to call it poverty. Reduced circumstances, she always said."

"Tell me about Paul Moreau. Do you know him?"

"Not personally, no. But I have seen him riding through the village, attending services at St. Denis. He joined the French Army in the summer of 1914. My old governess told me that he was at Verdun. He saw the Trench of Bayonets."

Verdun was for the French comparable to our Battle of the Somme in 1916, the bloodiest of fighting, and afterward the rallying cry of the French Army. The trench was a ravine where a company of French infantry had been cut off and killed, their bodies buried by a shift in the earth, save for the bayonets that marked where they still stood. It had had a profound effect on the Army and the country.

"I've met another member of the family, I think. Philippe Moreau. He had some connection with the branch of the family in Alsace?"

There was silence from the rear seat of the motorcar.

She had assumed—and I hadn't corrected her—that from the start I was talking about Paul Moreau, who lived in Petite-Beauvais. His wounding, his recovery. For that matter, I was still rather confused about which man I meant. There were similarities in rank, in background. But Father Robert had insisted that Philippe was not one of Paul's given names.

"I am not familiar with Philippe Moreau," the nun said curtly. "I did not know the family myself. Only what my governess told me. *Je regrette.*"

I could only take her at her word.

We drove in silence through the outskirts of Paris. The rain was still heavy and growing increasingly chill.

Once more I'd discovered nothing about Philippe Moreau, not from the priest, Father Robert, nor from this woman. I was no longer even sure that he'd been a prisoner of the Germans, had escaped, and was desperately trying to reach his own lines again. But he did exist; none of us who had rescued him, treated him, or sent him on his way to Paris had imagined him. Who, then, was he?

I pulled my coat collar up around my ears, for the heater in the motorcar barely warmed my toes. Beside me, Captain Barkley had a look of satisfaction on his face. I thought he was rather pleased that all my attempts to uncover information about Philippe Moreau had met with failure. I could be trusted now to convalesce as I should, quietly and responsibly, instead of dashing about in a cold rain without an umbrella.

As we crossed the River Seine and pulled up at the next intersection, I fumbled beneath my coat, looking for another handkerchief in my apron pocket, and something fell out between my seat and the Captain's, ending up on the floor in the rear.

Sister Marie-Luc bent down to retrieve it for me, saying, "If you please, I'm staying in a small hotel just behind the Church of the Madeleine. If you would be kind enough to put me down—*mon Dieu!* That man!"

There were still half a dozen pedestrians hurrying across in front of us as Captain Barkley waited for the intersection to clear. Heads bent against the rain, they were briefly caught in the brightness of the motorcar's partly blacked-out lamps.

She was leaning forward between our seats, and I thought she must be staring at the man with the black umbrella just passing the bonnet. The umbrella was tilted against the force of the wind-driven rain, his collar up, his hat pulled low. I couldn't see his features or judge his age, but he was hobbling painfully, leaning heavily on a cane.

A civilian—but with a cane—had she glimpsed his face before I'd realized where she was looking?

I turned quickly to the woman behind me. "Who is he? Sister Marie-Luc—"

She leaned back suddenly, where I couldn't see her face.

"*Mais non*. I was wrong. One sees ghosts after a while, you know. Faces that one half remembers. Faces of the dead. Wishful thinking, that someone may be alive after all. I am sorry. This is yours, I think."

And she handed me the handkerchief I'd been searching for.

As we moved on again I looked at those walking along the street. As in England, there were the wounded, some in Army great-coats, others in civilian clothing—some on crutches, others with canes. Empty sleeves, empty trouser legs, eye patches, and many with wounds that weren't visible beneath their heavy clothing. Gassed lungs, torn bodies, desperate minds.

Men she might have treated, men I hadn't, but their brothers in arms in England I knew all too well.

We found her street and the hotel at number 27. War had turned it into a *pension,* and as we pulled up in front, I saw another woman dressed very much as Sister Marie-Luc was, just stepping out of the door.

"You have been very kind," Sister Marie-Luc said. "*Merci* for rescuing me. Most certainly I'd have taken a bad chill. Thank you."

"I'll be in Paris for several more days," I said quickly. "Perhaps we could have lunch together?" Remembering that nuns took a vow of poverty, I added, "I would enjoy having you as my guest."

To my surprise, she smiled and answered, "Yes. It would be very nice indeed. Thank you." And then she was out of the motorcar, dashing toward the steps.

Captain Barkley watched her go. "Did you believe her? That she's a nun?"

I turned to him. "It's entirely possible. The nuns trained in nursing aren't always welcomed. Not where there are aristocrats clamoring to care for the wounded. I've heard stories of French soldiers being crowded into damp cellars or barns, no water, no food, their wounds untended, and only one or two nurses there, trying to save those they can. If it's true, that's rather horrible. I can imagine someone like Sister Marie-Luc might find it deplorable enough that she looks for other ways to serve. She spoke of the railway stations. Diana—one of my flatmates in London—told me much the same story about conditions at the start of the war. It must have been true."

"God help us," he said. He took out his watch. "I have a meeting in an hour, Bess. Will you be all right if I don't take you out to dine this evening?"

"I'm so grateful for the opportunity to go to that village," I said. "I couldn't possibly take any more of your time today. Besides, I ought to rest."

"I'd strongly recommend it. All the bouncing about on those roads must have tired you."

It had, but I didn't want to admit to it. Captain Barkley needed no added encouragement to treat me like a delicate violet.

CHAPTER SIX

CAPTAIN BARKLEY DROPPED me at my own hotel, and after several hours of rest, I dressed and came down for my dinner.

It was hardly better than the meal last evening, but I was hungry and ate the ham, potatoes, and onions, baked in a casserole whose tough crust had been extended with something I was afraid to identify, in place of the full amount of flour and butter. There was a watery flan for dessert, not enough eggs to thicken it properly, and the ever present non-coffee that tasted suspiciously like chicory. There was nothing that could be done about the shortages, and I was grateful for a filling meal. The carrots served with the casserole were surprisingly fresh, however, and I wondered how the cook had come by them. I didn't leave one on my plate.

Instead of a clear-cut victory, I thought, we were all going to be starved into submission. British, French, and Germans alike.

I was just preparing to leave my table when an English officer came into the dining room and looked around. I myself had come down late, and now all the other tables had been cleared and prepared for the next morning's breakfast.

"I say, are they closed?" he asked.

"I'm sure they'll serve you. I'm just leaving. Take my table. There's a place setting across from me."

"May I join you, instead? They might take pity on me then."

I smiled. "By all means."

His face was thin and drawn, pale with pain, and his left arm was strapped to his chest. I thought I detected a limp as well as he crossed the room to join me. He was probably in his early thirties, his hair fair and his eyes a dark blue.

"Major Anderson," he said, carefully inserting himself into the chair he pulled out. He went on to name his regiment—one of the Yorkshires—and his home.

"I'm from Lincoln," he said. "Louth to be precise."

"Sister Crawford. I'm from Somerset."

"Ah. My sister lives in Gloucester. Practically your neighbor." He had a nice smile.

"Indeed." I examined my memory for anyone I'd cared for in his regiment and found several names of patients who had survived.

"Yes, I know them all," he answered. "Good men too. I thought surely we'd lose young Bowen. That was a nasty wound. You and your staff must have worked a miracle there."

The waiter—one of the orderlies—came out from the kitchen, scowling to see a new guest in his nearly closed dining room, but I summoned him and said, "As you can see, the Major is rather late, but I'm sure you can serve him."

He reluctantly agreed, and after that was dealt with, I asked the Major how his own wound was progressing. "A shoulder, I think?"

"Yes. It's knit fairly well, but it isn't strong. The board in England cleared me for light duties and I came back to France barely a fortnight ago. The doctor at HQ took one look at my shoulder and sent me directly to Rouen. And they sent me here to do more exercises. I'm only allowed to take the brace off in my room when I'm resting. A blood— a nuisance, I can tell you."

"Surely you have someone to help you?"

"My batman died in the same action. They've assigned me an orderly. It isn't quite the same, is it?"

Officers grew comfortable with their military servants, and often a friendship sprang up between them as well that lasted beyond the Army. Simon Brandon, a very young hothead whose future was viewed dimly by everyone else in the regiment, had been taken on by my father. They had become fast friends despite the difference in rank.

"Not quite," I agreed.

The Major had ordered an omelet but they brought him the same ham and onion pie. With a sigh, he picked up his fork and dug in. "I miss being able to cut my food properly," he said. And then he added, "I saw you come in today with Captain Barkley. The American serving with the Canadians."

"Yes, he'd taken me for a drive. We were caught out in the rain as we came back."

"Where did you go?"

"Petite-Beauvais. Not the city. It's a small village just north of Paris."

His gaze was suddenly alert. "Petite-Beauvais?"

"Yes, as a matter of fact."

"Odd place to choose for a drive. Dreary little village."

"I'd had a patient from there. It was a spur-of-the-moment decision."

"My brother-in-law is a French officer. He was to sit on a court martial. The accused was from Petite-Beauvais. A capital case."

"Was he indeed?" I asked, making an enormous effort to keep my face blank. "Do you recall the name of the accused? Or his rank?"

"Sorry. I don't know that he told me. Claude was dragooned into service, because he was present on other business and they needed another officer. He only spoke of it because we were lamenting the damage Beauvais—the city, not the village—had suffered at the hands of the Germans. Claude had been married in the cathedral before the war. It's quite beautiful. He said he could only hope that Petite-Beauvais, wherever it was, had escaped a similar fate. I was surprised to learn there was another town by the same name."

The city of Beauvais was in Picardy, where some of the fiercest fighting had taken place.

"The church in the village is quite small. The fighting never reached there, but it hasn't been a very happy place, never knowing from one day to the next if the Front might collapse and pitch them into some rear-guard action." I tried not to toy with my knife and fork as I asked, "Was the accused convicted on the charges?"

"He probably would have been, if he hadn't escaped."

"That was fortuitous indeed. For him. When was this court martial?"

"I don't know that he told me. Some time ago, I expect."

There couldn't be a connection. How many soldiers could a village the size of Petite-Beauvais provide to the French Army? Ten, perhaps. No more than twenty, surely.

The accused could have been any one of them. And it also might explain the reticence I'd felt in the Curé and his housekeeper, or even in Sister Marie-Luc, to talk about the village to an outsider. It would be seen as a disgrace.

I wanted to ask more questions, but the Major took my silence to indicate that the subject was closed.

"You must be tired as well after your excursion. How were you wounded? Or is it something else?"

Something else usually meant dysentery, a scourge of the trenches and hospitals.

"I was shot by a sniper while trying to help a wounded man."

His face was suddenly stern. "And you're all right?"

"I will be, when my side has fully healed."

His expression didn't relax. "He knew who was in his line of fire?"

"At the last second, possibly. He could have killed me."

"Still," he said, and left it unfinished. *Hardly something an English sniper would have done* was what he must have been thinking.

We chatted while he finished his meal, but we didn't linger. He escorted me to the stairs, saying that he was stepping out to see if the rain had stopped, and I went up to my room.

If this court martial had taken place in the English Army, I could have asked Simon or my father for details. As it was, I was very much an outsider in Paris, and I could hardly count on Captain Barkley to find out from his own connections what had happened to the accused. I wasn't even certain it was an officer.

I checked my stitches and then changed my bandages before getting myself ready for bed. There was a little drainage on the old ones, and I cleaned the area carefully. I wondered if that had happened when I'd run for the motorcar in the rain.

It was difficult to reach around and make certain the plaster stuck across my back without twisting more than I liked to do, but I managed somehow. I could have sent for one of the nursing Sisters, but they were busy with the other patients.

Lying awake, listening to the sporadic traffic passing on the street outside, I considered what I had learned, and what Captain Barkley had discovered for me.

It appeared that his connections were useful but not getting me anywhere, and time was moving on. I needed another approach.

In England I would have had resources to turn to. My father's rank, Simon's ability to find out information, even my mother's friends and the wives of other officers from the regiment. Here there was nothing.

But there were nurses, women who dealt with the wounded, who sometimes found in their work that the Army was not their friend or even helpful. They had learned to search out other avenues to be sure their needs were met.

I'd met one. I could meet others.

It was an encouraging thought. And tomorrow, I decided, my side would be hurting too much to allow me to be entertained by Captain Barkley. Let him think that I no longer felt up to continuing my search. At least for the time being. What's more, we'd run out of options. The Captain would be happy about that.

*　*　*

He took my plea for rest in stride.

"Do you need a doctor to look at that wound?" he asked solicitously. "Should I take you to hospital? I wouldn't care to report to your family that there's any cause for alarm."

"There's no reason to worry," I hastily assured him. Then I smiled ruefully. "I should have taken your advice and not overdone. That's all. But it was so pleasant to dine out. I have enjoyed it."

"Then I'll leave you to it. But you must promise me to send me word at once if this is more serious."

I promised.

"I have my own work to attend to. It isn't happy work. I feel for the poor bas— poor devils who have deserted. The war is almost at an end. But there are those who stood fast and didn't desert. It isn't fair to them."

Even with my upbringing as my father's regiment moved around the world to India for its turn to serve the King and the Empire, I was also uncertain where I stood on the issue. Would I turn a blind eye, or carry out the letter of the law?

Then I realized what an opening he'd given me.

"You must know something about this matter. What do the French do about deserters? Are they shot?"

"Tried and shot or hanged, just as in the British and Canadian armies. Ever since the Army mutinied in 1917, there have been deserters, although it's kept rather quiet, for the sake of morale. And the French are severe with them. Mostly men in the ranks, I'm told. They have no place to go but their homes, and it's fairly common to find them again."

"And the officers?"

"They're quiet about that as well." He studied me, suspicious. "Why the sudden interest in French courts martial?"

"I dined—here in the clinic," I added hastily, "with a Major Anderson. One of his friends, a French officer, had served on a court martial. I found it interesting. It must be quite different from the way matters are handled in the British Army. Especially when the prisoner escaped before he could be tried."

"Not something the French are likely to be happy to talk about," he said severely. "I shouldn't bring it up with them."

"No, of course not. It's just that I hadn't heard my father ever mention that as happening in the British Army." Though of course it must have done. I wasn't naïve enough to think otherwise. "I did wonder what he was charged with."

Captain Barkley took out his watch. "I'll be late for my meeting. Shall I call on you tomorrow, then?"

"That would be very nice." I smiled and walked with him as far as the door of the convalescent clinic. The sun was coming out, watery but strengthening, and the air had lost its bite.

He left on foot, which told me he was no longer using the borrowed motorcar, and I heard him hailing a taxi just beyond the gates.

I went back up the stairs for my coat and found a taxi of my own. One of the staff had very kindly changed money for us, so I now had francs. I didn't care to walk as far as the Madeleine and the *pension* beyond it.

But Marie-Luc Daucourt was not in at the moment, I was told. Whether it was true or she was not inclined to see me, I didn't know. Glad that I had asked my taxi to wait, I went back to the Hôtel de Belle-Île, preparing myself for a quiet and possibly boring day.

Instead I was met at the foot of the stairs by one of the nursing Sisters.

"Ah, Sister Crawford. Do you feel well enough to read to a few patients? I hesitate to ask, but Sister Stevenson, who usually does it, is hoarse today. She was caught out in yesterday's rain, and it appears to have gone to her throat."

"Yes, of course, I'll be happy to."

Which is how I found myself in what must have been the library of the original house, amid a group of rather grumpy men, all of them recovering in one stage or another from their wounds. I counted one eye, both eyes, two lost limbs, a surgical patient, and three knees. Beside them sat a little white-and-black terrier.

"Corporal Thompson," one of the wounded men said, relieved that they were to have someone read to them after all. He pointed to the little dog. "He's the cook's dog, but he's not allowed in the kitchen. Nor is he allowed out in the garden. We've taken him on for the duration."

Corporal Thompson was better behaved than my audience. The book chosen for today was a French novel of manners, of all the choices, and instead they wanted to hear Wilkie Collins's *The Moonstone*.

"Something rousing," as one of them put it.

We found the book on the shelf of possible reading material, most of it left behind by former patients, and I began to read.

An hour later, I closed the book at the end of a chapter and promised to read again the next day.

The patient with both eyes bandaged said, "You're not regular staff. I don't recognize your voice."

"No, I was wounded, like you, and I'm here to convalesce."

They wanted to know more about me, how I came to be wounded, and what I thought about the war ending at long last.

I didn't tell them who my father was, but I was as honest as I could be about my training and experiences as a nurse.

They were respectful—each and every one of them had been tended by a nurse when they were brought in wounded and they knew how to behave. Which didn't stop some of them from flirting a little.

Major Vernon, I discovered, was an Intelligence officer. He had very little to say about what his duties were, but he seemed quite sensible and steady.

After the others had gone back to their beds for medication or exercises, he sat where he was. He was the officer with the patch, but his left eye, a very dark blue, was focused on me.

"Colonel Crawford's daughter, are you?"

"Yes, that's right. What have they told you about your eye?"

"Bits of shrapnel. They tell me it won't bother me after the lesions heal. I hope to God they're right."

"Career officer?"

"For my sins. Yes."

He toyed with a signet ring on his finger and then said, "Captain Barkley tells me you're looking for a French officer. Care to tell me why?"

I smiled. "He was one of my patients before he was sent on to Rouen. He cut quite a swath there, I'm told. I have wondered how he's managed with his feet so badly cut up." The words were hardly out of my mouth when it occurred to me that this was a man who would take them literally—and then wonder why. But it was too late now; I could only hope his questions were idle ones.

"Trench foot?"

"No."

"I'm curious. It's not a wound you see very often, is it? Lacerated feet."

I took a deep breath. "He was found wandering about in the night, dazed and bleeding from a number of wounds. Although none of them was life threatening, the accumulative loss of blood had left him quite weak, and he probably hadn't eaten for several days. His uniform was in tatters, he was cold and confused. It was when I put a hot water bottle at his feet that I saw what a state they were in. Apparently his boots had been stolen. He had walked on bare feet from wherever he'd been wounded. I was told later by a Sister at the British hospital that he had escaped from a prisoner-of-war column. His injuries were consistent with his story."

When he said nothing, still turning the signet ring, I added, "I don't quite see why Captain Barkley should have mentioned my interest in this man."

I didn't think he was going to answer me. And then he got up and shut the door to the passage before coming back and taking his seat.

"I should have palmed you off with some tale or other—that the Captain was jealous, that he thought your interest was too personal. Or perhaps that he had told me because he admired the courage of such a man. But as you are Colonel Crawford's daughter, and you've given me a fair account of your meeting with this patient, there's more that I must say."

He had my full attention now.

"I know nothing about this Frenchman who was found in the middle of the night, and near a British aid station. Let me be honest about that. But I've had several conversations with my French counterpart, and his people are actively looking for someone they want very badly. Do you know anything about the Paris Gun?"

"Yes."

"The French were always fairly certain that the Germans had a man here in Paris who could assess damage, give the guns better coordinates, and monitor the effect that this weapon had on the civilian population. You know that the shells appeared to come out of nowhere? Because they were hurled so high, there wasn't the usual scream of an incoming shot. They simply came out of the sky without any warning, and did quite a lot of damage. It was very bad for morale—the French had believed Paris was safe. That stopping the Germans on the Marne had prevented Paris from being taken, and the resulting stalemate in the trenches would preserve her in future. They were damn—very nearly right. But this new artillery piece changed all that. Paris was suddenly vulnerable, and it appeared that the Germans were making one last miraculous effort to outflank the defenders and bring the city to the point of surrender. And then the firing simply stopped. At the time, nobody knew why."

"And the officer—I presume he was an officer—was never caught? But what if he didn't exist? What if the speculation was wrong, and the gun was firing at random, for the greatest effect?"

"A very clever observation," Major Vernon said approvingly. "But

French Intelligence was adamant about this: He existed. And he must still be in Paris."

"And you are suggesting that Lieutenant Philippe Moreau just might be the man they were after? That he'd been trying to escape when our men found him? Or—conversely—could be the scapegoat for him?"

"You are most certainly your father's daughter," he said, smiling. "Captain Barkley tells me that you looked for one Pierre Moreau in some obscure hamlet near the Forest of Fontainebleau. And that you looked for a Paul Moreau in Petite-Beauvais. And it was fairly clear that neither of them was your man. What's more, you have a photograph of this elusive Lieutenant."

I was rather angry with Captain Barkley by this time. He had no business to tell anyone this much without even consulting me. And yet he had. To Captain Broussard, and now to this man.

"I do. But it was given to me in good faith by a fellow nurse who took it because she wanted to show her family at home what a handsome Frenchman she had met. If you don't even know if this spy exists, you don't have a photograph of him. Now, if I give you mine, it could become a witch hunt, and in the end, *this* Lieutenant Moreau could find himself facing a firing party. The French Army might not be too particular about that, if they needed to cover themselves with glory. There was the mutiny. And then the Americans came to do what they and the British couldn't do—bring Germany to her knees. Catching this spy would be quite a coup for the French."

"Yes, well, there's a great deal of truth in what you say." He turned as the door opened and an officer leaning heavily on a cane came in to search the shelves for a book. Major Vernon smiled at me, and we waited in silence until the officer had found what he was after and withdrew. "And I am not French Intelligence. Nevertheless, I am curious. It's curiosity that's kept me and many of our soldiers safe for four very long years." He grimaced. "And to tell you the truth, this inactivity is driving me mad."

I knew he was right. Eye patients were often the most difficult to keep quiet. They were well in every other respect, impatient for results, and had more energy than was usual in a hospital or convalescent clinic.

Still, I didn't trust him. If this began as a game for him, a way to while away the time he was here, what would he do with any information he found out? Put it all down to an exercise and walk away? Or feel honor bound to tell the French what they themselves might not have discovered thus far?

He seemed to know what I was thinking, for he said wryly, "You're not certain you trust me. Which tells me that you must know more than you've mentioned to Barkley, or perhaps to anyone else. What you've told me so far, while interesting, would hardly send a man to his death." He waited, then went on. "All right. Let me put it to you this way. You wouldn't, given your own wound, have rattled along these French roads in search of a former patient if you yourself didn't have some reservations."

True again.

"If you aren't in love with him, the only other possibility is that, given your upbringing, you have reason to suspect him—or at the very least, ask questions about him."

I smiled. "You must be very good at your work."

He didn't return the smile. "I am. I need to be."

I said, "What I know about this man—whatever you may think—could be explained away very easily. Which means I am not *protecting* him, so much as I'm making certain that I am not judging him unfairly."

"Well put. All right. I won't harass you with probing questions. But I hope you'll decide to trust me, if and when you *are* certain of your facts. Is that a fair request?"

"It is." Someone else was coming through the door, and I rose. "It has been interesting to talk to you, Major. And now I must return to my quarters for a rest."

He rose, accompanying me to the door, as a Lieutenant with surgical tape bulging around his middle walked in with the precise movements of someone who is afraid of waking up the pain again.

"I say," he asked, "I missed the reading today. Could you find the book for me, Sister? I'd like to catch up with the others."

I went to the desk near the windows and picked up *The Moonstone*. "Our place is marked," I said as I handed it to him.

"Will you be reading tomorrow?"

"I don't know. You'll have to ask someone. They haven't spoken to me about it."

"Thank you, Sister." He turned and walked stiffly toward the door again.

Major Vernon, quietly watching him, said, "He was bayonetted, poor devil. And very lucky the man doing it was not very good at it."

He escorted me to the staircase, nodded to me, and walked on.

I went up the stairs debating with myself whether I should have trusted him.

And I thought about what Major Anderson had told me last evening, about the man who had escaped the French court martial.

Spy? Prisoner? Or just a man who tried his best to escape from his captors?

There was no answer to that.

But it left me with food for thought as I propped myself up in my little bed and started to read a volume of French fairy tales I'd found in the little bookshelf against the wall. The illustrations were glorious and helped me with any uncertainties over the vocabulary.

But even as I read about glass slippers and handsome princes, I decided I'd done the right thing when I'd been wary of confiding in Major Vernon. Or even Captain Barkley for that matter. He meant well, the Captain, but his primary concern was my welfare, and given our past history, I didn't think I could convince him that I knew what I was doing.

With a sigh I went back to the travails of the kitchen maid who had fallen in love with a prince. They seemed far more surmountable.

The next morning I went again to the *pension* where Sister Marie-Luc had taken rooms.

Once more I was told that she wasn't in.

Was she avoiding me? Or out and about on her own affairs?

I walked down as far as the Church of the Madeleine in the hope of finding a taxi to take me back to the Hôtel de Belle-Île.

Just as I was about to step into one that had pulled to the side of the road, I heard someone call my name.

Turning around, I saw Sister Marie-Luc hurrying down the steps of the church.

"Have you come to see me?" she called. "I'm so sorry. I went to hear a recital on the great organ."

Holding the taxi, I said, "It's rather early. Still, will you have lunch with me?"

"Yes, but of course." She hurried to catch me up, and we got into the taxi together.

"I'm afraid I don't know the best restaurants for lunch. Do you have a suggestion?"

She did, and she gave the address to the taxi's driver.

I found myself in a small, rather dark little restaurant on a back street I had never heard of. The owner apparently was a friend of hers, because he came at once to seat us and ask what we would like. I had a little difficulty with his Breton accent, but we soon decided on our meal, and he left to give his orders to the kitchen, which was the domain of his wife and his sister-in-law.

The omelet was very good, with fresh onions and chunks of potato. The coffee was beyond even the owner's control. We drank wine instead, and talked about nursing, how it had changed as the war taught us more and more techniques to save men's shattered bodies.

"But for their minds," she said as we finished our food and sat back to drink the last of the wine, "there is often no cure. What they have seen and done—it is beyond medicine."

I had to agree with her. And then I said, "Would you know Paul Moreau, if you saw him walk through that door?"

Frowning, she looked at me. "You are obsessed with this man."

"No. Just looking for a friend," I said lightly.

I brought out my photograph of Philippe Moreau and put it down on the table between us.

Something in her manner changed, her eyes narrowing, color rising in her pale cheeks.

"Where did you get this?" she demanded. "And why is he wearing an American uniform?"

"Do you know him?" When she didn't answer, I told her an abbreviated version of my encounter with the nurse in Rouen who had a camera. "She gave me this photograph to take back with me to the hospital where the Lieutenant was treated. He charmed them all, it seems. But I was more concerned with his wounds."

"You should have nothing to do with this man."

"I'm sorry?"

"He is evil. You must put him out of your mind. And you would be wise to burn this photograph. It is not worth keeping."

"But who is he—and more to the point, what has he done?"

"Unspeakable things. I saw him in Belgium. He's a monster."

"Was he German? In the German Army?"

"No, I refuse to look at him another moment." She pushed the photograph back to me and summoned the Breton, who came at once with our reckoning. "*Alors,* my friend, we must go. How is your son? You have not spoken of him."

Her friend, as she called him, shook his head. "Jerome? He has dark days. I have hidden anything that could do him harm. But I fear that he will take his own life soon. If he has to throw himself into the Seine."

"I will come and see him. I will see what I can do."

"Bless you," the man said. "He is well in body now, and that's why I'm so afraid. While he couldn't do anything but lie there, I believed I could help him. Now—he's stronger than I am. And steady enough on his feet to walk wherever he wants to go."

"I will come," she said, nodding, and passed the reckoning to me. I paid it, as I'd promised I would, and we left the little restaurant.

"What's wrong with his son?"

"Shell shock is what you call it, I think. He remembers too much, and it has nearly destroyed him. His wife has already left him. His friends. But he is so tormented he can't turn away from what he sees in his head. It's rather terrible. I have done what I could. It may never be enough."

"No." I had dealt with such cases too.

She looked up and down the street. "I will go and see him now. You should be able to find a taxi at the next corner. Thank you for lunch."

And she was walking briskly away, not waiting for an answer. I called to her, but she never turned.

I realized then that she had had no intention of traveling back to the *pension* with me. Not after my questions. The restaurant owner's son had given her a polite excuse for avoiding any others.

In the end, I walked on toward the corner and eventually found a taxi.

Who was this man who called himself Philippe Moreau? And what in the name of God had he done that made a nun hate him so?

CHAPTER SEVEN

I WENT UP to my room when I reached Belle-Île, wanting to think, and with any luck, possibly rest. My side was burning rather badly, and the pain worried me.

But they called me down to read again, and I went, reluctantly.

I was relieved to see that Major Vernon was not among those who'd come to hear the next installment of *The Moonstone*.

The reading went smoothly, no interruptions, and there were questions at the end about the characters and the plot. I sat there and listened to my audience, smiling at their enthusiasm.

When the hour ended and patients went off to their wards, I put the book on the desk and started for the stairs.

Major Vernon was waiting there for me.

He smiled, raising both hands as if in surrender.

"I wondered if you would consider having dinner with me this evening. Not to talk about spies or wounded men. Just to enjoy the evening."

Hesitating for a moment, I said, "I'm rather tired . . ."

"Are you?" The smile changed to a grin. "Colonel Crawford's daughter in retreat? I don't believe it."

"We don't socialize with patients," I said primly, falling back on the rules of my service. "It isn't encouraged."

"I'm not your patient. In point of fact, there is nothing in the rules that prevents two patients from socializing."

I laughed. "Were you perhaps a barrister before the war?"

"Guilty as charged. I was trained in the law but found soldiering more to my liking."

"And you promise, no discussion of capturing anyone?"

"I give you my word."

I was still suspicious, but I nodded. "Very well."

"Good. I can't call for you at six, I'm not allowed near the Nursery. But I'll be waiting here."

I thanked him and climbed the stairs to my room.

When my bandages were changed, there was still a pink tinge on them, a little darker than it had been yesterday. I was overdoing, I knew that. With clean bandages and the curtains drawn against the day, I tried to sleep for a while, to give my body a chance to recover.

Instead I had to stop myself from tossing and turning—or at least what passed for it, considering how painful my side still was.

I was ready by a few minutes before six.

When I came down the stairs, Major Vernon wasn't waiting for me.

Thinking the watch pinned to my uniform might not be right, I walked to the door and looked out at the darkness.

He wasn't standing in the courtyard or by the gate.

I waited five more minutes, and then reluctantly went into the dining room where the ambulatory patients and some of the staff ate.

I was well into the main course, a casserole containing a starchy gravy, a medley of vegetables, and strands of meat that might be roast pork, when Major Vernon swept into the dining room and looked around. Spotting me, he came directly to my table.

He was still wearing his greatcoat, and I saw that the shoulders were damp with rain.

"I am so sorry," he said, standing before me, a frown on his face. "I wouldn't have missed our dinner plans on purpose. I was quite looking forward to it. The thing is, I'd gone for a walk at half past four, and I've only now come in. The police are looking for someone—they've blocked a number of roads, and are stopping every man to demand his papers. It was an hour or more, the first time, waiting my turn, and even longer the next. Will you forgive me?"

Everyone was staring at us.

"Yes, of course," I answered, smiling. "Do sit down, you might as well dine here with me. And you can tell me who the police are after?"

He took off his greatcoat, folding it over the back of an empty chair.

"God knows. Every male over the age of fourteen, or so it appears. Civilian or military. The police went through our papers meticulously, asking questions. Where are we from, why are we in Paris, where are we staying, how long we've been at that location, who could vouch for us there. And all the while they were watching our faces, as if they expected us to be lying. I was curious, and asked them why I was being stopped and questioned. They paid no heed. On the second occasion, I was asked to turn in profile while they conferred. I think they must know enough about this man that they're certain they'll find him before the night is out. God help him, whoever he may be. They're quite serious about this hunt. And rather careful about how it's conducted."

A Lieutenant by the name of Burrows had heard our conversation, and he leaned forward. "The last time there was a search like the one you describe, it was a spy they were after. I wasn't here, but a friend of mine was. Apparently they never found the man. Or if they did, it was kept very quiet."

"I expect we'll never know what was on tonight." Major Vernon looked at my plate. "Tell me dinner is edible."

"Mysterious but edible," I answered, and he laughed.

But I could tell his mind was still on his experiences at the police barricades. As an Intelligence officer, he might have gleaned more from the police than they had from him.

We were eating our pudding when Captain Barkley came in. Surprised to see him—the kitchen here fed patients and staff, not guests—I smiled as he came across the room to our table and, with a nod to the Major, took the chair next to me.

"I've finished my meal," I said apologetically. "If I'd known you were coming, I'd have waited."

"How are you this evening, Bess? Less tired, I hope."

"Yes, I'm feeling quite rested."

One of the staff started toward our table, a frown on her face, and I could see that she was uncertain about what to say to the Captain.

Forestalling her, I said quickly, "I'm afraid the kitchen is closed."

"Actually, I need to speak to you privately." He glanced toward Major Vernon. "If you'll excuse us? I won't be long." Rising, he held my chair for me, and I had no choice but to stand up and follow him out of the room.

There wasn't much privacy here. Convalescent clinics are busy and usually rather full, and Belle-Île was no exception. But for once Reception—where the orderly in charge usually sat in the wide marble entry with its grand staircase and high ceiling—was empty. There were several chairs against the far wall, and Captain Barkley led me there, waiting for me to sit down. So I did. But he remained standing.

"I've some rather bad news for you, I'm afraid."

My heart turned over. Simon? One of my flatmates? Surely not the Colonel Sahib. Or Mother, safe at home in Somerset?

"What is it?" I asked. "Tell me. Straight out."

"It's the nun. Sister Marie-Luc. I've just been told she was found in a back street along the Left Bank. She's been stabbed."

For an instant I couldn't take it in. My mind was so busy sorting through those I cared about that the sudden—to me—shift in direction was almost confusing.

"Sister Marie-Luc? But I'd just seen her—" I broke off. The Captain didn't know about our lunch. "—since we dropped her off at the *pension*," I amended quickly. And then I actually heard what he'd said. *She's been stabbed.*

That meant she'd survived.

I rose. "Where is she? I should go to her. What happened? Why would anyone wish to hurt a nun? They're respected, their habit would surely be protection enough." But even as I said the words I remembered that this nun had put aside her habit in order to serve in the military hospitals.

"Was she interfered with?" I asked, wondering if rape had been the motive. She certainly hadn't been dressed well enough to be taken for someone worth robbing. Her clothes were neat and serviceable, and she wore them with the air of a Frenchwoman, making the simplest clothing seem a little more elegant than it might have done on anyone else. Even so, there was nothing about her to draw attention.

Captain Barkley was shaking his head. "I don't know many details."

I remembered: she was going to see the Breton café owner's son. Was it he?

He went on, pacing before me. "The police are searching for someone. They've got barricades set up across Paris. Whoever he is, they're intent on finding him."

"So that's why people are being stopped and asked to identify themselves," I said. "Major Vernon got caught up in it. He told me about it."

"Yes, I've had a devil of a time myself," the Captain responded ruefully. "I'd have been here two hours ago."

"But how did you discover the search had to do with Marie-Luc?"

"I'm tasked with finding peo— deserters, remember? I thought it might have some connection with my own work. At any rate, I asked to see a senior officer. He told me what he knew."

"I must go to the hospital to see her. Someone should be there with her."

"Not tonight. It wouldn't be advisable. Besides, she'll have had surgery and won't be awake."

I'd been turning toward the door, but stopped at that. He was right. She wouldn't know I was there.

"Did she identify her attacker? Is that what the police have to go on?"

"They wouldn't tell me."

No, probably not, I thought. The police knew what—or who—they were looking for, and they had no need to ask anyone else for help.

"Someone heard her cry out," he went on. "By coming to her aid and getting her medical attention straightaway, whoever it was probably saved her life."

"But what was she doing there, where she was found?" Had she been coming back from visiting the Breton's son? Or was he the one who had heard her? Even possibly the one who'd attacked her? She had been so sure she could cope with him and help him.

"They wouldn't tell me that."

I sat down again. "This is terrible news. I really wish I could go to her."

"Your feelings do you justice, Bess, but she hardly knows you. Leave her to the care of the hospital staff. They'll see that she's properly looked after. You need to conserve your own strength. A long bedside vigil is the last thing you need just now."

He was right, of course. And considering how we'd parted, I had a feeling Marie-Luc might not be happy to see me.

"Could she tell the police anything that was helpful?" Was what I knew important?

"If she did, they didn't tell me. It's a civilian matter, after all. Once I'd discovered that it wasn't related to a deserter, I had no authority to ask questions."

"It might be your affair," I pointed out. "For one thing, it might have been a deserter looking for what little money he could find. If he was desperate."

Captain Barkley considered that. "Possible. But not likely," he said after a moment.

"Where was she taken? To which hospital?"

"She was carried to Casualty in one close to the Left Bank, then transferred to one just off Vendôme. A Catholic hospital. They will see to it that she's cared for."

I wondered. But I thanked him and asked if he would go with me to see her in the morning. He didn't seem very enthusiastic about that.

"You should put all your energies toward recovery. You're needed at the Front, Bess. All your skills."

"I don't think a visit to a patient just out of surgery will cause a setback. But perhaps you're right. Perhaps I should wait and see how I feel in the morning."

"I'm sorry to upset you over this, but I thought you would wish to know."

"Yes, of course. Thank you. It was considerate of you."

He left soon afterward.

I debated asking Major Vernon to escort me to the hospital, but if the barricades were still up, the police still questioning everyone, it might take hours to get there, and might result only in our being turned away. Tomorrow, then. I could go on my own.

I found the hospital with some difficulty. It was not a large facility, and indeed, I saw that for the most part, the patients were elderly nuns, older women, and a number of charity cases. The corridors were quiet, and the sisters walked down them with a *swish* of long skirts, their shoes making hardly any sound on the stone flooring. They nodded to me beneath the wide white sails of their head-dresses but didn't speak. Eventually I found the ward where Sister

Marie-Luc had been taken, and went down the row, looking for her bed.

I hardly recognized her. Without her woolen cap, her hair was short and a dark brown. Her face was too thin, her eyes too large. She stared up at me, and for a moment I thought she was too feverish to know me because there was no recognition in her gaze.

I stepped between the beds and smiled down at her. I could see now that she had been given something for the pain and was barely aware of her surroundings.

It would be unfair to bring her back to feeling pain. I was about to turn away, thinking I could come again, perhaps in the afternoon, when her gaze sharpened.

"Sis—" Her voice was a croak, barely intelligible. Clearing her throat, she said in a tentative tone, "Sister Crawford?"

"Yes, I've come to see how you are, if there is anything I might do for you. Captain Barkley told me where to find you."

"Did he? How kind." She seemed to lapse into a drifting sleep once more, but I stayed where I was. After a time she said, "It hurts." Her eyes opened again, and there was pain and anger in them now. "He did this to me."

"The Breton's son?" I asked. "Was it Jerome, Marie-Luc?"

She had drifted away again, and this time she didn't come back, her breathing deep and steady.

Jerome was shell-shocked. But somehow I didn't want to think of him stabbing her. As a rule, a man who suffered from shell shock was more likely to harm himself than those around him, unless he was so deep into nightmare that he couldn't distinguish family or friends from the figures that lived in his head.

But there were exceptions. There were always exceptions.

I stayed for a few minutes longer and then went to find the Sister in charge of the ward.

"You are a friend?" she asked, peering at me over her glasses. It was hard to judge her age, but the soft skin of her face told me she was at least sixty. Her brown eyes looked twenty years younger.

"Yes. I have only just heard what happened to her. How is she progressing?"

"The knife, it was not clean. We fear for infection. It struck her in the ribs just below the left breast, and then slipped on the cartilage, or perhaps she twisted away at that moment, for it cut a long gash down to her right side. There was loss of blood, but no organs touched. Only the muscles in the chest wall. We have done what we could. She will live. Barring, of course, infection. There will be a very bad scar. But she will be the only one to see it."

"I'm very glad to hear it."

"The wound could have been far worse, *vous comprenez*. It was intended to kill."

"I'm told someone found her in time?"

"As to that, there is nothing I can tell you. The police have not confided such information to us."

I thanked her, walked back down the long corridor to the stairs, and followed them to the ground floor.

Hesitating outside the hospital doors, I watched the traffic pass by for a moment and then made up my mind. Finding a taxi, I went back to the restaurant owned by the Breton family.

It was closed.

A neighbor, leaning out a window in the upper story of the house next door, called down to me. "There is illness in the family. They will not open today."

"Is it their son? Do you know? Is it he who is ill?"

"The police came, and they closed at once. I tried to hear, but *alors,* my ears are not very good anymore." She shrugged ruefully.

"Do you know where they live?"

"But of course, above the shop. Like me. That is my dressmaker shop below. But it is Sunday, I am not open."

I had lost track of the days.

"Does their son—Jerome—live with them?"

"*Non.* He has a small atelier, a studio, in the next street. Or is it two streets over? He was a painter, before the war. He stretched his own canvas, made his own frames. I liked his work. But the critics, they say he lacks a sense of light, but what do they know, the critics. They do not paint, do they?" Her voice was contemptuous.

I thanked her and was about to walk on when she added, "He has changed, Jerome. I have not seen him since he was sent home with bad headaches. He does not come to the café. But his mother cries sometimes at night, and I hear her. *C'est très triste*."

It *was* sad.

I asked again, "You don't know where to find Jerome? Where he lives?"

"*Non. Je regrette.*"

I smiled and walked on.

Why had the police come for the Breton couple? I still didn't know their names. I turned and went back to the restaurant. And there, in a corner of the glass window, was what I was looking for: AUGUSTE KARADEG, PROPRIETOR.

My side was hurting, but I took a taxi back to the Catholic hospital—it was called St. Anne's—and asked once more to see Sister Marie-Luc.

I was told she was still sleeping.

It was time to go to Belle-Île and rest. I was walking out the door when a voice called, "Sister?"

I turned to find a French policeman standing in the hospital doorway.

"Yes?"

"May I have a moment of your time?" His English was surprisingly good.

"Yes, of course."

He waited for me to join him, and then led the way to a narrow office just beyond Reception. He was fairly tall, dark hair flecked with gray, and his eyes were as blue as the sky. I could see at once why he had returned to serve with the police—his left sleeve was pinned to his chest.

"You have come twice to visit Sister Marie-Luc, the nun hurt in the street last evening?"

"I met her a few days ago, quite by accident. But as we're both nurses, I think we liked each other. We had lunch just yesterday." I was hoping by being so open that he would reciprocate.

"Yes, at the restaurant owned by Monsieur Karadeg. Madame Karadeg has confirmed this."

"I went there this morning. I'd wondered if they knew Sister Marie-Luc had been hurt. I found it closed."

I tried to make my expression questioning. Encouraging him to talk to me. But he was too professional to be drawn out.

"We are searching for their son. Jerome Karadeg. He was seen with her shortly before the attack. There is a witness. We are looking for more."

But no one saw the actual stabbing? I wanted to ask. It sounded that way.

"Is that who you were searching for last night? Several of the ambulatory patients at Belle-Île were caught up in your sweep. They didn't know why."

"For young Jerome Karadeg?" He was surprised. "I doubt it. He is dangerous, yes, but the police were very busy last evening. Crime does not wait for the war to end, Mademoiselle."

British police had told me much the same thing.

"One of them, a Canadian officer, has told me the search was for the person who had stabbed a nun."

He frowned. "Indeed."

I suddenly had the feeling I should extricate myself from this conversation as quickly as I could.

"Or am I wrong?" I tried to look flustered. "Was he the one who told me my friend was in the hospital?" I shook my head. "I'm recovering from a wound, and some of the medications I'm given confuse me."

His expression changed to one of concern. "Should I escort you back to hospital? It would be a pleasure."

"Yes, if you please. I'm rather light-headed. I expect it's from not eating properly with the sedatives. But I have had so little appetite."

Diana knows how to flirt and usually has any man wrapped around her little finger in a matter of a few minutes of conversation. I should have taken lessons. The best I could do was to plead frailty. But at least I'd distracted the police from Captain Barkley and his connection with the nun. Or our search for Philippe Moreau.

He helped me to find a taxi, gave the driver instructions, and took my hand before closing the door after me.

"*Au revoir,* Mademoiselle. You must not expend so much of your own strength to visit your friend. She will wish you to take every care of yourself first."

And with the closing of the door, my avenue to Marie-Luc was firmly shut off.

I let the driver take me back to Belle-Île, and he solicitously held my arm all the way to the door. I thanked him and went inside, leaning against the door after closing it behind me.

I couldn't find Jerome Karadeg, I couldn't find Philippe Moreau, and I couldn't visit the only person who was connected in some fashion with both men.

What was I to do now?

I could hear footsteps as the orderly came down the passage to return to his duty at the desk.

I straightened and went sedately up the stairs, in spite of my frustration.

CHAPTER EIGHT

I COULDN'T QUITE understand why I'd had that sudden sense of trouble if I continued asking the policeman questions. But I'd learned long ago to listen to my instincts. Whatever he was after, I had no business getting myself involved in his inquiry, and I had nearly done just that.

He was clearly investigating the stabbing of a nun. That much I understood. Which meant, with information in hand, that he was looking for Jerome Karadeg. I should leave that matter alone and go on with my own concerns.

But the key to that was finding out more from Marie-Luc about Lieutenant Moreau.

And so I was involved, like it or not, with the attack on her.

Sighing, I listened to the crackling of the fire, watching the heart of it burn red and orange.

Where had the elder Karadeg and his wife gone? Were they at a police station somewhere in Paris, trying to convince the gendarmes that their son wouldn't have hurt anyone? Or were they out searching, to find him and persuade him to give himself up? I wouldn't put it past them to try to spirit him away to Brittany before he was caught.

There was no Front grapevine here. The friends my parents had known in the past had moved to Nice and Provence, out of reach of the German advance. Simon was in England.

And then Madame Ezay came in with a cup of tea, and I thought, *Why not?*

She set the small tray on the table at my elbow, and observing me closely, she said, "You are too pale. You should not go out so much. Matron has said she is worried about you."

"I have a friend in hospital. She was badly hurt by someone, and the police are hoping she will be able to speak to them soon. The sad thing is, whoever attacked her could well be a man she knows—whose parents are her friends. I've tried to visit her, but she was in surgery to close the wounds, and still sedated when I came to see her. The nuns must wake her up very soon, or she will contract pneumonia. I very badly want to go back tonight. When the police have left. Will you help me?"

She was astonished that I should ask her to do this. And I thought surely she was going to refuse.

"But yes, I will do this. A friend, you say? A nun? It is too bad that someone would even think of harming her. I will do what I can."

Surprised in my turn, I said, "I don't want to cause trouble for anyone. But I could wait in a taxi, outside the hospital, while you go in, and if there are no policemen with her, if she's awake, it just might be possible for me to speak to her."

I'd concocted this plan on the spur of the moment, and I wasn't sure she would be happy about it. But Madame Ezay had the heart of a conspirator, and I think if I'd asked her to help me run away with my lover, she would have done it.

And so it was that after my dinner I slipped down the stairs while the orderly was eating his, and outside I found Madame with a taxi waiting.

"I have told Matron I am visiting my cousin. She did not object," she said to me in a whisper, and then I gave the patient driver the direction of the hospital.

It was quite dark now, and I sat well back in the taxi when we came down the seemingly darker street. I had removed my cap, because it would gleam too brightly in the shadows, and buttoned up my coat to cover my uniform.

"There's the hospital," I said to the driver as it loomed ahead of us. There was an almost Gothic look to it, and the dark shades, put up to shield the light in each room, gave it a blind air.

"I don't know this place," Madame said, and I wondered if she was about to refuse to go inside.

"It serves the poor," I told her. "You'll see."

She nodded, and after the briefest hesitation got out and crossed the street to the door.

"We will wait," I said quietly to the driver as a rectangle of light spilled out into the street, held her silhouette for a moment, and then vanished as the door was shut.

I tried to follow her in my mind. Up the steps, down the passage, into the ward, between the rows of cots, stopping at the right one.

It shouldn't take long, I thought. *Surely not.*

But I heard a church bell strike the quarter hour, and still she hadn't come out.

I was very uneasy now. The police would stop her—question her—and she wouldn't dare to lie to them.

And then the door opened again as someone hurried out and came toward the taxi.

Madame Ezay said breathlessly, "She is awake. The police have gone. But you must hurry. The Mother Superior will be making her rounds soon."

I thanked her, made my way as quickly as I could across the quiet street, and went through the door in my turn.

But there was a nun in Reception, come to collect the visitors' book. I smiled at her, nodded, and went on, as if by right.

She turned and I heard a door open and close somewhere behind me.

It seemed to take far too long to reach the ward. I opened the door, the familiar smells of disinfectant, illness, and soap greeting me as I stepped inside and shut it softly.

Walking down the aisle between patients, some of whom moaned in their sleep, others snoring, was familiar as well, except that these were all women, mostly surgical cases—gallbladder, appendix, tumors—the list was long. Not soldiers with their limbs missing or their faces swathed in bandages or their abdomens a mound under the sheets and blankets. I walked as quietly as I could until I came to the cot where Marie-Luc lay. Her eyes were open, dark in her pale face, and her fingers fidgeted with the coverlet over her.

"Hallo," I said quietly, smiling. "I expect you've had a very difficult time. Have the police been too bothersome?"

"They have been kind. But they don't believe me." She looked away, her eyes seeing something besides her neighbor, a white-haired woman of perhaps sixty-five, asleep with her mouth open, breathing loudly. The sound covered our whispers.

"Did you tell them—could you tell them who wounded you so badly?"

"I said, it was a stranger. I don't know who he was, but they asked about Jerome. Over and over again. They said he was seen with me just before it happened. But he wasn't with me. We had argued. He left. I was willing to swear to it. But they shook their heads. There is a witness."

"Perhaps Jerome did leave, and then decided to come back."

She shook her head restlessly. "He wouldn't harm me. I didn't see who it was. It was dark, just there, and he came at me. The knife was sharp. I felt it pull at my coat, and then it was through the cloth, into my body. I tried to fight. It was useless, he was too strong. Someone screamed. I think it was me. Or this witness. Possibly both of us. I don't know. And as quickly he was gone. I could feel the blood. And only then the pain."

Grimacing, she looked up at me. "It was terrible. I know now how brave my patients are. They don't scream, most of them. They are too quiet. I have never hurt so badly."

"What do the doctors say?"

"That it will heal. The cut. But there will be an ugly scar. They had to clean out the wound first. And then they sewed it carefully. But it will be there for me to see. Always there." Her voice was bitter.

"Are you protecting Jerome?" I asked.

She closed her eyes. "Sometimes it's better not to know. You understand?"

Which told me that she was afraid she did know.

"They will search for him. His parents must be out looking for him as well. If you know something that would make a difference, you must tell the police. Before it's too late."

There was fear in her voice as she answered me. "It wasn't *Jerome*. But they won't listen. And I can't explain."

She was tiring quickly now. I said, smoothing the sheet over her shoulders, "It's all right. You have done your best. I will try to come and see you again."

She closed her eyes. "No. It's best that you don't. I'd rather be left alone."

After a moment I turned and walked back the way I'd come.

Was she afraid it *was* Jerome? That he'd turned on her? What she said came back to me when it was too late to return to the ward.

I can't explain . . .

What couldn't she explain? The fact that he was too shell-shocked to know he'd attacked her? That in the dark, he'd seen one of his monsters and tried to kill it?

I could feel a mantle of sadness settling across my shoulders.

And I wasn't quite sure why.

We managed to return to Belle-Île undetected, Madame Ezay and I. As I paid the taxi driver, giving him a generous *pourboire* for his willingness to wait at the hospital, she went ahead of me, opened the clinic's outer door, peered inside, and beckoned to me. No one was about.

She was quiet as we walked up the stairs to our rooms. Someone had brought me hot water and fresh towels, and after making certain that I was well taken care of, Madame Ezay went off to her own quarters.

There was blood on my bandages when I got ready for bed. I scolded myself and promised I'd do better tomorrow.

Still, Marie-Luc was very much on my mind as I fell asleep.

It was nearly two o'clock in the afternoon when one of the staff came for me.

I had just finished reading to the wounded, and listened to their critique of the chapters we'd covered.

It was Captain Barkley who was waiting for me in the small lounge that had been a sitting room for the French family who still owned this house.

As I went in and closed the door behind me, he said, "Bess. I have some news of Marie-Luc. She's recovering in hospital, after surgery to deal with the knife wound. While the wound wasn't life threatening, it was extensive, I'm told, and because of blood loss, sutures were needed to close it, and hopefully to keep out infection."

I knew most of this, but I thanked him soberly for telling me about her condition.

"And have the police found her attacker?"

He stirred, as if he'd hoped I wouldn't ask that question.

"They've closed the case."

"What? They've arrested—they've arrested someone?" I had almost used Jerome Karadeg's name.

"In a manner of speaking." He looked out the window toward the street. "There was a young sergeant, son of friends. She'd known him for some time. The witness believed he must have attacked her. Marie-Luc refused to believe it, and the police have been searching for him. He turned up this morning."

"Have they told Marie-Luc?" I asked. "She will want to know. She has surely been waiting to hear. They will need her to identify him, when she's a little stronger."

The Captain took a deep breath. "She won't have to identify him."

Then Jerome had confessed. Was he even able to remember what had happened? Could he have realized that he had attacked the nun by mistake? Or perhaps she had got it all wrong, and he was indeed angry enough to kill, and now wanted to make amends.

"A sad business," I said, knowing she would be deeply hurt by the news. "Do the police believe him, then?"

There was something in his face that told me the answer to that before Captain Barkley could find the words.

"He's dead, isn't he?" I asked suddenly.

"His body was pulled from the Seine near dawn this morning. I just heard. Jerome Karadeg. That's his name. He's from Brittany. His parents own a small restaurant not far from Notre-Dame. I didn't want you to learn about this from idle gossip."

"Gentle God," I said, trying to take it all in. "How awful for them. How awful for her." The fear had always been that Jerome would take his own life. If he had realized . . . if he believed he had harmed Marie-Luc, he could have been driven to his death by self-loathing. "Oh, how horrible. How sad. Suicide always is."

"Well. As to suicide, the police aren't quite sure about that," he told me reluctantly.

For one terrible moment I thought perhaps that the elder Karadeg, Jerome's father, might have taken matters into his own hands. Might have preferred to see his son dead than in police custody. And then I realized that it wouldn't be possible. He'd have saved his son, gotten him out of Paris. Surely he would have?

Captain Barkley walked to the window and looked out at the street scene beyond. And then he said over his shoulder, "I'll take you to see her, if you like. She might be grateful for your presence."

Astonished that he would offer, I said, "I have only to collect my coat."

* * *

When we arrived at the hospital and were shown to the women's ward, I was told that the police had asked that Marie-Luc be moved to a private room for the time being. The staff was waiting for one to be cleaned.

A small kindness, I thought. She would have taken this hard. First the attack, then Jerome's death. It was all too much, surely, even for a well person to take in stride.

She lay with her face turned toward the far end of the ward, staring at nothing.

She didn't turn when I spoke.

I said, "Marie-Luc, I am so sorry."

She looked at me then. "Was it your doing? Did you tell the police, and they hounded him to his death?"

"No," I told her quietly. "I haven't spoken to the police. I only just heard. Is there anything I can do? For you or for the Karadegs?"

"No. He is dead, and that is all there is to it now. I'd rather be left alone, please."

I said, "On the other hand, if it wasn't Jerome who attacked you, then there is still work to be done."

"It won't bring him back."

"It will keep you safe."

I don't think in that moment she really cared. Jerome was a suicide. And his parents would be devastated, might even blame her. It was too much to take in, on top of her surgery.

I looked up at Captain Barkley. He wasn't happy about what I was asking, but he knew what I wanted.

With a brief word to Marie-Luc, he left the ward, left us alone.

I pulled up one of the chairs and sat down beside her bed.

For a while we said nothing. I don't think she wished to talk to me. But I could be patient.

Finally she turned to me and said, "I tried to tell the police. They wouldn't listen. Who is this witness? Who made them believe it was

Jerome?" Her eyes were incredibly sad. "I would not have hurt him for the world. I knew him when he was just a boy. He was a brave soldier. He didn't deserve to die a *suicide*." Her voice was hardly a whisper. "He would never hurt me."

"The police aren't sure—" I began. "I don't know why, but there is some question about what happened."

She stared at me. "What are you saying? That they don't believe Jerome hurt me? It's too late for them to apologize now. He's gone."

"I don't know. But I don't think it's that. It's the suicide. That's only what Captain Barkley told me. That they aren't completely satisfied, somehow."

Her gaze sharpened. "I must speak to his parents."

"They are dealing with the death of their son. I can't ask them to come here. I don't know where they are. The restaurant is closed. But if you wish to write a letter, I'll see that it's posted."

"Then I must be there, when he's buried. It will be in Brittany. They will take him home."

"You can't travel to Brittany. You aren't ready for such a journey. Even across Paris."

She intended to argue. And thought better of it.

"Then take me to Petite-Beauvais. It is a shorter distance than Brittany."

Completely confused now, I said, "I don't understand."

"I want to go there. My old governess left the house to me."

"For comfort? I don't think the hospital will allow even that. You know how much blood you have lost. How the tissue and muscles in your chest were slashed. It's too soon, believe me." I had only to look at her face to see that she didn't have the strength to walk as far as the hospital door. "If there is something in the house that you need or want, I'll try to go in your place and bring it back to you."

She considered me. "By the time I am discharged, it will be too late. But I must find a way to prove that Jerome isn't a murderer. You have to understand that. For his sake and that of his parents. I owe him that."

"Captain Barkley will take me. You have met him. You know he can be trusted. If it will give you peace."

I was beginning to see the steel in her soul. I'd glimpsed it when she sent me away there on the Left Bank, near the restaurant owned by the Karadegs. I could now understand why she had left her convent and gone out on her own to serve wounded and dying men after nuns were withdrawn from military hospitals. It would be impossible for her to do anything else, given her own character.

There was some reason why she was refusing me. It was present in her eyes, it was present in the way she held her shoulders. A physical resistance. Had she been arguing with Jerome when the witness saw them together? And now, because of that, because the police had been hunting him and he had had nowhere else to go but the river, she couldn't bear the guilt. And there was also the fact that she had used the excuse of going to see him to leave me outside the restaurant. She had used him. And he was dead. It was even possible she felt I should have a share in that guilt.

"I'm so sorry," I said. "I must go. I've kept Captain Barkley waiting much too long. But please, if you change your mind, you have only to ask."

"Thank you. There is an obligation, you see. I must do something about it." She leaned her head back against her pillows, exhausted.

Captain Barkley was standing by the waiting taxi, and he started forward at once as I came out the door of the hospital.

"What was so secretive that I couldn't be present?" he asked.

"I don't know that it was secrets I was after, or some feeling for what had become of Jerome. I didn't think she would talk as freely with you there. We are both women, and both nurses. That counts for much, since we can't really call ourselves friends." I held up a hand as he started to interrupt me. "She was upset over Jerome Karadeg's death. He died a suicide, and she feels she's to blame for that because he was accused of nearly murdering her and there was nowhere to turn. She's a nun, this weighs on her. And she wants to attend his funeral service. She's just not up to it, Captain. I tried to make her see that it was foolish even to consider traveling to Brittany."

He was taking my arm, guiding me across the street to the taxi. "She's a strange woman," he said. "I'll admit I don't know how to read her." As he opened the door of the taxi for me, he added, "It's not her fault, you know. Shell shock is the very devil to deal with. I've seen it at the Front, firsthand."

We were close to Belle-Île when he said, "I must ask. This Frenchman you've been searching for. Have you learned anything more about him?"

I remembered what Marie-Luc had called him. A monster.

Yet French Army records didn't show a Lieutenant by the name of Philippe Moreau. It was a common enough surname. *Who was this man?*

An image came back to me.

Bending over a shivering officer on a stretcher, reaching for his pocket as I examined the remnants of his uniform for a name. Instead, I found where a name patch appeared to have been ripped out of the pocket.

I'd wondered from that night in Base Hospital Three if this man had actually been German, masquerading as a Frenchman.

Marie-Luc had served in Belgian hospitals, nursing men who had been in the forefront of the fighting in 1914, who had watched their country come under German control.

The driver could hear my answer. If he understood English.

I said, "Would you care for a cup of coffee, bad as it might be, when we reach Belle-Île?" I longed for a cup of tea, but this was France.

The Captain started to speak, glanced at the driver, and smiled. "Yes, I'd like that, Bess."

We got down at the gates to the courtyard, and Captain Barkley turned to pay the driver. He waited until the taxi had driven away, then said, "There's a little café not far from here. Maybe that's best."

We walked the distance in silence. My side was aching as we sat down, and I waited until the coffee had arrived before speaking.

And then I said, "This man—it's wise not to give him a name in such a public place—may well be many things, none of them wrong. On the other hand, he could be someone dangerous, and neither the French Army nor the French authorities know where to find him. He could be a spy, a saboteur, using a false name. Or he could have escaped from the Germans and not yet found a way to cope with what he's suffered."

The Captain sat there, stirring his coffee, listening.

I took a deep breath. "My father would have found some of the circumstances of his rescue rather suspicious. He would have made it a point to learn just who this stranger was. Matron, in Base Hospital Three, didn't feel he was a threat. She was tired, overworked, and unwilling to take time from her other patients to look into this man's past. And yet when he was sent on to Rouen, such questions about his history didn't go with him. Rouen in turn allowed him to finish his convalescence in Paris. But why hasn't he sent word to the Army that he's alive and safe? And why don't they have a record of him?"

I was prepared for Captain Barkley to make light of what I'd just told him. When he didn't, I realized then that he had his own reasons for being interested. But he was a Canadian officer, not French. He could have turned his own suspicions over to someone here in Paris, and forgot Lieutenant Moreau.

Why hadn't he?

All this was going through my head, and when there was silence across the table from me, I knew my sense that there was something more to this business must have been right.

He was still toying with his coffee spoon, drawing little diagrams on the tabletop with the tip of the bowl. Thinking. When he spoke, I wondered if he'd been taking that time to choose his words.

"I've heard my French colleagues talk. Sometimes they seem to forget I'm there. They feel rather strongly that there was someone who was guiding or at least reporting on the shells that the Paris Gun was sending into parts of the city. He could very well have lain low for a time after it stopped firing, and then tried to make his way back to his own lines before he was found out and shot for spying. He could very well have been from the Alsace region, with a command of German and of French, so that he could pass as either. The thing is, no one *knows*. Paris has had its own spy fever—there was even Mata Hari, for God's sake. This one could be real or it could be hysteria."

"What do you think?"

He sighed. "There's not enough evidence either way to go to the authorities about Moreau, is there? Supposition, a handful of facts. My instincts tell me this should be left to the French. If he's here, they'll find him."

But would they? Would they even have a place to begin looking if they didn't know what we knew?

I was tired, in pain, and I recognized the fact that he was right. We mustn't throw Philippe Moreau to the hounds if there was even a chance that he was innocent. And yet—and yet.

He paid the waiter and we left, finding a taxi to take us to the Hôtel de Belle-Île. I was grateful, not wanting to walk.

We were just pulling up at the entrance to the hotel when I saw something white in the lengthening shadows by the door. All at once I realized that it was the sail-like cap of one of the nuns from the hospital.

Captain Barkley handed me down from the taxi, and I hurried toward her.

"Are you looking for me? My name is Crawford. Sister Crawford."

The nun smiled at me. "I had just been told you weren't in. Sister

Marie-Luc's fever has risen alarmingly. I think there's something on her mind. When I asked her how I could help, she begged me to find you, telling me that she had been wrong to send you away. Mother Superior felt that Marie-Luc will rest more easily if you come back and put her mind at rest."

I was surprised that a nun had been sent to tell me this. But I turned at once to Captain Barkley. "I must go back to the hospital."

He hailed the taxi in time to prevent it from driving on, and we got back inside, the nun sitting by me as Captain Barkley got in beside the driver.

When we reached the hospital, I discovered that Marie-Luc's fever had soared shortly after I'd left. Before she'd been moved to the private room. She stirred restlessly on her cot now, as if in pain, her face flushed and shivers racking her body.

"We've put a poultice on the part of the incision that is the possible source of infection. And we've cleaned it with antiseptic powder. Still, I fear the infection is spreading too quickly. We have sent for the doctor," the nun in charge of the case told me. "Quite frankly, I'm worried."

I went forward to the bedside, sniffing a little for any sign of the smell of infection, but there was none.

"Sister Marie-Luc? It's Bess Crawford. You wanted to see me?"

She didn't seem to hear me. I went on talking to her for a time, and finally she opened fever-bright eyes and stared up at me.

"Sister Crawford?"

Her eyes were narrowed, as if they were bothered by the light of the lamp on the table, but it wasn't very bright at all.

"Yes, I'm here."

"I was wrong. I'm so sorry. You must do something for me. I'm not going to live, and what I know will die with me."

"I'm told the doctors believe you'll recover. That they have caught the infection in time." I wasn't sure of that, but I'd known cases where patients were so certain that they wouldn't live that they died anyway. And there were cases where a patient had no hope at all, and somehow managed to live. State of mind was as much a part of treating patients as the medical care they were given.

"All the same, I can't be sure. Sister Claire could be wrong. My things. In the basket by the window."

Her clothing had been cleaned and mended and hung in what passed for a closet, a narrow alcove with a curtain that could be drawn across the opening. Her rosary and her ring and her shoes were in the basket I could see from where I stood.

"Keys. Do you see them?"

She was agitated now, pushing herself against the next round of fever.

Crossing to the basket, I looked inside. In the bottom was a small brass ring with several keys on it. I picked it up and brought it to her.

She fumbled with the keys, finally picking out one that was rather old-fashioned. "Here. The key to the house of my old governess. Go there. Bring me back a black lacquer box. Japanese. A gift to her. I don't know where she kept it. I didn't look for it after she died. I thought—it was safer where it was. Please. Go now."

I said, "I don't know if Captain Barkley can borrow a motorcar, but we'll find a way."

"He must," she said, her hands grasping my own so hard that it hurt my fingers. "It's my fault that Jerome is dead. I didn't tell the whole truth, and this is my punishment. Don't you see? Please! Help me."

"What truth? What should I be looking for?" I asked.

"No. Bring back the box. I beg of you. I must see to this myself. If I am dead, you must take it to the Karadegs. No one else."

She had been determined to go back to Petite-Beauvais on her own, but she was too weak. And somehow, as she grew more and more agitated in her frustration, her fever rising with her state of mind, she blamed herself for what had happened.

Across the bed, the nun in charge looked up at me, waiting for me to agree. I could read the urgency in her eyes.

"Yes, all right, I'll see what I can do," I said hastily.

"Bless you, bless you." Marie-Luc lay back against her pillows, exhausted now.

I stayed a few minutes longer, but she said nothing more, lapsing into that semiconscious state of the very ill. I turned and walked out.

Sister Claire, who was in charge of her care, followed me out of the room, shutting the door softly behind us.

"There is something on her mind, it won't allow her to rest. I have asked if she wishes to see a priest, but she only shakes her head." She bit her lip. "I hope I am not betraying a trust by telling you this. One of the other ward patients had a visitor shortly after you'd left. Her son, given compassionate leave. But his voice frightened Marie-Luc, and she became very upset, until one of the Sisters brought him over to her. She claimed he wasn't the same person as the owner of the voice, and I thought she was going to climb out of her bed to look around the ward. But he was the only visitor. He was very concerned for his mother, and this was too much for him. He was only nineteen, and he broke down when Marie-Luc called him a traitor and warned us that he was going to kill all of us. It was a very bad moment, you must see that. I was very grateful that this room was ready so quickly." She paused. "What is she afraid of, do you know? Or perhaps I should ask, *who*?"

"It's rather tangled," I answered. "The police believed the person who attacked her was the son of friends of hers, a young man she's known for ages and is—was—trying to help. She's adamant that he didn't attack her. The police were searching for him, and found him in the river. I think she blames herself." I was about to add that I was beginning to think she knew who attacked her, that this was part of her sense of guilt, when I remembered the policeman who had questioned me. The less I appeared to know just now, the better.

"Yes, when one is ill, and feverish, the mind plays tricks. Poor woman. I will keep an eye on her. As for this box she wants so desperately, it will worry her less when she is well enough to find it for herself."

"Yes, Sister, thank you."

She had a kind face, soft and caring, but she was also competent and well trained. I would have liked to help bring down Marie-Luc's fever, to be sure she would be all right, but it wasn't my ward, she wasn't my patient. And so with a nod, I left.

"Can you borrow that motorcar again?" I asked Captain Barkley as I rejoined him. "I've promised to go back to the village for Marie-Luc, and I don't think she'll rest quietly until I do. Her fever is high, they're treating her for infection, just as we were told, but I think it goes much deeper than that."

"A motorcar? At this hour?" He glanced at the sky. It would be dark in another quarter of an hour. "Do you think this is really important enough to try to do tonight?"

"I do." I longed for my own bed. I was tired, and my side hurt madly from all my exertions. The last thing I needed was a drive into the countryside. "I hesitate to go by taxi. We have no idea how long this search will take. Marie-Luc says she doesn't know where the box she wants might be hidden. But surely it shouldn't be too difficult to find—the cottage isn't large, and she really didn't look for it."

"I'll take you back to the clinic, then see what I can do." He looked closely at me. "You're tired, Bess. Are you sure you ought to do this? There's tomorrow."

"I'm rather curious about this box. I'd like to find it." I could feel the key in my pocket, under the handkerchief I kept there.

He took a deep breath. "I'll do what I can."

Poor man, I thought as he helped me into a taxi. I also didn't trust him. He might be as eager to find this box himself, to see what it contained.

Chapter Nine

An hour later the Captain called for me at the clinic, and with pillows and cushions to protect my side, we set out. If it was dark in Paris, it was even darker in the countryside.

The headlamps of the motorcar were dimmed as well, and although traffic was light, the road was not well defined, and we seemed to go at a pace that was just short of creeping along. Captain Barkley swore under his breath several times as we hit a puddle of water that concealed a very deep hole, and I feared for the axle.

It was going on nine o'clock when we found the first turning, and we wove our way through dark villages where unseen dogs barked at our passage, and an occasional curtain twitched or door opened to see what was afoot. Having lived in the shadow of invasion for so long, the inhabitants of these villages were wary.

Captain Barkley paused as we reached the outskirts of Petite-Beauvais.

"We can't just drive up to the cottage and unlock the door. Should we at least speak to the priest and tell him what we're about?"

A good question.

"I'm not sure how much we should tell him."

He said, "She's in hospital after a surgery, and there's something from the cottage that she would like to have."

I was dubious, but it was better than being taken up for house-breaking.

"Yes, all right."

He drove on to the rectory, and we found Father Robert just bringing in wood for the morning fires. He stopped, lowered the barrow he'd been pushing, and watched us approach. His face cleared when I called to him, and dusting his hands together, he came forward to greet his guests.

"What brings you back to us?" There was wariness and welcome in his voice.

"An errand of mercy," I said as we followed him into the house. "You must know Sister Marie-Luc. She was here recently. The woman who looked after her when she was a child lived here in the village, until her death a few days ago."

He had ushered us into the sitting room and was about to turn up the lamp when he looked across at us.

"Yes?"

It was a rather odd response, but I soldiered on.

"Sister Marie-Luc has been in hospital and she asked that we come here and look for a keepsake that would be of comfort to her. And we agreed. Her fever has risen dangerously. We are hoping this might help, a little."

"This is a surprise. She was quite well while caring for her governess. Not the dread influenza?" There was concern in his voice now.

"Unexpected surgery," I said, "with signs of infection taking hold. The nun in charge of her ward is worried."

"I'll pray for her tonight. Meanwhile, I'd be happy to take you to the cottage, but I'm afraid I don't have a key. And I hesitate to break down the door." He didn't add that he wasn't quite sure about us or our story, but it was there in his face: an uncertainty and unease.

I smiled. "She has given me her key. It won't take long. We must return to Paris tonight."

In the distance the familiar thunder of the guns resumed. It had been quiet as we drove north.

Father Robert raised his voice slightly, although it wasn't necessary. I thought it was habit, years of listening to the sounds of war and unconsciously trying to drown them out. "Fräulein Theissen was a very private person. I don't think she would care to have you going through her house."

Fräulein Theissen. One of the popular German governesses the French had employed to teach their children the language of their age-old enemy?

"I'm sure she would make an exception for the sake of her charge. I expect she left the cottage to her?"

That was a good move on Captain Barkley's part. It wouldn't have been possible to leave it to any surviving family in Germany. Not in wartime.

"Yes, I believe that's true. She was always very fond of Marie—Sister Marie-Luc. All the same—"

"I wouldn't think of putting you out," I said with a smile, cutting across his objection. "It's very kind of you to offer."

"Why didn't she take the keepsake with her when she left?" he asked then. "If it matters so much to her."

"She didn't have any inkling that she would be in hospital so soon. She had taken leave to care for Fräulein Theissen, and she intended to return to the Front as soon as possible. I expect she believed that everything was safer here under your eye, rather than dragged from post to post with her."

Defeated, Father Robert said, "Very well. But I must insist that you show me what it is you are taking away. I am responsible, you see, if anything goes missing."

"We'll be happy to do so," Captain Barkley said, offering his hand, and the priest had no choice but to accept it.

As we reversed the motorcar and turned back down the drive, he was standing by the barrow, watching us go.

"That was a near-run thing," I said when we were out of earshot.

"Yes, but what will we take back to show him? He might as well have come with us," Captain Barkley said.

"We'll find something."

We had no trouble finding the cottage the nun had come out of on that rainy day to beg us for a lift. It stood a little apart, and was well kept up. The door unlocked with ease, but the interior was dark and cold, with an odor of mustiness mixed with age and sickness.

Without a word, the Captain went back out to the motorcar and rummaged in the boot. He returned with a torch that had a low battery but was just bright enough to let me find a lamp and the match holder beside it.

The wick was trimmed and the bowl clean. It caught straight-away, and I looked around for another lamp as it brightened the room.

It was a typical cottage, with four small rooms: a parlor, a kitchen, a bedroom, and an unfinished room that had become a box room. There was no upper floor.

"It shouldn't be too difficult to find a black lacquer box," I said, for the cottage was spotless, clean, and well kept.

There was another lamp in the bedroom. The furnishings were simple enough, with a colorful quilt on the wooden bed, a chest for clothes, a chair, and an armoire. In one corner was an old wooden cradle with a peaked hood and a pretty floral design around the edges.

I wondered if the cradle might have been a gift from the mother of one of her charges, or perhaps she had brought it from Germany, a tool of her trade, so to speak.

In the other room, Captain Barkley was standing in the middle of the floor, an uncertain look on his face.

"Is everything all right?" I asked.

"Now that we're here, I am feeling some qualms about going through the fräulein's possessions. I think I'd have felt better if she hadn't been named. Anonymous and impersonal."

"You must hurry. Father Robert might well take it into his head to walk down here and see what we're about."

I turned back to the bedroom. There was a framed photograph hanging above the bed. I looked at it now. Although it was faded, I could see the man with a luxurious beard, a stern face, and sterner eyes. People of that era seldom smiled when their photograph was taken. Cousin Melinda had an album of similar faces, standing still for the photographer with unsmiling expressions as the long count before the flash began. Unlike the more modern cameras.

I began my search, carefully opening the drawers of the chest and delving into the possessions I found there. The fräulein's identity papers were in one corner, and her birthplace was given as Alsace. Her mother's name, to my surprise, had been Moreau. I put them back. There was a small case of jewelry, a ring that must have belonged to someone in the family, for it was kept in a tissue with a lock of very fair hair. Her mother's wedding ring? A string of pearls, not of the best quality but nice, with a gold clasp; a small watch to be worn with a uniform; and beneath that another photograph, this time of a younger woman I took to be the fräulein, with a very young child in a frilly white dress, still in leading strings. Was this Marie-Luc?

I pocketed it. This would serve to placate the priest.

From the chest I went to the wardrobe. It didn't take very long to search, because there were no more than half a dozen black dresses in there, with matching boots and two hats, one summer and one winter, and two purses.

I made certain there was nothing on the top of the wardrobe, and then looked in and under the bed.

If there was a lacquer box in this room, it must be invisible.

Captain Barkley was just finishing with the parlor. He straightened up from peeling back the carpet, and shook his head.

"Nothing here."

We moved on to the box room and the kitchen. In the box room

I had to move several older pieces of furniture, a crate full of dishes, and other long-forgotten items to search thoroughly. Setting aside a chair with a torn cane seat, I dislodged another box holding gardening tools. They made a racket as they fell to the floor. I was about to put them back in the box when I saw something in the bottom.

It was a packet covered in oilcloth and tied with string. I opened it, thinking it might hold the box I was after, only to discover it contained letters. I put them back where I had found them, and then on second thought, put them into my pocket as well. What if there had been no lacquer box for ages, and the contents had gone into this room with the rest of the past?

My hands and feet were cold by this time, and my side was burning like fire. I went back to the kitchen.

"No luck," the Captain said, closing the door to a cupboard.

"Is there any way into the attic, above us?"

"No, I looked." He took out his watch. "It's late. What are we to do now?"

I was about to mention the letters when the front door opened. We stood where we were, and then I walked toward the parlor.

It wasn't the priest standing there. It was a tall man with a raw scar across his face and his right arm in a sling. And he wore the uniform of a Captain.

"Who are you? What are you doing here?" he demanded.

"We're friends of Sister Marie-Luc. She's in hospital in Paris and very ill. She asked us to bring her this." I reached into my pocket and pulled out the photograph I'd found.

He crossed the room, limping heavily, and took it from me. "That's not Marie-Luc," he said.

Scrambling for something to say, I replied, "But she said there was a photograph of her as a child." Improvising, I added, "With her mother."

"That's not her mother."

"Well, how was I to know?" I snapped.

"It isn't even a female. The child. That's a boy."

It was customary to put both male and female babies in such flowing garments, although I was never quite willing to believe my father had ever had his likeness taken in ribbons and lace.

"If you know so much about the fräulein's history, tell me where to find the photograph I'm looking for."

"There never was one. I'd have known if there was."

"Then who are you?"

"Paul Moreau. They just brought me home to recover. But the house isn't open. I thought I might come here. Where is Fräulein Theissen?"

I was still trying to absorb what he was saying. It was Captain Barkley just behind me who replied.

"She died. A week ago. Father Robert can tell you."

He swore. "Then it's the rectory. You've got a motorcar. Will you run me up there? This infernal knee. I shouldn't walk that far. Not yet."

"I didn't hear a motorcar," I said, looking beyond him through the open door.

"It took me to the house. When I found it nearly uninhabitable, I had no choice. Now I must go all the way back again. I'd seen the lights on, after all."

"I understood that Paul Moreau was a Lieutenant."

"I was due for a promotion but never received it. I was listed as missing. Actually I was taken prisoner, and yesterday I was exchanged for a German officer. His father is dying. Someone in the German High Command. I was badly wounded but recovering. It wasn't likely I would be returning to my regiment. Not with this knee. It was a safe exchange. A useless soldier for an active one." His tone was bitter.

"Why do you know so much about Fräulein Theissen's affairs?" I asked.

"Look. I'm tired. Take me to the house. Whoever you are, get out. I don't know if Sister Marie-Luc sent you here or not."

"Father Robert knows why we're here," Captain Barkley said. "You might speak to him. I'm sure he'll offer you a room for the night."

Captain Moreau's mouth tightened to a thin line. "Be damned to all of you."

He turned and limped to the door, disappearing in the darkness.

"Well, well," Captain Barkley said softly.

I walked over and closed the door. "We haven't found anything resembling a lacquer box," I said. "And Marie-Luc didn't see it when she was here nursing the fräulein. I think someone else has it. Or Fräulein Theissen gave it to someone for safekeeping."

"I agree. Do we go back to Father Robert?"

"I expect we ought to." I carried the lamp I'd been using back to the bedroom, intending to set it in its place before turning down the wick and putting it out.

The light passed across the photograph of the bearded man, and I stared at it.

The only place I hadn't looked was there.

The Captain helped me move the bed aside so that I could lift the frame off the wall. And there, caught in the back, was an envelope. Not brown with age the way the paper backing of the frame was, but relatively new.

"I think we've found it. Whatever it is," I said quietly, for his ears only. "And I think we should go, quickly."

He helped me replace the frame, saw to it that it was properly leveled, and then restored the bed to its former place beneath it.

I turned down the lamp, made certain that it was safely out, and we hurried back to the parlor. Captain Barkley put out his, replaced it on the table by the window, and ushered me out the door.

We passed Captain Moreau, still struggling back the way he'd come. We slowed to ask if he wanted a lift, but he ignored us.

When we reached the rectory, there were still lamps burning downstairs. I hurried to the door and knocked, while Captain Barkley stayed with the motorcar.

Father Robert answered, staring out at us.

"It took you long enough to find what you wanted," he said.

"It took us a while to be certain what it was she wanted." I retrieved the photograph of the woman and child from my pocket. "I've taken this from the house."

He looked at it, frowning. "Why should she want that?"

"I don't know. She's feverish, I told you. Perhaps she feels it's somehow comforting."

"But it isn't—" he began, then leaned forward, staring into the darkness beyond the motorcar. "There's someone walking up the road. At this hour."

"It's Paul Moreau," I said. "He's been exchanged for a German prisoner. He said. He's been wounded, and he was brought back here to recover. But the house is closed, and Fräulein Theissen is dead. I thought he might be coming here."

"*Mon Dieu*," the priest exclaimed under his breath. Handing the photograph back to me, he shut the door as quietly as possible, and the next thing I knew, the lamp glowing from the front window was turned out, and even as I watched, the only other light, in the hall, was extinguished.

I hurried back to the motorcar.

"What happened?" Captain Barkley asked. "What did he say?"

"He was about to tell me that the photograph wasn't of Marie-Luc when he glimpsed Paul Moreau walking back to his house. He wanted to know who it was, out on the road, and I told him. That's when he closed the door and the lamps went out."

Captain Barkley was already reversing, but that done, he stayed where he was, the bonnet pointed toward the road, the headlamps off, the motor idling softly, until we could no longer see the dark shape of the Frenchman.

And then we hurried down the drive, turned toward Paris, and I think we both felt a flash of relief.

Even though neither of us could have possibly said why.

Chapter Ten

IT WAS AFTER hours at the clinic, and there was nowhere we could talk, no quiet lounge or the like. Nor were we ready to go to the hospital.

We had traveled back to Paris in silence, the sound of artillery accompanying us most of the way.

Captain Barkley found a café that was open, catering to men who worked at night. Most of them were over fifty, tired men who had done heavy labor on the roads or the Métro.

We sat in a corner in the back. Captain Barkley ordered wine for both of us, though it would be watered, and we waited until it had been brought to us before having a look at what we had taken from the Theissen cottage.

The letters, I quickly realized, had been written to the fräulein by her charges over the years. Grateful letters, for the most part, and affectionate in tone.

After I had quickly skimmed through the first four or five, Captain Barkley said, "These aren't important. The envelope."

Casting a quick glance at the men at the other tables, I took out the envelope and then said, "Perhaps we shouldn't open it. Perhaps we should just take it on to Sister Marie-Luc."

"Not on your life," the Captain said in a low, fierce voice. "I want to know what the hell this is all about."

And so I slipped my finger under the flap of the envelope and gently, carefully, opened it.

Inside were several pieces of paper.

One was the deed to the cottage. I set that to one side. Next, there was another photograph, this time of a woman in front of the Eiffel Tower, still under construction. But not the same woman. I set that aside as well. Under that was what appeared to be an official paper in German. It was written in script, and neither my companion nor I could decipher it.

"A baptismal record?" I asked. "See, that appears to be the word for 'church.'"

"I'm not sure that's what it is." He examined the sheet more closely. "I can't tell. The script is so ornate, I can hardly make out a single word, never mind decide what it might mean in English."

We set that aside as well. There was another sheet in German, and this appeared to be a letter.

After that was another photograph.

And this time I recognized the man, if not his surroundings.

"It's Philippe Moreau," I exclaimed in a whisper.

"It is, by God." He took it from me and studied it. "Taken before the war? He's not in uniform."

"Possibly. But who is he? And why did Marie-Luc's old governess have a photograph of him?"

"I expect that's what she wants. To show it to the police and tell them that it wasn't Jerome Karadeg who attacked her? It would make sense. You've said she feels guilty over what happened to him, and wants to make it right somehow."

"But I had a photograph. She could have used that."

"And who would believe her, when the man was wearing an American uniform?"

"That's true," I said slowly. "She called him a monster."

"Who? When?"

"I went to see her. I thought she might tell me whatever it was she knew about Philippe Moreau. She refused to talk about him, save to tell me he was a monster."

"What else have you got?"

"A cutting from a newspaper. French this time. Something to do with a murder." I read on. "A murder, but no one had been taken up for it. At least not by the time this was printed." I looked for a date, and found it on the reverse. "1900?"

"Makes no sense. The whole lot. I don't see anything here that will clear Jerome Karadeg's name."

"No. Perhaps not directly," I said after a moment. "But there may be something that Marie-Luc understands." I gathered the bits we'd taken out and put them carefully back into the envelope, then tried, wetting my fingers, to make it seal again. "Well. Perhaps she won't know that it was sealed to start with."

"It's too late to be allowed in the hospital."

"I don't think it is. If we tell the porter at the gate that this is in regard to Marie-Luc."

He was tired, eager to return the motorcar. And I was fighting pain with every breath I took. But I was worried about her. If she was agitated, her fever wouldn't break.

In the end he agreed. Then, as we were walking out of the café, I glanced up at his face. And it struck me suddenly that he was disappointed by what the envelope contained.

What was he expecting? Or more to the point, what was he hoping for?

The porter, sleepy and claiming that he couldn't comprehend our French, finally let us in, as much to be done with us as to be helpful.

Sister Claire was summoned. She greeted us and took us to the room we'd been in before. And she said, as we walked there, "There's little change. I hope you were successful in finding whatever it is she wanted so badly."

"I'm not sure. We tried, that's what matters."

She opened the door, and I could see for myself that there was no change. Captain Barkley waited outside while I walked up to the bed and took Sister Marie-Luc's hand.

"It's Bess Crawford," I said softly. "I've come back. There was no lacquer box, although I looked very carefully for it. But behind the framed photograph above the bed was an envelope. I hope that's what you wished me to find."

At first she didn't respond. I continued to talk to her. At one point Sister Claire spoke from behind me. "The infection hasn't spread. That's a blessing. But she's very ill."

I could feel the heat of her body as I held her hand, and her hair was clinging damply to her forehead where someone had been bathing her face with cool water.

I was about to give up when she stirred, her eyes fluttering before opening, and she looked around blankly until she was able to focus on my face.

Gripping my hand, she said, "You must tell them I can go there. You must. I need to look for myself."

I didn't think she'd understood a word I'd said to her.

"But I have gone for you. You gave me the key," I said gently. "Remember?" I put it in her hand. It was cold from the night air.

"Please, make them understand. I owe it to Jerome, it's all my fault. Please, *for the love of God, tell them.*"

I took the envelope out of my pocket and with difficulty extricated my own hand from her viselike grip and put the envelope in its place.

She felt it, lifted it, looked at it. Then she let it slide through her fingers.

"The box. I want the box. It's Japanese, you can't miss it," she begged, reaching out for me again.

I caught her hands to stop them.

"It's very late. In the morning, Marie-Luc, I promise you, in the morning."

That seemed to reach her.

"Yes, in the morning. I'll be stronger then." And then the worrying note returned to her voice. "You won't forget? Tell me you won't forget!"

"I won't. Sister Claire is here, my witness to that promise. But only if you sleep. You must be rested before we will be allowed to go."

"I understand. I'm very grateful." She lay back against the pillows, exhausted by the effort she'd made. Her next words were slurred as she drifted into sleep. "I need to rest. It's true."

I waited another quarter of an hour, knowing that Captain Barkley would be pacing the floor and wondering what was happening. And then I retrieved the envelope from the sheets, put it back in my pocket, and left the room.

Sister Claire escorted us to the door. "You do know that she won't be traveling tomorrow," she said, concern in her voice.

"It was the only way to convince her to rest," I said. "I hope she'll be more coherent tomorrow, and can see reason."

"What is in that box?" she asked me at the outer door. "What is it she wants so desperately?"

"I wish I knew," I said, remembering the sharp-eyed policeman. "I'm just trying to keep her from fretting herself to death."

"And the envelope?"

"I have no idea. But it feels like photographs. See for yourself." I gave it to her, and she held it in her hand, weighing it as she looked at it.

"Yes. The church teaches us that when we enter the convent, we leave all earthly things behind, and give our devotion to God. But when one is ill . . ." She left the sentence unfinished.

"Sister Marie-Luc has served her country," I said. "And to do that she had to leave the convent behind. It wasn't her choice, it was forced on her."

"That's true. Thank you, Sister Crawford. I hope that I'll have better news for you tomorrow."

We drove in silence back to my clinic. Then, as the Captain helped me to bundle up my pillows and cushions, he said, "Why did you lie to Sister Claire?"

"Because I'm sure the police have already questioned her about Jerome Karadeg, because they've talked to Marie-Luc, and they will question me if they believe that I know whatever it is that Marie-Luc knows. Thank you. I am so sorry to involve you in her plight, but there's nowhere else to turn."

He held the door for me, then bent to kiss my cheek before I crossed the threshold.

Upstairs in my room, I changed my bandage, then lay down on the bed for a few minutes to rest, intending to go through the envelope and the letters again.

Instead I fell fast asleep and woke up only as the fire sank to embers and I felt the night's cold drifting in.

The nursing staff wasn't best pleased that I was spending so much time out of the Hôtel de Belle-Île, and I shamelessly told Matron about Marie-Luc's condition. "I've sat with her," I said, "trying to give her the will to fight. I don't tend to her, but I do try to keep her spirits up."

That placated Matron for a while, but I knew that I ought to be more careful.

Later that morning, as the sun came out from behind the clouds, Major Anderson asked if I'd care for a leisurely walk. "We won't go far, it's just to stretch our legs a bit."

I accepted, found my coat, and we set out to stroll down the street. He gave me his arm, and we talked of the weather, several of the improving patients, and the prospect for peace.

"I heard the guns last evening," I said. "They didn't sound like an end to the war."

"No." We turned a corner. "You were out with Captain Barkley last evening. I believe he borrowed Broussard's motorcar again."

"We drove out into the country, a little."

"Only a little?"

I dropped his arm. "What is it you wish to know, Major?"

"I expect I'm a little jealous," he said ruefully.

I didn't believe a word of it. "A little curious perhaps. All right, I'll tell you. A friend is very ill in hospital. We did what we could to make her more comfortable."

"Her?"

"She's a French nurse."

"Ah." He offered me his arm again, and we walked on. After a while, he said, "Bess, whatever is worrying you, I'll help in any way I can."

"All right. Tell me about a murder here in France, some years ago. Before the war. It was never solved." I had managed to decipher the cutting, enough to be sure of my ground. "Five people found dead in a house out near the Bois. Four women, one man. Why did the police never catch the killer?"

"Good God, Bess, that isn't something I'd know very much about. How did you come to hear of it?"

"My friend's old governess kept the cutting about it."

"Did she, indeed? And somehow it's just come to your attention?"

"She's delirious, rambling. People remember odd things when in the throes of a fever."

"True."

"Then tell me about your court martial."

"It wasn't mine."

"You mentioned it to me, you must know something. Who was the man who escaped custody before he could be tried? Do you know his crime?" I smiled. "With my background, I must say I'm curious."

We were sparring with each other.

"Just that it was a capital case. I told you."

Check. And mate.

We walked in silence again for a time, turning back at the next cross street. By then I'd made up my mind.

I said, "Major. The patient I have been visiting has a connection with Petite-Beauvais. I think it might be important that I find out about this court martial. *Something* is worrying her. And the reason she's in hospital is that someone tried to kill her. The police believe they know who it is, but she's adamant that it was someone else. I want to help her, but I don't know where to begin."

"Did she see the person who attacked her?"

"I don't know. Possibly. At least she has some reason to believe she knows who it is. But she won't tell the police. I don't know why. She keeps saying she must wait until she can prove it wasn't the man the police suspect."

"Interesting. Still, I don't see how this is connected to the court martial?"

"I don't know that it is. I wouldn't even question it, if it hadn't been for the fact that the village is too small to have so many monsters living there. Her word, not mine."

"Hmmm. Which is why you wished to know about the murders that took place before the war. I hardly think the Army would deal with him, if this man is in fact guilty of them. He'd be turned over to the police. It was a civilian crime before his service in the Army. That's to say, if he isn't a career soldier. I'll see what I can discover. My brother-in-law might recall it."

"That would be very kind of you."

He looked down at me. "Why are you so involved in this matter? Just because it's a friend who is in trouble, and you want to help?"

"I don't think whoever stabbed her expected her to live. And once she's healed, and he finds her again, he may try again. It's possible he watches the hospital every day to see if she's been released. Or perhaps he's bribed someone inside to alert him. I have no way of knowing." I took a deep breath. "I really have no reason to interfere in her affairs, but she did ask for my help."

"Yes, well, it's hard to walk away in that case," he said sympathetically. "I'll write to Claude and see what I can learn. It will take time. He's at the Front."

"Captain Barkley has told me he was sent to Paris to search for deserters. I would have thought the Army would send someone in the Military Foot Police, instead of a line officer. Are there that many deserters in Paris? I find it hard to believe." I tried to sound innocent in the hope of learning more about what the Captain was actually doing here. "He seems to have an inordinate amount of free time. Of course that might be because he's often up half the night attending salons, leaving his days free."

The Major's eyebrows went up. "But I thought—of course, I'm convalescent, I'm not current with what's been happening."

He had covered up his surprise very nicely, but I'd seen through the swift redirection. I let it go for the moment, having found out enough to know that I'd been told a very convenient lie by my American friend.

We reached the clinic at the end of our walk, and as I turned to go through the gates, I thought I saw someone across the street duck behind a passing taxi, but when the taxi had gone on its way, there was no one. Where could he have gone? There was another house very like the Hôtel de Belle-Île, with gates that were a little more ornate, the tips of the spears forming the pattern painted a gold that had dulled over time and was in dire need of repair. The only place he could have gone was the courtyard, but I could hardly walk over to look.

"What is it?" Major Anderson asked as I lingered by our own gates for a moment too long.

"I'd have sworn I saw someone across the way—I thought I'd recognized him," I said, still watching the street. But the Major was already striding toward the main door, and I had no choice but to follow him, knowing I could stand there for an hour, and if someone had indeed been watching the clinic, he could outwait me. But as soon as we were inside, I pleaded fatigue and went up to the first floor, in search of a window that overlooked our courtyard. The rooms there had been turned over to the patients, and I had no excuse for going inside any of them. By the time I reached the Nursery, there was no one in sight.

Fifteen minutes later I slipped outside and took a taxi to the hospital.

It was a wasted journey. Sister Marie-Luc's fever had broken, and she lay in an exhausted sleep.

I sought out Sister Claire and asked, "Can you tell me? Did Sister Marie-Luc ask again about going to that village?"

"Truthfully? I don't think she remembered it when her fever came down. But it's odd. That policeman—the one who interviewed her after the attack on her—was here again this morning, and when I told him that the patient was resting after suffering from a fever, he asked me what she had said in her delirium. I gave him an account, and he asked if she had told us why this box was so urgent. I explained as best I could."

"And what did he say to that?"

"He just listened to me, and nodded when I'd finished. I couldn't really be sure what he thought about it."

"If the person who attacked Sister Marie-Luc killed himself in remorse, I don't quite see why the police should still have an interest in her case."

She shook her head. "I can't answer that. Perhaps he was concerned for her."

Or perhaps whatever had seemed odd about the body fished from the Seine was still worrying him.

But I said nothing of that to Sister Claire. Just then someone down the passage called to her, and after making her excuses, she walked sedately away, the wide white wings of her coif giving her the air of a bird about to take flight. Concerned about encountering the police, I hurried outside and two streets over found a taxi.

* * *

When I reached the clinic, I went up to my room and lay on my narrow bed, an arm behind my head and my eyes fixed on the ceiling, thinking.

Surely the police hadn't set someone to watch me, I told myself. And whoever was across the way this morning as I came home from my walk might have had nothing at all to do with me. There could be any number of reasons why that policeman had come back to the hospital. He might even have been there for another reason altogether, and politely inquired about Marie-Luc. After all, she hadn't made a formal identification of her attacker, but it was always possible that in her fevered state she might have remembered some important detail that would help him close the inquiry.

But a nagging suspicion moved me to get up from the bed and take the envelope, the letters, and the photograph from the table where I'd set them last night, and hide them.

More easily decided than carried out. Where in a nursery does one hide anything? The first place anyone would look would be the small chest where I'd put my belongings, or the armoire where I'd hung my coat and my uniforms.

But digging around in the nursery, I found a box of toy soldiers, in French and British uniforms of the period of Waterloo. There was a Wellington, a Napoleon, and even a General Blücher, and a company of Black Brunswickers. It was a battle I knew well. My several-times-great-grandmother had waited not far away for news of her husband that fateful June day in 1815.

I upended the box on the bed, scattering infantry, horse, and cannon every which way, and put my cache from Petite-Beauvais in the very bottom before replacing the figures. Then I returned it to where I'd found it.

Satisfied, I came back to my bed and nearly lay down on an Old Guard, which had to be marched back to the toy box before I could resume my contemplation of the ceiling.

Where was Philippe Moreau, and why had Paul Moreau's return from being taken prisoner so upset Father Robert?

I found no answer to those questions and turned instead to what Captain Barkley was doing in Paris.

I had first thought he might be supporting me in my search for Philippe Moreau to keep me out of trouble, but he was beginning to show signs of a more personal interest in the village of Petite-Beauvais now, giving himself away.

Had he known about it before I arrived in Paris, or had he discovered it while helping me?

I had hardly rested, my mind was too busy. But my side had appreciated the quiet half hour.

Making a decision, I got up and smoothed my uniform.

Going in search of Madame Ezay, I found her folding sheets in the laundry drying room. There was no one else about, so I smiled and said, "Let me help you."

"You shouldn't be doing any such thing, not with your injury."

"I can sit over there and find two ends of every sheet, then hold them while you do the rest. I'd like your help."

"But of course, Sister Crawford. What is it you need?"

I wasn't entirely sure.

"The Mayor's office, *la mairie,* registers all births and deaths in a village, does it not?"

"*Bien sûr.* It must be done."

"But if a village is too small for a *mairie?*"

She smiled. "The smallest village has a mayor. Someone always steps up."

"Are there church records as well? As there are in England?"

"Yes. If the marriage or birth is reported to the priest."

"Why wouldn't it be?"

"If it is not a legitimate birth, one has only to move to another village, and it would be assumed that the birth had been registered properly where the child was born."

"Is this a large problem?" I asked, surprised.

She shrugged. The pile of folded sheets in the basket at her feet was growing quickly, with my help.

"Who knows? It is possible, certainly. But why do you ask?"

"There's someone I can't seem to find. I wondered if his birth had been registered anywhere. The French Army appears not to have any such person on its rolls. I thought perhaps he didn't use his first given name. Possibly he didn't care for it."

"Ah. I had a cousin who was given the name of his grandfather, whom he detested. As soon as his grandfather died, he used his next given name, Aristide, instead. It was not his legal name, but he refused to go back to Hieronymus."

I smiled. "I can't say that I blame him."

"Yes, his grandfather was Flemish. And very unpleasant, from all reports." She reached for the next sheet. "Mind," she said, "you must know where a person was born. Or you don't know where to begin."

Alsace? Ruled by the Germans since the 1870s? A needle in a haystack. And even if Petite-Beauvais had such an office as a *mairie*, no one would be willing to let me search it. Nor would Father Robert be persuaded to let me see the church records. That was certain.

"If a village is too small, would I look in the next larger town?" I asked.

"Possibly. But it would have to be very small indeed."

Like the hamlet in the Forest of Fontainebleau?

"Is there someone in particular you want to know about?" She looked up, as if afraid she might be prying. "Perhaps if I knew why you wish to know all these things? Or who it is you want to find?"

"I don't really know myself," I said wearily.

"But you have asked. You must know a little?"

"A French officer, one who was wounded and brought into our aid station. I thought he might be from Alsace. He spoke fluent German, I'm sure."

"That's likely. If he went to school there, they would not have taught him French."

Perhaps this whole quest was mad.

"Yes, I'd thought of that."

The pile of dry sheets had been replaced by a stack of freshly folded ones. There were only pillowcases left, and Madame Ezay could deal with those herself.

I thanked her and went back to my room.

Sister Marie-Luc had called Philippe Moreau a monster.

It was time to find out why.

Marie-Luc was exhausted, still, from her long ordeal with fever, but she was awake when I walked into her room.

She tried to focus on my face as I came up to the bed, and for a moment she couldn't quite place me. Then she said, "Sister Crawford." Her voice was hardly more than a thread.

We chatted for a few minutes—or to be honest, I talked to her about trivial matters, the weather, war news, the gossip I'd heard at the clinic about the Armistice that was being proposed, while she listened without comment.

Was she too weak to tell me what I wanted to know?

I said, "I'm aware that it's not something you wish to discuss. But I have an obligation of my own, and I have no choice but to ask you. What do you know about Philippe Moreau? Is that his real name? Where does he come from? You called him a monster once, and you led me to think it was he who attacked you, not Jerome Karadeg."

Not all of that last was true, but I asked the questions fast and without any time for her to think, in the hope that she might answer at least one of them, if only in anger. Instead, she turned her face to the wall, refusing even to look at me.

"Please. This is no longer a matter you can keep to yourself. You must tell me something."

I waited, giving her time to reconsider. I hadn't brought the packets with me. I hadn't expected her to have the strength to look at the contents. Now I was wishing I had, that they might force her to talk rather than withdraw.

And then without warning she turned her head and met my gaze, anger in her eyes. "You don't know what you're meddling with. Let it be."

"I know something. That you know who attacked you. That the priest in Petite-Beauvais is afraid of Paul Moreau. I know that Philippe was in Paris a matter of days ago, and most likely is still here. I think the police are following me, but I don't know why. My side is slowly healing, and I must go back to the British lines soon. There isn't much time."

"The war is almost over—let it alone, I tell you."

"What has he done? What is it you know about him, that he would wish to kill you, and let Jerome Karadeg take the blame? And then send him to his death in the Seine?"

I really didn't think she would answer me.

And then to my surprise, tears filled her eyes, and she said, "I know the truth."

Chapter Eleven

There was silence in the room for a time. I could hear voices in the distance, and somewhere a church bell striking the hour.

"The woman who lived in that cottage. Juliane Theissen. She was a cousin of the Moreau family. Her mother was living in Alsace when the war broke out that would give the province to the Germans. They couldn't get away. Her father died in the fighting, an officer in the French Army. Some years later, when her mother died, Paul Moreau's father went to Alsace and spirited her out, bringing her back to Petite-Beauvais without permission of the authorities. He told everyone that she was a German fräulein who had come as a governess to the young boy, his cousin, he had also rescued, and no one guessed it wasn't true. It was the thing then to have a German governess. As for the child she brought with her, I don't know that Mrs. Moreau was ever certain whether the boy was actually the girl's younger brother or even Moreau's natural son. He was desperate for an heir."

She took a deep breath. "Soon afterward the child, Philippe, was adopted by the Moreau family. There had been no other children in that family, you see. And then Mrs. Moreau discovered she was pregnant. When Paul's father died, his widow, Paul's mother, sent the governess away. That's how I came to know her. My parents hired her to care for me, and soon she was making her living as a governess. It wasn't until years later, when I was older, that I learned about the child. Even so, she wouldn't tell me who he was. I have suspected he was Monsieur Moreau's natural son."

Her voice faded, and I thought she'd finished, that she wasn't going to tell me the rest of the story.

I was about to ask her to go on when she said, "What happened next is not clear. Philippe and Paul were in school; Philippe was twelve, Paul nearly ten. They went to spend a weekend in the house of the Lavaud family, near the Bois. The family's son was a classmate of theirs. Paul went out riding in the afternoon. He said later that there was an argument in the family that had upset him. He came back at four o'clock to find everyone dead, and Philippe dazed, with blood on his hands. The police believed he'd killed them all, except for the Lavaud boy, who was in the kennels, and so he was taken into custody."

"The Moreau children were connected to this murder?" I sat back stunned. I'd been prepared for anything except this. I had assumed that the newspaper cutting had been kept because the fräulein had known the family, yet she hadn't kept any cuttings from the ensuing inquiry or trial, which was curious. I'd thought by understanding that, I would have more insight into the other papers she'd hidden, and any connection between the murders and the Moreaus. It was even more shocking now that no one had saved the rest of the story.

Marie-Luc was still talking. I tried to concentrate on what she was saying.

"—it doesn't matter what happened next. Suffice it to say that somehow Philippe escaped before he could be tried. The police searched without finding any trace of him. I've always believed that he went to Alsace. He couldn't have remembered his early years there, he was no more than two. But he must have heard Fräulein Theissen speak of her home."

I realized what that must mean. "Are you saying that when war broke out in 1914, he was still in Alsace? He must have been of an age to join the German Army. Did he take part in the invasion of France?"

"I have seen him for myself, in a German uniform. Now you know why I want no part of him. He is a killer and a traitor."

"But where is he now?" And was he the same man who'd called himself Philippe Moreau?

"I don't know. I'd thought he was dead, you see. The fräulein spoke of him as if he were. But somehow he managed to visit her. Just before I arrived to care for her. As she lay dying, she told me. Not until then."

I stared at her. "That's why you believed you'd seen him on the streets of Paris. Because he'd just been to Petite-Beauvais."

Had he taken that black lacquer box? Was that what had become of it?

"But how could he have attacked you? The man I knew as Philippe Moreau could hardly put one foot in front of the other. He could barely stand."

And yet I'd seen him in a taxi just after I'd arrived in Paris. I was certain of that. All I could think of was that his wounds must have healed faster than anyone had imagined.

She turned away from me again. "He came at me from behind, that one. It wasn't Jerome. He never wears his uniform—he wasn't wearing it that afternoon. But *he* was wearing one, I'd swear to it." She closed her eyes, as if to shut out the memory. "He struck me on the back of the neck, and then as I raised my arms to protect my head, the knife came. It was there, sharp and ripping from one side to the other with such force that I reared back into him, one hand clutching at the arm driving the knife, and I felt the fabric of a uniform. Then he was gone, and my knees buckled. I was kneeling there, watching the blood run down my clothing into the gutter. Someone was calling to me, but I don't remember much after that."

I sat there, letting the silence lengthen between us.

I could hear her breathing. Ragged and unsettled.

"Now, God help us, I have told you everything. What good will it do you, or me?"

Her voice was so low I could barely make out the words.

"I don't know," I answered. "I wish I did."

After a time, I said, "Why would Philippe Moreau risk everything to kill you, a woman he hardly knew?"

"Because I had seen him in Belgium. And I never told Fräulein Theissen that I had. Not even the last time I had come to visit her. That was months ago, before she took ill."

The door opened, and Sister Claire bustled in. "Ah. You have a visitor," she said, smiling. "And we are much better this morning, are we not? The poultice helped to stop the infection." She came around the bed, intending to take Sister Marie-Luc's temperature. "What is it?" she asked sharply. "You're as pale as your sheets."

"I'm very tired. I have asked Sister Crawford to go."

"And just as well, if you're feeling this low."

I rose, said farewell, and walked to the door.

Sister Marie-Luc turned her head to watch me go, but didn't say good-bye.

I had a great deal to think about.

In the taxi on the way to the hotel, I went over in my mind what I'd just been told. But as we pulled up in front of the clinic, I was still trying to absorb it.

It struck me suddenly that if what Marie-Luc had told me was true, Philippe Moreau was indeed from Alsace, just as Matron had suggested at Base Hospital Three. And that was something to consider. When the attack on the family living near the Bois had come to light, France was in the midst of "L'affaire Dreyfus."

The Dreyfus Affair was a notorious scandal involving the Army and the government and the Catholic Church. An innocent man, a Jewish army officer, was found guilty of treason for passing Army secrets to the Germans, and sent to the infamous Devil's Island prison in French Guiana—as it turned out, on falsified charges. In the midst of the uproar that ensued, the truth came out, and finally he was given a new trial five years later, in 1899—and found guilty a second time. The judges managed that only because he was sentenced to time served. Even the great writer Émile Zola had fought for him, as well as Georges Clemenceau, later one of France's most popular wartime prime ministers. This fight kept French politics in an uproar for ten years, making and breaking reputations. And the fact that Dreyfus was Alsatian had made his spying seem even more plausible, although it was his religion that had made him a target. Any reason for showing sympathy toward Germany was enough.

Had Philippe's background played any part in the boy's being charged with the murders? It must have been discovered—the newspapers would have found it out if the police had not—that he'd been adopted by a French family.

At any rate, there had never been a trial that might have cleared Philippe's name—or sent him to the guillotine. What had become of the child Juliane Theissen had brought to France with her? Where had he fled to? A place where the family's former governess might still have relations? She must have helped—*someone* surely had spirited him away. He was only twelve at the time. How could he have survived on his own, even if he got away from the place where he was being held?

I dug into the bottom of the box of toy soldiers and brought out the envelope for another look.

I read it with renewed interest.

There had been five people in the house that day: two housemaids; an older woman, Madame Lavaud, the mother of the owner; and her son Georges and his wife, Thérèse, parents of the boy whom the two Moreau children, according to Marie-Luc, were visiting. The son of the house, Victor, was in the kennels with the dogs. He was not aware that anything had happened. A groom had seen him there, playing with the puppies. A friend of the family had gone riding—this must have referred to Paul Moreau.

Five adults, alone in a house. How had a twelve-year-old boy managed to kill them?

And why was he in the house with the adults, and not out riding with his brother or visiting the kennels with his host? Had it been a matter of bad luck? Or of intent?

In this account, another guest was found dazed and wandering, and this must have been Philippe.

The two maids had been in the kitchen. It was the cook's afternoon off, and they had been making coffee. One was found in the pantry, next to a shattered jug of milk, the other by a kitchen table. The owner was in his study, and his wife died in their sitting room; the older woman, the man's mother, in the passage outside. The murder weapon was a large hunting knife taken from the room where the shooting rifles and shotguns were kept. It was found in the hall near the older woman.

A knife.

But the cutting, while it named the Lavauds, didn't give the names or ages of either of the guests, who were unharmed. The shocking story was complete without identifying them. And this made it all the more curious that the fräulein had kept it but none of the later articles that must have appeared.

For that anonymity was about to change.

I searched again through the papers, just to be sure there were no more cuttings or other references to the crime that I might have missed.

How on earth was I to find out more about these murders?

In Paris, away from all that was familiar and understood, where the language was one I could speak reasonably but not well enough to expect anyone to take me for a native, I was at a disadvantage.

Where to turn?

I went to find Madame Ezay.

She was paring carrots for our dinner.

"The scullery maid's mother is ill," she said when I walked into the kitchen. "I have been asked to help."

There was a pail of carrots by the table.

"I'll wash them while you pare," I said, taking the pail out to the pump. It was far heavier than I'd expected, but I soldiered on, washed the thick orange vegetables, and brought them back. She handed me another knife and I removed the tops.

"*Alors*," she said with a smile. "There is something you wish?"

We had the kitchen to ourselves. On the cooker a tall pot was simmering quietly, and I could smell chicken broth with onions. We had had roast chicken last night, and I would not have been at all surprised if the bones were in that pot.

"Something occurred eighteen years ago. An account of it appeared in a newspaper, a Parisian one, I should think, although there's no name on the cutting I have found. I need to know more about what happened on that date. How the story ended."

"Ah. Newspapers and periodicals came and went for some years. A man would start one up, declare his principles, write editorials in support of them, and then public interest would wane and the paper would go away. It was more about politics than what was happening that might be news. Unless of course it was a scandal."

"We call that a nine days' wonder," I said, grinning at the carrot top I'd just cut off.

"Yes, of course, nine days. Absolutely." She chuckled, a merry laugh. "Very well, what is the subject of this cutting? Is it about that poor man Dreyfus? I was in the school at Rennes when the new trial began. I saw him myself, a broken man physically. Did you know he is an officer now? Fighting for France, after all France did to him?"

"No, I didn't know," I said, surprised. I knew he'd been pardoned—accounts reached us in India, and letters from friends living in Paris had been full of the story. I'd heard my parents discussing it in 1906, when Dreyfus was given back the rank he would have held but for the trials and his imprisonment. My father, an officer himself, had been surprised that Dreyfus would accept reinstatement in the Army that had turned against him.

"If it is not that, then what? It was all the news there was for ten years. Everyone had an opinion. One could start an argument with a word, and there would be a fight in the street before it was done."

"A murder," I said, gauging her interest in the subject. "In fact, five murders. A man, his wife, his mother, and two housemaids."

She stopped working and stared at me. "In one house? God in heaven, who would do something so monstrous?"

Sister Marie-Luc had called Philippe Moreau a monster too.

"The cutting was only about the discovery of the bodies. I have no idea if the police ever solved it."

"Here in *Paris*?" she asked, as if expecting me to tell her it was in Berlin or London. Somewhere that such things could happen.

"The house was near the Bois. A large house, I should think, because it had grooms in a stable yard and puppies in the kennel."

"*Zut alors.*"

We had begun to chop the carrots into short lengths. For a moment there was only the sound of our paring knives slicing through them with a *crunch* and *thump*.

"Where would I go for such information?" I asked.

"The booksellers along the Left Bank. Many are gone, the war. But you will find books and old copies of papers."

I thanked her, finished helping her with the carrots, and hurried upstairs. Catching up my coat, I went out to find a taxi.

Down the street from our gates a man loitered at the corner of a building. I couldn't see him well enough to judge whether he was minding his own business or minding mine.

When the taxi had crossed the river and stopped where the stalls lined the walk under the trees, I got out, asked the driver to wait for me, and began my search. The air was chilly, and I pulled my coat collar closer. The booksellers looked up with expressions of bored interest.

The men standing in the stalls were all older, past the age of military service. One seller was a woman, her hair cropped short and her coat oversized, as if it had been her husband's or father's. Her hands were jammed into the pockets, her cap pulled down.

Most of the books on display were in French, as one would expect, although I found a surprising number in English and even Russian.

Many people in England had burned all their German books in the first days after war had been declared in 1914. I thought it must have happened here as well, because I didn't see any. Still, they might have been kept out of sight unless someone knew to ask for them.

I spoke to each seller in turn, asking if the stall sold newspapers from 1900. One asked if I actually wanted 1899, when the second trial of Alfred Dreyfus had taken place.

"*Non, merci.* For something that happened in the Bois. A serious crime."

He brought out an assortment of newspapers. I didn't recognize the names of most of them. There were old issues of *Le Mot*, *L'Illustration*, and *L'Aurore*. I thought perhaps they were important enough to keep because of their articles. I remembered what had been said about newspapers reflecting the political controversies of the day, and I could see that it must have been true. Some of the papers had lasted only a matter of months, others several years.

I thanked him, shaking my head. "This was a murder."

He said, "The stall there, the man with the beard. Ask him."

I moved on, still speaking to the owners. When I reached the man with the beard, he grinned. "If you have not found it so far, Mademoiselle, you are in luck. What is it you seek?"

I told him, and he went to the back of the stall, dug around in boxes for a time, and brought me a half dozen yellowing newspapers.

"Could I look through them?"

He shook his head. "Mademoiselle, I am earning my living here. Do you wish these papers?"

The price was higher than I'd expected, but I had very little choice in the matter. I bought them, left them in the waiting taxi, and continued my search.

The last stall but one was owned by a very old man, his hands blue veined, his eyebrows like thickets, but his eyes were a sharp gray.

He had no newspapers to sell me, but he told me he remembered the murders.

I wasn't certain whether to believe him, but he sucked at an unlit pipe and narrowed his eyes for a moment, then said, "Lavaud."

It was the name of the family that had been murdered.

"What happened? Did they ever find the killer?"

"They suspected the man who had been walking out with one of the maids. He had a temper, jealous. But the doctor who examined the young boy who was visiting could find no injury to account for all the blood on his clothing."

"He was taken into custody?"

"His mother was sent for, and the boy was interviewed again. He was taken up, the date was set for the trial. But it was never held."

"What happened?"

"There could be no trial without someone to try." He said it as if it were the most logical thing in the world, and I should have considered it myself.

"But where did he go, this boy?"

He shrugged, that Gallic shrug that can say so many things.

I was about to thank him and turn away when he said, "Why do you want to know, Mademoiselle?" His eyes had narrowed again, as if judging me.

"I found an old newspaper used to line a cabinet," I said, unwilling to tell him the truth. "It was an horrific crime. I wanted to know if whoever had done it had been caught and punished."

He was still weighing me up, and I felt myself flush under his scrutiny.

"When one is a patient, and healing is slow," I said quietly, "one longs for anything that will make the time pass more quickly. Even an eighteen-year-old murder."

To my surprise, he nodded.

"Then I will tell you one thing more. This inquiry was never closed. How could it be? There was even a reward for information. More money than I'll ever see in what's left of my lifetime. It was never collected. Whoever he may be, he's had eighteen more years of life than they did, the dead. There is no shame in turning him in. I ask you to remember who told you about the reward." And he gave me a mirthless grin.

I hurried back to the taxi, glad to be inside, glad to be away from here. Even the glorious lines of Notre-Dame couldn't take away the feeling I was left with, that if I knew where Philippe Moreau was and turned him in, everyone would think I had done it for the reward.

I returned in time to read another chapter of *The Moonstone* to my circle of listeners. The group had grown, and I didn't know whether it was the reader or the tale that brought others to listen. But they were an intent lot, interested in the story, and there was always some discussion afterward about whether Franklin Blake or Sergeant Cuff would find out who had stolen the Moonstone.

Sitting there listening to them, I myself was thinking about another crime, the murder of the Lavaud family. Juliane Theissen was dead. But as she lay dying, had she confided in Father Robert? Or even confessed to him? Did he know what she knew about Philippe Moreau?

There had been no time to search through the newspapers I'd bought. But after tea, I went up to my room and spread them out on my bed, drawing up a chair so that I could look through them comfortably.

The papers were old enough to need care in turning the pages—I don't think anyone had unfolded them in years, if ever.

Then why had the bookseller kept them?

The reward, surely. Like the old man's dreams.

I had a headache, after reading through the first paper. If it had been in English, I could have scanned the columns more quickly. I set the stack aside where Madame Ezay wouldn't find them and toss them out, and was about to delve among the toy soldiers again to find the envelope when there was a tap at my door. I hastily shoved the box out of sight and called, "Come."

It was one of the staff, reminding me that today I was to be examined by one of the staff doctors. This was a routine matter, initially begun to make certain that no soldier was malingering, trying to use his wound to keep him in comfort when he was well enough to return to the Front. Most officers were more than eager to return to their men, and in the ranks, there was a strong sense of letting the side down by not rejoining one's regiment as soon as possible.

And yet all these men knew what they were returning to. They knew their chances of survival were slim at best. They knew what wounds looked like, what gas and shrapnel and machine guns did to the human body, the very real danger of amputation or burned-out lungs. They had struggled to rescue the wounded who had fallen out of reach in No Man's Land, dragging men back at the risk of their own lives. And still they wanted to go back. They could not betray the men who were still out there, dying in their place. It wasn't courage or heroism, it was a strong sense of duty to men they were closer to than brothers or parents or wives. A comradeship of shared fear and blood and determination that surpassed anything else they had ever known.

I tidied my cap and my apron and went down to the small room where men were examined. I was the only person there other than a Dr. McDevitt.

He was older than most of the doctors I'd worked with, sidelined to clinics and hospitals where his skill would serve his patients but his age would not be a factor.

He smiled as I walked in. "A pleasant change to see a pretty face instead of a line of ill-tempered men. How are you, Sister?"

"I'm progressing quite well, I think."

And it occurred to me as I said those words that he might well send me back to work before I'd found out anything more about Philippe Moreau.

I suppressed a sigh. My duty was there, with wounded men, and anything else would have to wait.

"Yes, most of my patients tell me they're faring very well," he said dryly, "as if they could convince me of that fact without any further ado."

After peering at my wound, he went through a list of questions: Any discharge? Bloody or clear? Had there been any redness or swelling of late? Was the incision healing regularly, or were there pockets where it was not, soreness I could feel but he couldn't see? Had I noticed any odor of infection? How much pain? How was my gait—could I walk normally and without pain. Stand? Stoop? Bend over? Lift normal weight? Demonstrate, if you will, Sister.

By the time I was finished with Dr. McDevitt, I had the strongest feeling he was going to send me back. But he said, peering at me over his glasses, "Another few days, perhaps. The food is not the best here, and no better in British hospitals. You will need to be at full strength when you return."

I didn't tell him how little rest I'd been getting, nor how tired I was at the end of the day.

"If I am careful, and go to one of the base hospitals instead of forward aid stations?"

He shook his head. "We'll talk again in a few days."

I thanked him and left, only to turn around. Surprised, he looked up at me. "Something else, Sister?"

"Sir, no. Not in regard to my case. How many French clinics are there, similar to this one? If I'm to stay a bit longer, I'd like to look up a former patient to see how he's progressing. He was French, brought in to us by a stretcher party. I had to translate for him. It was a very serious case." Not completely the truth, of course, but very close.

"My dear, Paris is full of them. Fifty? A hundred? I couldn't begin to tell you how many there are. Finding him will be nearly impossible, even if you had the time."

"Thank you, sir."

"It does you credit, Sister, to want to know the outcome. But our duty ends when men leave our care. We can only say prayers for their well-being, whether they return to their regiments or are invalided home." He took a deep breath. "I daresay the outcome is often much the same."

Another avenue closed to me.

I went back to my room and read through two more of the newspapers, without any luck. One was dated three months after the murders, which meant that there was nothing more worth printing about it, or the killer had long since been taken up and was awaiting trial. The other was two weeks later than the previous one.

I went down for my dinner and found a table by myself, near the back of the room. I must have looked as cross as I felt, for no one came to ask if he might sit in the other chair.

Afterward, I found a taxi to take me back to the hospital. I didn't see my watcher, but I knew he was there. I could feel eyes on me as I stepped into the Renault.

Sister Marie-Luc was just finishing her meal. I could tell she wasn't very pleased to see me.

And I saw too that she had not remembered sending me to Juliane Theissen's cottage in search of a black lacquer box from Japan. I had expected to offer the envelope to her, but bit off what I had been about to say and instead asked how she was feeling.

"There is so much pain," she said, "and whichever way I move, I seem to pull at stitches somewhere. Still, I'm grateful."

I could see that her dinner had consisted of a broth and a dish of carrots. There must have been a glut of carrots at the market today.

"Is there anything I can do for you?" I asked.

She looked away. "I have heard nothing from the Karadegs. They will blame me for what became of their son. It's not surprising. But I tried to explain to the police."

She went on in that vein, and I could see that what had happened to Jerome still weighed heavily on her conscience.

Apparently the police had refused to listen to her, and instead believed the witness, claiming that the shock of the attack had left her with no useful memory of it. "I have asked the nuns to light candles for me in the chapel. But it will never be enough."

"You can't feel guilty," I said. "You did what you could."

"The policeman is not a practicing Catholic," she said. "He doesn't understand."

I wasn't quite certain what that had to do with her deep-seated sense of guilt, except that he had not believed her, had not tried to find another answer.

"I know you are certain the man wore a military uniform. But can you be certain that it was Philippe Moreau who attacked you?"

"I didn't see his face, I tell you. But I know Jerome. It wasn't *Jerome*." She was suddenly agitated. "Why must everything come back to that monster?"

"Did Juliane Theissen believe her son had killed all those people in the Bois?"

Her eyes held mine. "You know nothing of this. You will do well to say nothing to anyone about this. Now you must go, and I would prefer it if you didn't come to visit me again."

"He's in Paris, Marie-Luc. And someone has been following me. Had he followed you before you were attacked? Should I be afraid of shadows in the dark?"

But she ignored me, folding her napkin and setting it beside her plate.

I had one last question for her. "Had Fräulein Theissen ever worked for the Lavaud family? Could that have something to do with why Philippe might have killed them?"

I think that if she could have got out of her bed, she would have physically shown me to the door and shut it after me.

Instead she did the next best thing. She pulled her rosary from her pocket and closed her eyes, her lips moving as her fingers threaded the beads between them.

Chapter Twelve

A light rain had begun to fall while I was in the hospital. I had to walk to the next corner before I could find a taxi, and I wondered as I strode as quickly as I could up the dark street if there was someone behind me biding his time. I'm not usually given to such fears, but there was no one else about at this hour, and my footsteps echoed against the high walls on either side. Windows were dark, their shades pulled against the possibility of a German air raid, and my feeling of being alone and vulnerable was very strong.

I told myself quite firmly that there was no way that Philippe Moreau could know I was in Paris, a nurse he'd last seen in a base hospital in the British sector. It seemed more than likely that the police might have an interest in my comings and goings, because I had come to see Marie-Luc so often. But even that was not a satisfactory explanation for the watcher outside the Hôtel de Belle-Île.

For a moment I even wondered, as the taxi came toward me and slowed, whether Captain Barkley had put someone on to watch me, thinking that I might find myself in trouble running about Paris while I was healing. It wouldn't do for a British nursing Sister to faint on one of the boulevards.

Arrived back at the clinic, I found Captain Barkley waiting for me, as if conjured up by my own thoughts.

"You've been out," he said, gesturing to the raindrops on the shoulders of my coat and the damp curls struggling to escape from my cap.

I wanted to reply that I had just come through the doors, and so it must be fairly obvious that I had been outside. Instead, I answered, "I needed a little fresh air."

"There will be fog tonight, if I'm not mistaken. I'd not go walking on my own after this. I'm late coming to offer you dinner. Have you dined?"

"I have."

He looked disappointed. "I'm sorry to hear it."

"The truth is, I went to call on Marie-Luc. There's still a good deal of pain—well, the incision is a long one, running right across her body. But the fever seems to have broken."

"You shouldn't be wandering around Paris after dark all on your own."

"The days are so short already that if I must only step out in sunlight, I will not see very much of the city before I'm sent back to work."

"I'll arrange a tour tomorrow if you like."

"I'd really prefer going back to question Father Robert."

"You should leave that business alone. There's nothing in that cottage left to be found. There's nothing more you can do. It's not your place to search for this missing officer. If he is missing, and not just recovering in a flat or a clinic. For all I know he might be next door to this house, or in the Sixth Arrondissement—or the Seventeenth."

"In that café you were eager to sort through the contents of the fräulein's envelope with me. Now you want no part of it. Or anything else."

We were on the verge of quarreling. Looking more closely I could see that he was tired, and heaven only knew how long he'd been waiting for me. And I was still stung by Sister Marie-Luc's refusal to talk to me. She had every right—and yet it seemed that no one wanted to say anything about Philippe Moreau, even though he was more often than not the elephant in the room.

Then it occurred to me that if the watchers were the captain's, he knew very well that I'd visited the nun again, and he wanted very badly to find out what more I'd learned. Small wonder he was cranky after I'd refused his dinner invitation.

"No, that's unkind of me. I'll go with you to dinner, if you like, and perhaps have a glass of wine. We can enjoy the company and talk of something else."

He was glaring at me, not yet ready to make peace.

"I saw the doctor this afternoon. He says I'll be fit to leave in a few days."

That changed the atmosphere considerably.

"I must say I'll be happier when you are under the Army's eye rather than wandering about Paris, ill and lost."

Hardly ill, and very definitely not lost. I bit back my answer and smiled.

We set out for a restaurant he'd wanted to try, and my amusement nearly got the better of me when I saw that carrots were on the menu. I had a small glass of wine, and we talked about England, mostly, and the island of Mackinac, where he'd spent so many happy weeks as he was growing up. It was a cheerful meal after all. And then, as he was dipping a spoon into a very odd-looking tart (the crust gray but the apples thinly sliced and fanned out in perfect symmetry—the French, trying to cope in spite of the war), he commented as casually as possible, "What does Marie-Luc have to say? Is she still convinced that Jerome wasn't the man who attacked her?"

"She is certain he wasn't. But she didn't see the man's face, worst luck. Or claims she didn't. Still, she knows it wasn't Jerome." I thought about that. "People are distinctive. In feel, in odor, in manner," I went on slowly, lowering my voice as I considered the problem. "If you came up behind me and put an arm around my throat, and tried to stab me while I struggled to stop you, ending up slashing me across my chest, something about you would register, surely. I might not see your face, but I could honestly swear that I knew it was you. Or conversely, if it was a stranger, that it couldn't have been you, that something about him was quite different."

He set his spoon aside, looking down at his plate. "I know what you are referring to. I have two young cousins. Sometimes when they arrive unexpectedly, one will put her hands over my eyes and disguising her voice, ask me to guess which one it is." He lifted his gaze to meet mine. "Cynthia favors lavender scent. But Nan is more adventurous, likely to be trying a scent of her mother's or buying a new one she thinks she might prefer. I hadn't realized it, but I always guess it's Cynthia if I catch the fragrance of lavender. If it's any other scent, I always guess it's Nan."

"Yes, exactly. If she thinks it wasn't Jerome, I'm almost prepared to believe her."

"Then who attacked her?"

"That's just it. She thinks it must be Philippe Moreau. But I'm not convinced he could have brought it off, that vicious stabbing. Not in his condition."

"He's had time to heal."

"I know. I'd thought of that." Shaking my head, I added, "It's impossible to sort out."

"Even if it was Philippe. For the sake of argument. Why would he attempt to kill a nun?"

"Because he's in Paris, and so is she?"

"It still doesn't explain why he should want to kill her." He picked up his spoon again and finished his tart.

Tell him all the rest? Or not?

Across from me at the next table a woman laughed, silvery and provocative. She was wearing a satin version of a Hussar's tunic, a turban on her head. It was pinned, I realized, with the brass shell casing from a rifle cartridge. There was a design on it, giving it the appearance of a vase, and from it sprang beautifully dyed silk violets. I wondered if they had been made from the tiny silk parachutes that kept flares over the trenches from descending too rapidly, allowing the maximum amount of light for the maximum amount of time. War or no war, French dressmakers had managed to keep women looking chic, and I thought of the clothes my mother had lovingly refurbished for four long years. England was dowdy, France—even with the war so much nearer—was still fashionable.

Changing direction, I said, "Captain. I think you've been holding out on me. I think you may know more about what's going on than I do. After all, you can speak to the French Army. I can't."

He nearly choked on his wine and lowered the glass, regarding me over the rim.

"Damn it, Bess."

"Fair is fair," I said firmly. "Have you been having me followed? I need to know whether someone out there is intending to keep me safe, or to do me harm. I don't want to be worried every time I step outside the clinic."

"All right, Bess, yes, those are my men. I should have known you'd spot them. But I couldn't be there all day every day. And I was worried. What am I to tell your father if something happens to you? Or God forbid, your mother?"

I didn't add Simon Brandon to that list. But I had a fair idea of what he would do. The surprising thing was that he hadn't already found a reason to come to Paris, on his own or as my mother's surrogate.

"I don't mind," I said, "but I wish you'd told me." I did mind, but I also knew that he meant well.

I'd successfully distracted him from asking what I knew.

He called for the bill, and then helped me with my coat. Outside the wind had picked up, blowing bits of newspaper down the street outside the restaurant, and people hurrying past us had their collars up, hats low. Even the beggars had called it a night.

It happened so fast that neither of us had time to react.

I was turning to say something to Captain Barkley when someone bumped into me, and I sucked in my breath as it felt like an elbow caught my bandaged wound. I stumbled back against the door of the restaurant just as the Captain cried out, swearing on the heels of it, and jerked back against me. And then he was running after someone, other pedestrians caught off guard and trying to get out of their way. Even as I watched, he stopped, staggered, and went down.

I rushed toward him, and bent over to take his shoulder.

"Captain? Are you hurt? Tell me where."

He groaned as he rolled over on his back. I could see blood, and I ran my hands down his greatcoat until I discovered that it was coming from his arm and his side.

A knife? Like Marie-Luc?

I knelt there, people beginning to collect around us, reaching inside his coat.

Then he was shoving my hands away. "Help me up. *Now.*"

I started to argue, realized what he was telling me, and as he rolled over to his other side, fighting to get to his feet, I gave him my shoulder, and he managed to stand.

"I'm sorry," he said in halting French. "Drunk. Too much wine."

The gathering crowd stared at us, and I laughed, saying, "He is celebrating the end of the war too soon."

They looked askance but began to turn away and go about their business.

"A taxi," my companion said roughly. "Hurry."

I lifted one hand to hail a taxi coming our way, the other arm bearing a good deal of his weight.

The driver slowed, staring at us. I smiled. "Too much wine," I called, and he stopped.

I got the door open and helped the Captain to drag himself inside. His face was grim in the little light there was, and I gave the direction of the clinic, thinking it was a better choice than a hospital, where questions might be asked.

It seemed to take an eternity to reach the Hôtel de Belle-Île. I couldn't tell how badly the Captain was bleeding, for he was hunched over in the far side of the vehicle.

And then we were pulling up before the gates. I handed the driver a fistful of francs, then with clenched teeth got my companion out of the taxi, all the while scolding, "I told you not to drink that fourth glass. What is Matron going to say about this? Really, Captain, it's too much. I have never been so *embarrassed.*"

He grunted something that would pass as an apology. Shutting the door of the taxi with some force, I gave him my shoulder and somehow we got through the gates and across the courtyard before he collapsed on the steps in front of the door.

I saw with relief that the taxi had driven on, then said, "It's all right, he's gone."

Moving around him, I managed to get the door open, and called to the orderly, praying that he hadn't gone off duty already.

He was there in a matter of seconds—I thought he must have caught the urgency in my voice. Between us we got the Captain inside, and then the orderly was calling for members of the staff.

I looked up to see that there was blood on the orderly's hands. Just then one of the Sisters came running, and Dr. Wallace was at her heels.

Between us, Sister Franklin and I got his greatcoat off and, with more difficulty, his tunic. As the doctor cut away his shirt, I could see that the knife had slashed across his arm and gone on to open up the flesh over his ribs. It was bleeding profusely, but I didn't think there was any serious damage done.

More orderlies came, and Captain Barkley was carried to one of the free beds and laid carefully on the sheet that Sister Franklin had pulled across the mattress. Dr. Wallace was busy trying to clean and close the chest wound while I attended to the arm.

Captain Barkley, back with us now, looked up at me and said, "How bad?"

Dr. Wallace, his hands busy, answered for me without even looking up. "You'll be all right. Sore as hell, but all right."

Another Sister had come up behind me to take my coat. "I'll sponge it before the blood dries," she said, but when she had helped me out of it, she gasped. "Sister—"

I looked down, and saw that my apron and my skirt had been slashed. But when had that happened? When whoever it was appeared to bump into me?

I turned away and quickly put my fingers into the gaping tear. It went through my undergarments and there was even a long rip in my bandage. In fact, there was a thin red line oozing blood in my side.

The bandaging had saved me.

"Nothing," I said, turning and smiling at the doctor and Sister Franklin, who were waiting to hear how badly I was hurt.

They went back to the task of washing and closing the Captain's wounds, sprinkling antiseptic powder on them as they worked. Dr. Wallace began making small tidy stitches, drawing the edges of the wounds together. There was never time for such things at the Front. The doctors sewed up a wound quickly, even though it would leave a heavy scar, because there were more men waiting for care, and one did the best one could.

It took nearly half an hour to finish working on the Captain, and when Matron came to see what all the fuss was about in her quiet clinic this evening, I gave her a brief account of what had happened.

"There was no one about as we stepped out of the restaurant— that's to say, everyone was walking along, head down against the wind, minding their own business. And then someone bumped against me, hard, knocking me back into doorway. I heard Captain Barkley cry out, and then he gave chase. But whoever it was got away. I managed to get the Captain this far, thinking it was best."

"Yes, of course, far better," Matron said. "Was it an attempted robbery?"

"I don't think it was. He never spoke, and I've wondered if he was waiting out there for us—or for someone," I amended hastily. "The next person to come out? I don't know."

We were just settling the protesting Captain into his cot—he wanted no part of staying the night, angrily assuring us that he was well enough to return to his own flat—when there was a resounding knock on the clinic door.

The orderly who had let us in had lingered to hear what had happened. He turned and walked swiftly out to Reception to answer the summons.

We could hear voices, but not what was said. And then the orderly, protesting, was following someone into the room where we'd put the Captain.

I looked up to see the cold-eyed policeman who had dealt with Marie-Luc's stabbing, and my heart sank.

His eyebrows went up as he recognized me, but he turned to Matron, greeted her politely, and said, "My name is Duplessis. There was a taxi driver who discovered blood all over the rear seat of his Renault. He reported this to the police, and told us where he'd dropped off the man and the woman who had taken his taxi from a restaurant to this place."

If I'd been alone, I might have succeeded in convincing him that the patient who had taken me out to dinner this evening had had his wound reopen while trying to stop a thief who had attempted to rob us.

Instead, Matron, indignant over the whole affair, and Dr. Wallace, who was just drying his hands, gave the police a full account of the evening's events. And the Captain, lying there listening grimly to what was being said, looked as if he would have gladly disappeared under the pillows.

The policeman insisted on viewing the wounds for himself, and

I thought at first he was going to insist that the bandaging be removed. Nodding to the Captain, he waited until the bedclothes had been pulled back and the remnants of the bloody shirt that Captain Barkley was still wearing had been opened to show the site and extent of the knife's work.

He asked the Captain if he had recognized the man.

"I did not. It happened too quickly. That's why I went after him."

"But failed to catch him."

I intervened before the Captain could say what was obviously on his mind.

"He could hardly leave me. What if this assassin had somehow doubled back? I was frightened and called to Captain Barkley not to go too far."

"Did you indeed?" the policeman asked dryly.

Captain Barkley, for once, said nothing.

"I should like to know," Matron said firmly, "what the police intend to do about this matter? Captain Barkley and Sister Crawford were clearly English, and I am hoping this is not going to be allowed to happen again to another of our people."

The patient, about to claim he was an American, thought better of it, and his mouth snapped shut.

Dr. Wallace said, "If you're finished with my patient, kindly take yourselves elsewhere. I'm about to give him something to help him rest."

Sister Franklin, casting a last glance at the patient, hurried to usher the rest of us back into the lobby.

Matron was speaking to the policeman, but his eyes were on me. He remembered me all too clearly from St. Anne's, and here I was, involved in another knife attack. I kept my arm close by my side to hide the rip in my uniform, and stood a little behind Sister Franklin.

After the orderly had given his evidence, the policeman nodded and said, "Thank you all. And now I wish to have a word with—Sister Crawford, is it? Yes, thank you—Sister Crawford, if you please."

Matron said, "Inspector, if you wish to interrogate one of my nurses, I shall remain."

But the others quietly left us alone.

"You are a friend of the nun Sister Marie-Luc?"

"I am," I said evenly, as if I was in no way perturbed by the question.

"And here you are, attacked tonight by a knife. You and the Captain."

"I was not injured," I said.

"Then why should this unknown assailant be lying in wait for *him*?"

"I don't know the answer to that." I realized he was goading me.

"A busy street, and not a single witness?"

"It wasn't busy, but I'm sure people were aware that the Captain was chasing someone when he collapsed in the road. They came to stare at him. No one offered to call the police or find a doctor. My first thought was not to take their names but to get medical care for Captain Barkley."

"No one has come forward to report a disturbance on that street."

"They were there, Inspector. You found a witness to Marie-Luc's stabbing. I'm sure you'll find one here."

"He was an impeccable source. We aren't always so fortunate."

"Impeccable or not, he was wrong. Marie-Luc knew her assailant wasn't Jerome Karadeg, and you wouldn't believe her. You haven't even asked me for a description of our assailant. Medium height, and compactly built. I could see that much as he ran away."

"A description that could fit anyone in France," he said, almost with a sneer.

"Sister Crawford has just had a shocking experience. I must insist that you treat her with courtesy and let her rest," Matron snapped.

"I will leave you with one piece of information, Sister Crawford. We have come to the conclusion that we might well have been mistaken in our identification of the body taken from the river and identified as that of Jerome Karadeg."

With that bombshell, he turned, thanked Matron for her cooperation, and without glancing at me, walked out the door, nearly slamming it behind him.

Matron, staring at it as if she could still see the man who had just left, said, "There's more here than meets the eye, Sister Crawford. What is there between this policeman and you?"

I told her the truth, about Marie-Luc, about Jerome Karadeg, and the nun's certainty that he would never have harmed her. "But the police prefer to believe it *was* Monsieur Karadeg. To be honest, I don't know. But there has been some sort of history with a French Infantry officer, and he is the one she blames. I don't think the police cared very much for the fact that I believed her."

"Who is this other man? "

"He appears to be someone her former governess knew."

She considered that. "Why should he wish to harm her? A nun?"

"I don't know. Perhaps she knows something about him that he doesn't want told."

Thinking about that, I wondered how much Fräulein Theissen might have told Philippe Moreau about Sister Marie-Luc.

"Or because you are also a nursing Sister, if not a nun, and English, if not French," she said pensively.

I hadn't thought about it from that point of view—that someone might be targeting nurses. As a rule our work and our rank as officers kept us safe. But what if someone blamed a nurse for a treatment gone wrong or a report to doctors that changed his life, like identifying him as shell-shocked? It was sobering.

When I didn't answer straightaway, she added, "And do you, as well as Captain Barkley, also know what this nun might know?"

That was difficult to answer.

"I don't think it's a matter of what we know. It may be a matter of his fearing it."

"And that could be as dangerous. Guard yourself. Well. Go up and change your clothes. Yes, I've seen the rip in your apron and your uniform. Madame Ezay can help you mend it. You are certain there is not also a rip in you?"

I grinned sheepishly. "I was just in the way."

"We don't know that yet. Good night, Sister Crawford."

And she waited as I climbed the stairs and turned down the passage.

It was well after midnight, and I hadn't been able to sleep. I got up, dressed, and walked down the stairs, thinking I might look in on Captain Barkley. The house was dark, save for a small lamp in Reception that burned all night, and I had brought my torch down with me.

When I tapped lightly and then opened the door of the room he'd been given—it was one Matron kept for use as a recovery ward for surgical patients—the low lamp on the table beside his cot showed me an empty bed.

Where had he gone? He'd been given a sedative to help him rest, and he appeared to be in some pain when I last saw him. He couldn't have improved enough to be sent on to his flat at this hour. When the orderly in charge of Reception went off duty at eleven, the main door was locked. A clinic full of recovering patients considered a late night on the town to be most unwise, although a few officers were allowed to dine out on occasion, as a test of endurance. Major Vernon, with his eye patch, for one. Not fit to return to the fighting, but not precisely an invalid either.

I closed his door softly and tiptoed on to the library in case he'd gone there, where he could sit more comfortably. It was empty.

I went back to the hall that served for Reception. Even with the lamp it was shadowy at best, especially under the stairs. But I heard an odd sound, and shone my light in that direction.

There was a door leading to the kitchens behind the staircase and I was moving toward it when something seemed to uncoil, just visible out of the corner of my eye, and I whirled.

"Bess—for God's sake, don't scream," the Captain said in a harried voice.

Far from screaming, I was prepared to use my torch as a weapon if this were an intruder. "What are you doing out of bed?" I demanded quietly.

"I've been looking for you," he said, frustration in his voice. "Where the devil have they put you?"

"Upstairs," I said shortly. "Are you in pain? Feverish?"

"No. I want to know what is going on."

We could hardly hover beneath the arch of the stairs, looking guilty at every sound. And it was one thing to be found in a patient's room late at night while one was on duty. Quite another to be discovered there when one was not. Matron would not be pleased.

"The library. But quietly."

He was about to protest, but I was already on my way, moving with care in the dim light of night lamps.

We closed the door. Even in the gloom I could see that he was pale and sweating. "Sit down," I said softly. "Before you fall down. I won't be able to get you up again before the house arrives to see what the clatter is."

He did. "What's been happening, Bess? I think it's time I knew."

He was right, now that he'd been attacked.

"Very well. Remember the cutting about those murders in the Bois district?"

"The one we couldn't determine why it had been kept. Yes."

"I've learned from Marie-Luc that Philippe Moreau and his brother Paul were there at the time. Visiting another student from the school the three boys attended." I went on to explain about the Moreau family, the murders, who was in the house, who was not, and what had become of Philippe in the aftermath of the inquiry.

Captain Barkley was frowning, trying to concentrate. "You're saying that he was taken up for murder. But what about other servants, the groom, for one, or even the son of the house? Or the other brother, Paul? It seems to me that whoever investigated the crime, did a damn— did a very poor job of it."

"That's the problem. We have the cutting that Fräulein Theissen kept. But I've been unable to find any subsequent reports. I even went to the booksellers on the Left Bank, and while I found a few newspapers from that period, they seem to be either before or after the crime. There's not a single mention of it."

"You're certain of that?"

"My French is passable," I said, "but now that I know the names of the victims I could search for any mention of them. And Marie-Luc refuses to see me now."

"There's one person who can help us. Get your coat, Bess. I know where Captain Broussard keeps his motorcar. I can't drive but you can."

I'd been taught by Simon Brandon, and a few of my tennis friends.

"Where do you think you're going?" I demanded, striving to keep my voice low.

"Father Robert will know something. And if he doesn't, there's Paul Moreau."

"Do you have any idea what time it is? You have no authority to drag people out of their beds in the middle of the night and order them to answer your questions."

"It's barely midnight."

"It's going on two o'clock in the morning."

His eyebrows went up. "It can't be."

He was still wearing what was left of his bloody shirt and trousers. Someone would have taken any personal possessions, including his watch, and put them securely away until he was able to keep up with them himself. And the tall case clock here in the library wasn't working.

"You've been sleeping. Unfortunately I couldn't seem to. That's why I've come down, to look in on you."

He regarded his bandages for a moment, then looked across at me. "Did he stab you as well? I don't remember anyone looking at you or taking you away to be examined."

"He tried. Luckily it wasn't very successful, as stabbings go." But I'd washed away the thin trickle of blood where the knife had tracked and said nothing. I didn't want it reported to the police that I'd lied about being wounded as well. It was of no consequence, and I could tend it myself, such as it was.

The Captain's mouth tightened.

"What's more, the Inspector was rather mysterious about Jerome Karadeg. Hinting at the identity of the body. He was fishing, and I don't know what for. You yourself had told me that there was some question about his death."

"I only know what the rumor was, that there was some doubt about the suicide. The man might have tried to make it appear to be an accident, to save his parents from distress."

I nodded. "That's true. Yes, 'the accidentally shot while cleaning his revolver' story." It was a fairly common diagnosis by a local doctor, when a man shot himself, to stop gossip and the resulting pain for the family. "I need to pay the Karadegs another visit. And I need to find out about this talk of a witness to the attack on Marie-Luc. Was it the same person who came to her rescue? I don't know what the Inspector deems to be 'impeccable.'"

Captain Barkley grinned. "His *beau-frère*." His brother-in-law.

I wasn't sure that anyone short of the Prime Minister would do, but then it would still depend on which political view the Inspector followed.

I got the Captain back to his bed and slipped up the stairs myself, disturbing no one on my way.

The next morning I didn't wait for breakfast in the dining room. I let myself out and found a taxi to take me to the café where Marie-Luc and I had quarreled over Philippe Moreau and she had gone off on her own to find Jerome Karadeg.

I wasn't even certain that the café would be open. There would have been a service for Jerome, and his parents might well have decided to keep a period of mourning for their only son.

But when I got there, the doors stood wide, and I could see workmen and shopgirls eating breakfast. Madame Karadeg was there, serving. She wore the severe black of heavy mourning, a small black lace cap on her dark hair, and her eyes were red-rimmed, as if she hadn't slept in days.

I hesitated, and then stepped inside. She looked up, and the ready smile for a new customer, the practiced and professional expression of welcome, faded into a glare.

I stood there, not knowing what else to do.

She set down the dishes she was carrying, said a brief word to the men at that table, and crossed to the door to meet me—or cut me off before I could take a table. I couldn't be sure.

She took my arm in a painful grip and ushered me out into the foggy morning. "I can't believe you would show your face here. My son has scarcely been put in the ground." Her voice was low, almost a hiss of dislike.

"I was here with Sister Marie-Luc—" I began, but she cut me off.

"*Bien sûr*," she said. "I know who you are. The two of you quarreled just there, and she went to find my son. And what happened? He was hunted by the police, for something he didn't do. Why should he harm a nun? I ask you!"

"I know nothing about that, except to say there was a witness. Ask the police. They will tell you. But Marie-Luc begged them to listen to her, she tried to make them understand that it wasn't Jerome who'd attacked her. She still denies it."

Madame stared at me. "You are lying."

"Why should I lie? I've never even met your son."

"They told me the witness was a woman. I thought it was you. You were with her, and I was certain you'd followed her, to make up your quarrel."

A woman?

I'd been told it was a man.

Had Inspector Duplessis invented the witness? But someone had pointed him in the direction of Jerome Karadeg, which made me wonder if *he* had followed Marie-Luc, only to run away when the screaming started. Looking guilty . . .

"I went back to the clinic where I'm recovering. I didn't know what had happened to her until much later. She's still in hospital. The wounds are deep. I wanted to ask you why your son would turn on a friend, and a nun at that. That's why I came. I want to find answers to what happened."

"Why?" Her eyes narrowed with suspicion. "My son is dead. We took his body to Brittany, and buried him there. What can you do now?"

"Take away the black mark of suicide, and find out if he was murdered."

"Murdered? When it was the police hounding him that drove him to kill himself? *Zut alors.* You are mad. Go away and leave us to make sense of our loss. He was an only son, do you understand that? Now, go. And don't come back. Or I will summon a gendarme and tell him you are harassing us."

"Madame, last night I myself was attacked with a knife, and my friend, an officer in the Canadian Army, as well. Your son is dead. *He* couldn't have harmed us, could he? Then who is it? Who has a reason to try to kill *us*? If I knew the answer to that, it might go a long way toward clearing your son's name. It won't bring him back to you, but he will no longer be a suicide in the eyes of the world. Because it might well be the same person, you see, who is doing this."

She stared at me, her eyes filled with something I couldn't read. I didn't think she could see beyond the loss of her son. Beyond watching him being put in the ground. What happened to Captain Barkley, whom she'd never met, was of no importance to her. Sadly, I couldn't blame her.

And then she said, so much venom in her voice that I stepped back away from her, "*I hope God punishes you for the vile woman you are.*"

With that she turned on her heel and marched back to the café like a soldier setting out to do battle. If it hadn't been for the patrons in the café, I think she would have slammed the door, to emphasize that she had shut me out.

I stood there, thinking how unfair it was to blame me, and yet all too aware of the fact that she was grieving.

Monsieur Karadeg came to the window just then and peered out at me. Then he lifted his fist and shook it, his face dark with anger.

I turned away and walked swiftly toward the nearest street where I could hail a taxi and go back to the clinic.

The staff was still serving breakfast when I got to the Hôtel de Belle-Île.

Major Vernon was there, and he looked up as I walked in.

"Your friend is a patient now," he said in greeting. "What happened to him?"

"A madman. Just outside a restaurant near the Boulevard." I sat down, although I wasn't certain I could swallow food. I was still very upset about what had happened at the café.

We talked for a few minutes, Major Vernon and I, before it occurred to me that he might also have access to Captain Broussard's motorcar.

I said, as we were finishing our meal, "You don't by any chance know Captain Broussard well enough to borrow his motorcar for the morning, do you?"

He considered me for a moment, then said, "I could probably manage it. Where do you wish to go? Versailles? Have you ever been there?"

"Some years ago, with my parents," I answered. "We came through Paris on our way home from India."

"Chartres, then? The great cathedral there?"

I smiled. "Actually, I want to go north."

"Where the fighting is? Are you quite serious?"

"Not that far. I can drive myself, of course. It's just that I don't believe the Captain would agree to my borrowing his vehicle."

Major Vernon grinned. "You would probably be right in guessing that he would be concerned. I hear he's very careful with that motorcar. The surprising thing is that he lent it to Captain Barkley. The Americans—the Sams, as they call them here—have a rather Wild West reputation."

"Worse than the Australians?" I asked, thinking of my friend Sergeant Lassiter.

"I wouldn't go that far," he said dryly. "I don't believe the French were quite ready for Paris to be taken by the Allied armies, rather than the Germans."

It was true, I thought. Everyone on leave wished to come to Paris. Even the Russian émigrés preferred to live in Paris, since most of them spoke French.

"Would you ask Captain Broussard? Without mentioning me, unless you must. I really need desperately to go to Petite-Beauvais."

"Finish your coffee, such as it is, and I'll see to it."

An hour later, we were on the road.

I had said nothing to Captain Barkley about our journey when I had looked in on him before I went to the kitchens to fetch my coat. It had been sponged and dried by the cooker, and Madame Ezay had done a remarkable job getting out the bloodstains.

CHAPTER THIRTEEN

WE MADE GOOD time to Petite-Beauvais.

The sun was out, pale and watery. The village looked no better in daylight, and the women on the street were not the fashionable ladies of Paris but drab in black with black scarves over their heads against the chill. The old men wore coats of another era, with the omnipresent black beret. It was as if the village was waiting for the war to end before making itself more habitable, in case the Germans won after all.

Major Vernon had been curious, asking questions all the way here, and I had tried to put him off to some extent, saying nothing about the murders.

We found Father Robert in the tiny church. The stone floor was cold, and I doubted it ever really warmed up even in high summer. I could see my breath when I called to him. He looked up from the lectern, where he was turning pages in the large, gold-edged Bible, readying it for Sunday's service. Even at this distance, I could see it was the handsomest thing in the plain little church, and must have cost the parish dearly.

He didn't appear to be happy to see me, and he examined Major Vernon as if trying to decide whether he was the same officer who had accompanied me the last time.

"Sister Crawford," he said politely, and came up the aisle to meet us.

"*Bonjour,* Father." I waited until he was closer, then said, "I have come about a matter that distressed both Sister Marie-Luc and myself. We found a cutting in the late Juliane Theissen's papers. It was rather frightful, what we read there. I was wondering if you might have more information on what happened—if there were other mentions of the murders in the press. Was the killer ever caught?"

I could read the shock in his face as I spoke, and he shook his head, as if to say it was not something he wished to discuss.

"I've looked for newspapers of the period. But it's been eighteen years, Father. I expect most of them were used to start kitchen fires or line cupboards. You were here at the time, weren't you? You must know how the case ended." I didn't add that I knew some of it from Marie-Luc.

"It was a tragic business," he said finally, "and best forgot."

"Yes, I know. I agree. But you see, something has happened that has brought it all back. I've seen Philippe Moreau in Paris. He claims he's a French officer, but he's not in the Army's records. How can that be?"

I could feel the cold seeping into my boots as we stood there, but Father Robert seemed to be oblivious to it.

"I know nothing about this man," he said. "As for the murders, no one was ever tried, as far as I recall. We are rather out of the way here in Petite-Beauvais, and news seldom reaches us."

"Philippe Moreau grew up here. He lived here to the age of twelve. Surely you remember him? Or should I be addressing such questions to his brother, Paul Moreau?"

"No!" he said quickly, and then took a deep breath. "Why must you bring up matters that are best forgot? Let the past alone."

"I can't. You see, I don't know where my own duty lies. Should I report what I've seen to the police? The Army? I don't know. And someone has tried to kill Sister Marie-Luc, and last night, Captain Barkley was attacked. Do I put these things out of my mind? Tell myself it's none of my business, only to find that I'm the next victim because I know what they knew?"

He stared at me. Then he said, "There are beggars in Paris. Deserters too, I'm told. Some of them are desperate. Starving is a painful way to die."

"And yet Sister Marie-Luc's crucifix and her rosary weren't taken, and Captain Barkley still has his purse and his watch."

"Perhaps he was frightened off, this poor man, before he could rob anyone?"

"These were knife wounds, Father. Very painful ones that could easily become infected. They were intended to kill."

Where did this man's loyalties lie? With Philippe Moreau? Why? *Did* he remember the small boy that Juliane Theissen had brought here with her from Alsace? Did he know the truth about his parentage? And why the elder Moreau adopted him?

Major Vernon touched my arm. I knew what he was saying, that it was useless to ask the priest for his help. I'd tried everything I could think of to reach him, to make him understand that we needed answers. Because if Jerome Karadeg was dead, he couldn't have attacked the two of us last night. And Marie-Luc must be right, that he hadn't hurt her. If Philippe Moreau had already killed five people, taking a knife to three more wouldn't stir his conscience.

In the end, we left Father Robert in his church. I considered speaking to his housekeeper, but it was unlikely that she would tell us anything he didn't want her to gossip about. A priest's housekeeper, like a vicar's wife, knows how to keep secrets.

We did go to the house where the Moreaus lived. It still had that air of abandonment, the brass knocker sounding through empty rooms.

If Paul Moreau was living there, alone and without staff to help him, he had no intention of opening the door to us.

I did wonder why it was that the priest was so afraid of him.

*   *   *

As we walked back to the Captain's motorcar, Major Vernon said thoughtfully, "You wanted to know about that court martial. And now you want to know about murders that took place years ago. What does one have to do with the other?"

He was in Intelligence. He was not someone who could be palmed off with a few lies.

"I don't know," I told him honestly. "There's this, you see. I think Philippe Moreau has a secret, and I don't know what it is. Did he kill five people when he was twelve? And why isn't he on the French Army rolls, either as serving, missing, captured, or killed? They must know something about him. When I saw him as a wounded man wearing a ragged uniform that hardly kept him warm enough to survive, it was a *French* uniform. If he'd been court-martialed, he wouldn't be listed on the active rolls, would he? Have you learned anything more about the court martial?"

"The French must be embarrassed about the outcome. They are not talking."

"Yes, well, they've had a mutiny in their own army—hanging some of the ringleaders. It's not surprising that they don't want to discuss court-martialing an officer."

"We're not happy about that ourselves. But now I think it's time you told me all there is to know about this man Moreau."

He asked a lot of questions as I explained everything I thought he needed to hear. The Major had a logical mind, and I could see that he was carefully cataloging every fact.

When I'd finished, he turned to me. "Dear God, Bess, you've got yourself in the middle of something that's dangerous. You're damned lucky you weren't hurt as well last night."

I didn't tell him that it wasn't for lack of trying on our assailant's part.

"I can't see why an old murder should be responsible for all that's happened. But I can't find any other connection between the nun, her old governess, and Philippe Moreau." I hesitated. "I did think, in that base hospital, that he might be a German spy. But Matron suggested that it was his upbringing in Alsace that made him so fluent in German. You had to be, once Germany took over. Everything—church services, business matters, schooling, even at home—everyone had to speak the language of their new masters. You could be in serious trouble if you didn't."

The day had faded, early dusk falling with the heavy banks of clouds that had moved in from the west.

"Well, yes, that's true," the Major said, slowing as a woman on a bicycle came weaving her way out of a side road and turned in front of us. On the back of the bicycle was a cage, and in it were two hens, staring at us with gold eyes. "But I'm finding it hard to believe that there's no record of a French officer by that name. Had you considered that he might have been called Philippe as a child, but now uses his full name? He could be François, Armand, Georges, Louis—it would be impossible to look up all of them and learn which he might be."

"I had thought about it," I said ruefully. "And another possibility has just occurred to me. He was not a Moreau when he first came to France as a child. He was adopted, given that family's name. After what happened in the Bois, when he was accused of murder and disappeared, he could very well have decided to use his birth name." Frowning, I added, "But how do you reconcile that with giving us his name as Moreau when he was interviewed in hospital?"

"Perhaps his birth name was German, not French. He might have feared he couldn't explain that away, and chosen the easier way out of the problem."

I sighed in frustration. "I don't suppose we'll ever know what the truth is. Unless he's found. I'll be going back to the Front very soon. That means it could remain a mystery."

"Well. It helped to pass the time while you were recovering," the Major said, smiling across at me. His black patch, in the glow of the headlamps, looked sinister. And then he turned his gaze back to the road, and I saw only the profile of his good side.

* * *

The silhouettes of Paris loomed ahead, and soon we were back at the clinic. Major Vernon dropped me at the door and went on to return the motorcar to Captain Broussard.

I was crossing the courtyard when a man's muffled voice said, "Sister Crawford?"

I spun around, realizing that I couldn't reach the door before whoever it was reached me.

"Don't scream, for God's sake."

I saw him then. A darker shape in the deep shadows by the thick square gateposts.

"Who are you? What do you want?" I asked, keeping my voice low in spite of the pounding of my heart.

"I don't intend to hurt you."

French. His English was French accented. But he must have been wearing a scarf around the lower part of his face. And the way he was hunched, it would be impossible to judge how tall he was, or how slim or compact his body might be.

"Who are you?"

"Leave Paris. Leave me alone. You don't know what this is about."

"It's about the murder of five people," I said. He jerked at that, and I went on quickly, "Move toward me and I will scream. There's an orderly just on the other side of that door." At least I hoped he was on duty, and not at his dinner.

After a moment he said, "Yes, all right. Murder, if you like. One more won't matter."

"You nearly killed Sister Marie-Luc."

He replied, surprise in his voice, "Why should I want her dead?"

"She knows who you are and what you did. I think Juliane Theissen told her a long time ago what you did."

"That's probably true. Go back to your own people, Sister Crawford, and let the past stay buried." His voice changed, rough and chilling. "You won't see me the next time. You won't know I'm there."

He turned and walked swiftly through the gates, moving with a twisted gait, and I couldn't tell whether it was exaggerated or an indication that his feet were troubling him.

I raced for the gate, looking to see where he was going. But there was no one on the street. Surely he couldn't have disappeared so quickly, if his feet hadn't healed?

He could have turned into another courtyard, or concealed himself in a doorway, lying in wait and hoping I would follow him. An attack that would take me by surprise and allow him to strike before I could even scream. I hesitated, standing there in the street.

I had no weapon, and if I went into the clinic and persuaded an orderly to come out with me, there would be no one to find.

I was still standing there when I heard footsteps fast approaching from the other direction.

Wheeling, I was poised to race for the clinic's door when I realized it was Major Vernon, returning from dropping off the motorcar.

"Bess? What are you doing there in the middle of the street?" he demanded. "Why aren't you inside? You haven't been standing there waiting for me all this time, have you?"

"You've already returned the motorcar?" I asked, confused. It hadn't been long enough, had it?

"Broussard is at the Café Rouge this evening. I was instructed to leave the motorcar there, where he could take it back to barracks himself."

"Oh," I said, and as he caught me up, we turned and went through the gates up to the door.

"Why were you in the street?" he asked again.

"I thought I saw someone I recognized," I replied. "I must have been wrong."

We had hardly reached the door when a wall of rain came down the avenue, spreading fast. Major Vernon flung the door open. I was inside, and then he was at my heels, shoving it shut behind us.

I could hear the heavy drops of rain striking the paneling like the sound of distant machine-gun fire.

The orderly at the desk looked up, surprised. "Rain?" he said, then, listening, "A nasty night out there."

He was more right than he knew.

We left our coats under the stairs and went in to dinner. Our conversation was stilted, with long spaces of silence, because we couldn't talk about what we were thinking. And afterward I went up to my room.

Was the man in the courtyard tonight Philippe Moreau?

He hadn't been able to kill me last night. Instead he'd wounded Captain Barkley. But why had he come to try to frighten me away? Perhaps that was much less dangerous than a murder, attracting the attention of that cold-eyed policeman. Especially since he'd already failed once to discourage me.

I slept restlessly, trying to work out the answer.

I wished for my father, or Simon, someone I could talk to about what was happening here in Paris. A clear eye, uninvolved, someone I trusted.

But there was no one to turn to for advice or explanation.

I could always go to the staff doctor here at Belle-Île and tell him that I was fully recovered, that I was ready to go back to my post in one of the forward aid stations.

That would be to retreat from what I'd started. And my great-great-great-grandmother who had shown such courage on the eve of Waterloo would disown me.

I was smiling as I finally drifted into a deeper sleep.

Somehow in the night I'd taken a decision about what to do next. It was useless to try to pass on to the French Army the little information I possessed about Philippe Moreau. Who would listen? I couldn't go back to St. Anne's—I didn't think Marie-Luc would speak to me. But there was the police Inspector. The problem was finding the police station he was assigned to. Was it in the area where Marie-Luc had been found stabbed? Or in the district near St. Anne's? He had also come here, which meant that he was handling this inquiry as well.

After breakfast, I looked in on Captain Barkley, who was fuming about his enforced stay in the clinic.

"I have no fever, the stitches are clean, and I see no reason I can't go on about my business. Speak to them for me, Bess. Tell them I'm not a fool, I know how to take care of my wound."

"I'm a patient here myself," I told him. "My word doesn't carry much weight. Matron will decide when you can leave."

He grumbled on a bit longer, and then said, still quite annoyed, "I understand you went to Petite-Beauvais again. With Major Vernon."

Ah, I thought, that was his problem. And men tended to gossip as much as women did, sometimes.

"It was a wasted trip," I said. "Father Robert wouldn't talk to me, and we couldn't raise anyone at the Moreau house. I don't know if Paul Moreau is still in residence or not."

He seemed pleased that we hadn't made any progress.

"What I don't understand is why Father Robert is so afraid of Paul Moreau."

"He's the equivalent of the local squire. And he probably wouldn't be best pleased to discover the local priest was telling strangers about his family's skeletons. He wasn't the pleasantest person to deal with, when he came to the governess's cottage that night. I'd wager he has something of a temper."

"That's true. We're probably the first to come knocking on the rectory door asking about the family's history in nearly twenty years. Monsieur Moreau wouldn't care to remind everyone in the village about what happened."

We talked for several minutes longer, and then one of the staff came in with his breakfast, and I took that as an opportunity to leave.

I had every intention of seeking advice from Madame Ezay about finding the French policeman. She was not upstairs making up beds, and I'd come back down, crossing Reception to look in the kitchens or laundry for her, when the outside door opened, and who should step in but the Inspector.

With him he had a short, sturdy man in workman's clothing who looked rather frightened, his eyes wide as he glanced nervously around him.

"Sister Crawford," he greeted me. "Well met. I have with me this morning a well-known miscreant who favors the knife to cut purse strings and pockets. I thought perhaps you might recognize him."

At this, his prisoner turned to stare at me, surprise in his face.

I was feeling as surprised as he was. He looked nothing like the man I'd seen running away from the restaurant where we'd been attacked, the Captain and I.

But I paid both men the courtesy of taking my time before shaking my head and saying, "I'm so sorry, Inspector. I don't believe he is the man."

"Turn around," he ordered his prisoner. And he did, showing me his broad back.

Again, I could only shake my head.

"I will speak to the Captain, if you please. He was chasing his assailant, he might well know him again."

By this time the orderly had come up from his own breakfast. Seeing the newcomers, he hurried to his desk and asked how he could be of assistance.

I didn't think the man the Inspector had brought with him could speak or understand English. He was looking more and more ill at ease, and when I'd told the orderly to take the policeman to the Captain, the man struggled in the Inspector's grip.

The Inspector ignored the impediment and strode after the orderly. I followed behind, and the prisoner cast me a frantic look.

We were admitted to the Captain's room, and the Inspector repeated his questions.

Captain Barkley studied the man, front and back, then shook his head.

"He was taller, slimmer, I think. Sister Crawford, does this person look familiar to you?"

"I don't believe it's the same man."

"Nor do I."

The Inspector thanked him and, with a nod, left. By this time his prisoner had decided he wasn't to be hanged—or guillotined—and he followed meekly.

I went after them, and in Reception, as the Inspector was preparing to leave, I said quickly, "May I speak with you privately?"

"I'll take this person out to one of my men," he agreed, and after a moment, he returned alone.

The library was empty at this hour, and I led him there. As I shut the door behind us, I said, "If you please, I'd like an honest answer. If Jerome Karadeg stabbed the nun, Sister Marie-Luc, and he's dead, then who tried to stab Captain Barkley and me? It's important that I know. I've never met Jerome Karadeg, I wouldn't know him if he walked through that door. I didn't recognize our assailant, what little I saw of him. Have you had any luck speaking to witnesses?"

"I have found only two. A man and his wife, walking across the street, who saw the Canadian officer chasing someone and then collapsing. No one else has come forward."

"Who was the witness to the nun's stabbing?"

"I don't have to tell you that."

We were still standing, and he was growing impatient with me.

I took a deep breath and then plunged in. "I was only a child myself in 1900, but I have been told that there were murders in a house near the Bois. Five of them, and a twelve-year-old boy was suspected of the crime. It's this twelve-year-old, now a man, whom the nun believes stabbed her. I don't know the details of this earlier crime—I only know about it at third hand, so to speak. It was before your time as well. But I haven't been able to find anything in old newspapers, and I don't know anyone who was involved."

He was interested in spite of himself. "And you believe this grown man, who tried to kill the nun, has also tried to attack you and Captain Barkley. Why? Because you know Sister Marie-Luc? Or because you believe he knows that you are aware of what he's done?"

"I can't answer that. But it does seem odd, does it not, that the three of us have been attacked in a matter of days. And if Jerome Karadeg stabbed Marie-Luc, who stabbed us? This person took nothing from us. It wasn't robbery. What was it? And the man you brought here today isn't anyone we know."

"Are you in possession of the names of the victims in this earlier crime?"

"I believe so. It was sometime in 1900, and I would guess during the summer. The man and his wife were a Monsieur and Madame Lavaud. His mother, also Madame Lavaud. There were two maids in the house at the time, but I don't know their names."

"Lavaud," he repeated, half to himself. "Why is that name familiar?"

"It went unsolved. The boy who was charged never went to trial, although everyone at the time must have been convinced that he was guilty."

"This was the son of the house?"

"Someone visiting that child."

"How did the nun know of this affair?"

"Her former governess, an old woman who died recently, had also at one time served the Moreau family. She had moved on to care for other charges by that time, of course, and one of them was Marie-Luc. But surely she would have felt the shock and horror personally, having known the accused."

"Of course," he echoed. "I shall have to look into this matter."

"There's one more thing. You've hinted that there was some question about the death of Jerome Karadeg. Something that cast doubt on the fact that he'd committed suicide. Can you tell me what that was? It might be important, you see."

He parried the question. "Why do you care? I understand you are convalescing and will be returning to your post very shortly."

Who had told him that? Matron, the other night when he was here? Had he been looking into me and into Captain Barkley as well? It was an unpleasant thought.

"It has nothing to do with me. But I should like to know, since the Captain and I were attacked, that I can safely put this man Karadeg out of my mind. This will allow me to see what happened outside the restaurant in a different light."

"He was a coward to the end." It was said contemptuously, and I remembered all at once that Jerome Karadeg was a victim of shell shock. "He even tried to cut his own throat before he went into the water, dreading drowning."

This was news indeed. "Are you sure he did this? That he tried to cut his own throat?"

"Yes, Mademoiselle, we are quite satisfied. It was a shock to his father, I can tell you, when he was brought in to identify the body. The doctor who examined it has said the slash was not well done. It is not easy to do this to oneself."

I thought to myself that it might have been more horrific to try than to drown. I shivered, understanding now why the Karadegs were so upset. Not just at the suicide of their son but also at the manner of it. No wonder they believed he'd been hounded to the point of desperation.

When I said nothing, the Inspector commented, "You need not fear the dead, Mademoiselle."

"No. But you are telling me that it was not Philippe Moreau after all, that Sister Marie-Luc was wrong about that. It also tells me that what happened to Captain Barkley was another matter altogether."

"Very likely."

I left it at that. I'd already told him too much about the Lavaud family as it was, but I'd hoped he would help me.

He nodded to me. "If that's everything you wish to discuss, I will say *bonjour* and take my leave."

"Yes, thank you, Inspector. I appreciate your listening to me."

"Not at all."

And then he was gone.

I stood there, staring into space, thinking about our conversation. And then I left the library and went up to my room.

Was it true that Philippe Moreau had nothing to do with what had happened to Marie-Luc? She was obsessed with him, she had called him a monster, and when she had thought she saw him on the streets of Paris, she had been almost driven mad by her anger. It would have made her happier to believe that her attacker was Philippe Moreau and not Jerome.

Had Juliane Theissen fostered this obsession, because the child had been her brother or possibly even her own son? She wouldn't have wanted to believe that the boy she'd given up to the Moreau family had become a killer, but she would still protect him.

Then why had she come back to live in the same small village where the Moreau family lived? To remind them every day of every week what she must have believed they had done to the boy? If he was indeed her son, and she had been forced to allow them to adopt him, her bitterness must have known no bounds. And yet, as a woman alone in a strange country with a small boy to care for, what sort of life could she have given Philippe?

It was an interesting perspective, and I sat there by the window, looking down on the courtyard of this house, considering a very different direction.

What had become of the boy who had been called a monster, a murderer?

And what effect had these charges had on the other child in the Moreau family? How had Paul Moreau dealt with this? After all, he was only a child himself. I was beginning to see why he was a man with a temper.

Perhaps that was where to begin, not with Marie-Luc's view of Philippe Moreau.

I got up and went to the small desk here in the nanny's room. I wrote a short letter to Paul Moreau, and then went down to the orderly in Reception and asked him to post it for me.

And then I had nothing to do but wait.

The trick would be receiving an answer before I was ordered to leave Paris.

There was nothing to do, it wasn't time to read to the other patients, and so I spilled the toy soldiers out across my bed and took out the envelope that had come from Juliane Theissen's house.

This was all there was. I hadn't pulled up the floorboards or tapped at the walls, ripped open the mattress or the seats in the chairs. I wasn't convinced that the fräulein had hidden more than this envelope. I hadn't found the lacquer box, of course, but it would hardly be concealed in a mattress or a chair seat. Very likely I held in my hand the contents from it. The hinges could have broken or it might have been dropped—such things were fragile. Or perhaps too many people knew about it and she had got rid of it after choosing the photograph on the wall as a safer place.

So why, I asked myself, had she chosen to keep these few pieces of her past out of sight, where no one would think to look for them?

Turning the envelope over in my fingers, I wondered again that there was only the one cutting. Why not follow the account to the end of the inquiry? Or at least keep the final news story, however it ended? Had she feared that her employer at the time might find them and connect her to the Moreau family? But they would already have known whom she had worked for in the past.

Then why keep the beginning, the first account?

Paul Moreau was the child of both his parents. When they adopted

Philippe, before Paul was born, *he* became not only the elder son of the house but also an heir. The interloper taking precedence.

How did Paul feel about it? More to the point, how did his mother feel?

Had she seen this adopted son through his incarceration? Was it she who had put up the money to spirit him safely to Alsace? I hadn't really thought about her role in all this. Paul, at ten, was too young to help anyone. Had she come to care for Philippe? Was that why she had sent away his governess?

It was an interesting thought.

There was a knock at my door.

"A moment, please," I called, and hastily shoved the envelope and the soldiers back into the tub, putting it under the bed out of sight.

It was Madame Ezay.

She looked frightened.

"There's someone at the door, asking for you."

"For me?" I repeated, surprised.

"He's an English staff officer. *Très formidable!*"

I reached for my coat and ran out the door, only to remember the healing wound in my side. I walked down the stairs more sedately, smiling with excitement, my heart beating fast.

My father had found an excuse to come to Paris.

CHAPTER FOURTEEN

I COULDN'T SEE him as I came down the last flight of stairs—he must have stepped into an adjoining room—but I thought he'd heard my footsteps because someone was returning to Reception, long strides across the tiled flooring echoing up the staircase. I hurried down the last few steps and turned to greet him.

The height, the uniform, the dark hair just threaded with gray were right. The face was not.

And then I recognized him, and my greeting died on my lips.

It was Colonel MacInnes, one of my father's friends.

"Hallo, Sister Crawford," he said, holding out his hand.

I took it, summoning a smile.

He grinned. "You must have been expecting to see your father. I'm sorry. I didn't think. But I'm his emissary. He discovered I was being sent to Paris, and he asked me to call on you and find out exactly what he can do for you."

I could think of a dozen things, if it had been my father standing there. But Colonel MacInnes, a fine officer and a good man, couldn't be dragged into my problems.

"I'm well," I said. "They're talking about sending me back to the Front in a few days."

"That's good news indeed. Your mother will be pleased to hear it, and I can tell her myself that you are looking fine. She's been worried, you know."

"I expect she has." I should have written, I scolded myself. But I hadn't. "I am feeling stronger every day."

"Excellent. And Captain Barkley? I'm told he hasn't reported to your father for several days."

Oh, dear. No word from me, none from the Captain. No wonder my father was worried.

"Um, he's had an accident, but he's recovering nicely. Would you care to speak to him?"

"There's no time. I have a meeting with Marshal Foch in an hour."

We chatted for several more minutes, and then he asked me to walk with him to his motorcar. He helped me with my coat and nodded to the orderly still standing behind his desk, then opened the door for me.

The wind was cold after the rain. "I'm only here for forty-eight hours," he said, "but I've brought someone with me. At your mother's insistence. My God, I wish I had an officer on my staff like her. She could field an army without turning a hair." He chuckled, and as I looked up, I saw Simon Brandon standing by the Army motorcar's door.

"My father's Sergeant-Major," I said, trying not to give myself away, but I was nearly as glad to see Simon as I would have been to see the Colonel Sahib.

"Tomorrow at noon, I need him to meet me at the embassy. Any messages you may have for your family you can give to him."

"Thank you, sir."

We had reached the gates, and Simon turned, nodding to me as if we were strangers.

"Sergeant-Major," I said, formally.

"See that she writes her mother," Colonel MacInnes said to him as he stepped into the vehicle.

"Yes, sir. I will, sir." He closed the door, then watched the motorcar drive away and disappear around the corner. I waited as well.

Then he turned to me, grinning. "I expected to find you in an invalid chair, drooping amidst your blankets. Where's the Captain?"

"Drooping in his blankets. Someone tried to kill him. And narrowly missed me."

"Good God. Your mother told me you were up to your ears in trouble. I should have believed her. I only have twenty-four hours, Bess. But if you're in danger, I'll find a way to convince Colonel MacInnes to take you back to England. He appears to be under your mother's spell."

"I think he'd have married her, if my father hadn't got there first," I said, taking his arm. "There's a café in this direction. Not very far. We can talk there."

"How is that wound?"

"Much improved. I think they may have erred on the side of caution because I'm my father's daughter. But it has been slow to heal. There was infection, to start with. They were quite worried about that." Which probably explained the appearance of Captain Barkley, I thought. Unless my father had learned that he was here and sent his own orders. "Simon, I need to find out if a certain Lieutenant Philippe Moreau is known to the British Army. As a German spy. Or if he'd been court-martialed but disappeared. For that matter," I added, realizing what I'd just said, "it may well be that he's got a habit of disappearing."

We found the café, the windows steamed from the warmth inside, but we had it nearly to ourselves. I warned Simon against the coffee, and instead he had a glass of wine.

He gave me news of home as we waited to be served, and when the waiter had left us, he changed the subject. "Tell me the story."

"Oh, good heavens," I said, struck by a realization. "This afternoon I must read to the convalescents. Please don't let me forget."

And I launched into an account of everything that had happened, holding nothing back. He listened intently, watching my face as I talked. It was good to be sitting here with him. I knew I could trust him, I knew I could depend on him. The only thing I had to fear from him was being kidnapped back to England, if he was worried enough.

The woman behind the counter had been eyeing him, examining me as if to wonder how I had attracted such a handsome escort. I was well into my account when she walked over to ask if he'd care for another glass of wine. He smiled at her and told her he would. When she brought it, she lingered by the table, asking if he was English, and if he intended to stay in Paris very long. She was attractive, possibly thirty, and had very pretty eyes. She knew how to use them too.

I sat patiently waiting for her flirtation to end, then finished what I wanted to tell him. Simon digested it for a time, looking out the window at the passersby. Then he turned to me and said, "I don't like this. Whatever is happening, whoever is behind this business, he's prepared to kill. Let it go, Bess."

"I was hoping for more practical advice."

"I know. And I know you. You'll see this through to the end, if you can. I'm not likely to distract you."

It was nearly noon. We ordered lunch, much to Madame's delight. Simon asked me for clarification on certain points, making sure he knew exactly what had been happening.

"It seems to me that Barkley is in no condition to confront this man Paul Moreau. And you can hardly drag Major Vernon further into this business. You shouldn't have taken him to this village in the first place. If anyone learns that he's involved, and he's attacked, it could cause an incident. Did Barkley report what had happened to him?"

"I don't think he's had a chance. And that's another point, Simon. I'd give much to know why he's in Paris to start with. I can hardly imagine that an officer of his experience is here to hunt deserters, although he makes it sound reasonable enough. He was telling me about the salons he'd attended. Most deserters can barely feed themselves."

"You're right. That duty is generally left to the Foot Police. He's been dispatched to Paris on other business. I had that from the Colonel."

"Did he also tell you what he's doing here?"

Simon smiled. "No. Above my rank, I expect. But if I had to guess, I'd say the Captain is looking for someone."

"Perhaps he thinks he's found him," I said, finishing my potatoes. They had been the best part of the meal, although the onions had been well cooked too. The meat was gristly and tasteless. "That's why he's so willing to give me his help."

"You say you've written to this Paul Moreau?"

"If he answers me. I expect he won't."

"And you'll go back there, to meet him if he asks it?"

"He's recovering from wounds. I don't believe he'll come to Paris to see me."

"Very well. I'll walk with you as far as the clinic, and I'll see if I can commandeer a motorcar. I don't care for the possibility of your walking into trouble. You know nothing about the man."

I felt an unexpected surge of relief. With Simon at my back, even a furious Paul Moreau was no threat.

"Captain Broussard has one, but I don't think you'll have much luck there."

"We'll see."

He paid for the meal and we returned to Belle-Île. The wind cut through my coat, and I shivered. "I hope the war ends soon. I don't know how we'll survive another winter of fighting."

"There's an ambulance at your door. Look."

He was right, it was just pulling up. Hurrying, we got there in time to see that there were new arrivals being brought into the clinic. Simon walked on as I stopped to help with the task of unloading the stretcher cases. Matron and several of the Sisters came out to meet the newcomers a moment later. We got them inside and sorted rather quickly, and then I went to the library to read once more.

"There's fierce fighting at the Front," one of my regular officers said as he came in and took a chair by the hearth. "I just spoke to a Lieutenant Raymond. From Gloucester, he says. The Germans aren't going quietly."

"I've heard the French are bickering over what terms they'll demand as reparations," another man commented. "That's going to delay any chance of an early end."

I wondered if that was why Colonel MacInnes was here, to keep the French from fighting amongst themselves.

Picking up my book, I was surprised to see Captain Barkley being wheeled in, in an invalid's chair. He was pale but seemed to be alert and eager to get out of his bed.

I read for the assigned hour, and then, giving everyone to believe I was tired, excused myself quickly, before Captain Barkley could wheel himself across the room to where I'd been sitting. They were still talking about the chapter as I shut the door. I hurried to Reception and looked out at the street.

A motorcar was sitting there, waiting.

I'd left my coat and a rug, among other things, behind the stairs, and so it took no more than a matter of seconds to collect them and leave.

Simon got down to hold the door for me, then turned to the crank. "I hope you know where you're going," he said.

"There shouldn't be any trouble," I assured him. "Is this Colonel MacInnes's motorcar?"

"I was afraid you'd notice." He got in, gave me a grin, and we set out. I had no trouble finding our way out of Paris, and then we settled down for the journey to Petite-Beauvais. We talked very little. I asked for news of Mrs. Hennessey, and was surprised to hear that Simon had stopped in to see her only last week.

"She sends her love. And she's concerned about what's going to happen to her lodgers when the war is over. I told her it's likely that you'll keep the flat."

"Yes, I expect I shall," I said slowly. I hadn't thought about that aspect of the war ending. After four long years, it seemed as if this was what was normal now, and that what had been before was no more than a dream of a distant time. How it would be afterward, I don't think any of us could imagine. "I'm fond of her," I added. "Were any of my flatmates in London? Diana? Mary? Lady Elspeth?"

"Not when I was there. Mary was in France, Diana had stayed in Dover, and Lady Elspeth had just left for Folkestone."

"I've hardly seen them for months," I said. "And Melinda?"

She was a Crawford cousin who had married another Crawford cousin—an Army man like so many of us—and was now a widow living in Kent. When she was a child, she and her mother had survived the bloody Siege of Lucknow during the frightful Indian Mutiny of 1857. She had been quite the heroine, in fact.

"Your mother had a letter from her only recently. She's well. I gather she knows more about the war than the Prime Minister. Your mother tells me your cousin keeps up a correspondence that includes half of Parliament, most of the Army, and a good part of the Navy. You might write and ask what Captain Barkley is doing in France. I've no doubt at all that she could tell you."

I laughed. Still, he wasn't exaggerating.

We fell into a comfortable silence, except for the occasional direction that I needed to give.

We had always been comfortable together, although I could hardly remember the angry, stubborn boy who had come out from England as a private soldier. My father had seen something in him that others hadn't, and the dire predictions that he'd be cashiered or court-martialed before he had served out his first year hadn't proven true. And in the end, well liked by officers and other ranks, Simon had become the youngest Regimental Sergeant-Major in the history of the regiment. My father had also privately called him one of the best soldiers he'd ever come across, and had tried to persuade him to go back to England to train as an officer. Simon had steadfastly refused.

There was an overturned hay wain at the crossroads, and we lost half an hour as farmers tried to right it. Simon got down and organized the effort, or it would have been midnight before we were on our way again.

It was dark, well past the dinner hour, when we reached the village. There was no one about on the streets. We drove directly to the Moreau house, and I pounded on the door, to no answer.

"Leave it to me," Simon replied when I voiced my frustration.

He disappeared into the shadows, and I stood there in the cold wind waiting for him to return. But he didn't. The minutes ticked by, and I began to feel distinctly uneasy. What was keeping him? Had something gone wrong?

I was on the point of going around the house myself when the door opened, and Paul Moreau stood there, outlined by a lamp on a small table behind him. His face was twisted with anger and a frustration that went far beyond my own.

"Come in, then," he said without any politeness or courtesy, and stepped aside. It wasn't until I was well inside the door, uncertain whether or not I should have waited for Simon, that I saw him just beyond the lamplight, near the stairs.

Without another word, our host led us down the passage to a sitting room. The dustcovers had been taken off one of the chairs, and a table had been cleared. The remains of a dinner occupied it now. I saw a crust of bread and what appeared to be an omelet. There was also a half-full bottle of wine and a glass with a little left at the bottom.

"You're the woman who was in the fräulein's house. With an officer," he went on, not offering us a seat. "What is it you want now?"

"I am so sorry, Captain—"

"No, you aren't, or you wouldn't be here," he threw back at me.

"You're wrong. I have come to your door twice, and you refused to speak to me. I think you know why."

"The affairs of my family are no concern of yours."

"That's true, in other circumstances. But there have been several recent attempts at murder now. Sister Marie-Luc, and Captain Barkley, the man you saw with me at Fräulein Theissen's cottage. By the grace of God, I escaped serious injury. That makes your family's concerns my own. If you like, we'll leave. And I will speak to the police. Let them sort out what's been happening."

I turned to go, and I'd almost reached the door when he relented. I'd thought he might, but as my hand reached for the knob, I was afraid I'd guessed wrong.

"Yes, all right. You're here. We might as well get it over with. What do you want?"

"To clear up a mystery," I said. "The police sought a man in Paris, for the attack on the nun. But Marie-Luc stubbornly insists that it was the wrong man. She glimpsed your brother in Paris, and she's convinced that he has found her and tried to kill her."

I could see that he hadn't known that Philippe Moreau was in Paris. Recovering quickly, he said, "Why should he wish to harm her? And he is not my brother. He never was."

"I don't know whether that's true or not. Legally he must still be. As to any blood ties, certainly Fräulein Theissen knew what the truth was. She brought him to France. I have no idea what your mother was told. Or even how she felt about it when your father insisted on adopting Philippe." I walked back into the room and took one of the dustcovers off the nearest chair to the hearth, sitting down in it and holding out my hands to warm them. Simon remained standing by the door.

"I didn't know he was adopted. For years, I believed it was true that he was my elder brother. And my mother dared not say anything while my father was alive. She was a bitter woman by the time he died. She told me later that the child was his bastard, foisted on us. I didn't *want* to believe it then. Philippe was barely two when he came to Petite-Beauvais. He couldn't remember any home but ours. She made his life wretched, all the same. I've always thought that's why he—" He broke off, turning to pour himself a little more wine, but then he set the glass down without tasting it.

"Why he murdered the Lavaud family? Because they were making their own son unhappy?"

He spun around. "How did you know about that?"

"There was a cutting in the fräulein's possession. It was the first newspaper account of the murders. I think Marie-Luc knows how that ended, but I've not been able to find out for myself whether Philippe was charged or not. Still—*something* was wrong that afternoon. You went off riding. The Lavauds' son was in the kennels. Philippe was found dazed and wandering."

"My mother sent her that cutting. With a note that informed her it was her son they were taking into custody. She told me years later."

It was the ultimate cruelty. The woman who had taken in the boy, however reluctantly, abandoning him now.

"And did they arrest him?"

"He was charged. My mother refused to go back to Paris for the trial and fight for him. I didn't understand why at the time. She said only that he was guilty and there was nothing she could do. I don't know that she ever saw him again." He sat down heavily in the chair by the table. "You can't imagine my shock. When I returned to school at the beginning of the next term—it was just a few weeks later—I was taunted unmercifully. By the end of term, I was convinced I hated Philippe. That he was the monster my mother assured me he was." He twisted the stem of the wineglass in his fingers, watching the contents swirl around.

"What became of him?" It was Simon who asked that question.

"The newspapers claimed that on the first day of his trial, he took violently ill. It was thought that he might have taken some poison.

It only added to the perception that he was guilty. They rushed him to hospital, and on the second night that he was there, he escaped. There was another boy in the ward. Philippe simply took his clothes and walked out."

"Where did he go? Did anyone help him?" I tried to picture a twelve-year-old child, forsaken by his mother, his brother, and everyone else, walking out into the dark streets of Paris, with nowhere to go, no money, nowhere to turn. How on earth had he survived?

"I don't know. I wondered, years later, if Fräulein Theissen had come for him and helped him to escape. Although how she would have managed it, I don't know. He was not allowed visitors, he saw no one but the staff. I did ask my mother, once, if she had spirited him away to save us all the nightmare of a trial. It might have occurred to her that the endless news coverage would stop if he vanished. It was difficult for all of us."

"How did she answer you?" I asked.

"She laughed in my face. Victor Lavaud, the murder victims' son, never believed it was Philippe. He told the police it couldn't have been. But there was some sort of evidence. He found the bodies, you know. The police thought that very clever of him. It accounted for the blood on the soles of his shoes and on his clothes."

He took a deep breath. "After that, it was as if he had disappeared into thin air. There was a search, of course, but with no leads, the police gave up. They felt he'd died on the streets."

"Do you think he went back to Alsace?"

Paul Moreau took a deep breath. "It had occurred to me. Not in the beginning. Fräulein might have helped him. She must have had a few family members left in the province. I don't know that the police ever looked for him there, if it even occurred to them. At any rate, interest in the murders soon waned, and I could get on with my life."

"You never heard from him again?"

"Not from him. I did hear of him."

I waited, almost holding my breath. Fearing what he might have to tell me.

"The war. He must have enlisted under Theissen. I remember someone asking me if he was any relation to my old governess. I had no idea if it was true or not, I just denied it vehemently. In late 1915, no one wanted to be related to anyone who was German. And then Karl Theissen was taken up on a charge of treason. I didn't want to know if that was Philippe. I didn't want anything to do with him, or this man Thiessen. I told myself the fact that this was also the name of our governess was no more than an unfortunate coincidence."

"And he was court-martialed," I said, before I could stop myself.

He looked up at me in surprise. "Yes. But he escaped again. It was thought that he fled to the German lines and gave himself up. Where else could he have gone?"

"When was this?"

"In early 1916? Yes, I believe that's right."

"But I thought—there was someone from this village who was court-martialed in the spring of this year."

"That wasn't anything to do with me. The man came home to help his pregnant wife plant a crop on their farm."

I'd been told he'd escaped. Someone must have felt sympathetic toward him and turned a blind eye.

Hurriedly collecting my thoughts, I could see that the time difference helped explain how Sister Marie-Luc had seen Philippe Moreau in Belgium in a German uniform.

And here, at the end of the war, Philippe—no longer Karl Theissen—was back in Paris. I'd seen him, and so had the nun. Small wonder he had tried to kill us. Not because of the murders a long time ago, but because he was wanted by the French Army.

It was finally making sense. A terrible kind of sense, if he had spied for the Germans in Paris, and when we found him, he was trying to reach his own lines before the war ended.

"You can see why I wanted no part of his resurrection," Paul

Moreau was saying. "It will all be raked up again. The murders, the trial, the court martial, his escape to Germany. I'll be dragged into it, sooner or later. The newspapers will find me. They have before." He picked up the glass and emptied it, swallowing hard, as if he didn't care for the taste. His gaze swept us, me sitting by the fire, Simon still standing by the door. "Do you see why I didn't want any part of you?"

I did. All too well.

"I'm so sorry," I said, for the second time that evening. "But you must see as well that we can't simply let him go on killing."

"He hasn't killed," Paul Moreau retorted harshly. "You and the Captain and the nun are still alive."

"Not for want of trying," I responded, cold in my turn. "Do we just wait, and hope that once his feet are healed, he's finished with us and intent on whatever new life he hopes is waiting for him?"

It was Simon who spoke then. "Conditions are very bad in Germany. He speaks French. Now that he's in Paris he could go anywhere in France, claim to be anyone. He could emigrate to Quebec. Or Martinique."

"I have no idea where he is or where he will go. I don't care. You must ask this nun, since she seems to know more about him than I do."

"She believes he killed the Lavaud family. I don't think she is aware of the court martial. *Did* he kill them? You were there. You must remember something about that day, and what happened to him."

He'd been flushed, whether with anger or wine or both, I couldn't tell. Now he shrugged. "God knows. He was accused. They took him away, and that was the last time I saw him."

"What was the evidence against him?"

"I don't have any idea. The police wouldn't tell me what was happening. Why should they? I was nine—almost ten at the time. Someone sent for my mother, and she came at once. When she took me home, she told me never to mention Philippe or the Lavaud family ever again—to anyone. Nor was I to acknowledge that Fräulein Theissen had ever been our governess. When the fräulein bought the cottage here in Petite-Beauvais, my mother was furious. She always believed Father Robert was somehow responsible. She never went to services at the church again."

"Did you think your brother was guilty?" I asked.

"After a while, when everyone else believed it, I accepted it as well."

"Who else could have killed them?"

"I have no idea. I understood later that the police had spoken to the groom, and to the man who was courting one of the maids. I'd quarreled with Victor Lavaud, the son of the house. He was Philippe's friend, but I'd been invited to stay as well. And so that afternoon I took out one of the horses. I'd been told I could. Victor was sulking, sitting in the kennel playing with the new puppies. Philippe was upstairs in his room. When I got back from my ride, there were police everywhere. I was taken to the gardener's cottage and left there for hours—they fed me my dinner, and I asked where Philippe was, or Victor. I asked why they couldn't serve me dinner in the house, as they had before. The gardener's wife kept weeping. I was asleep on their daughter's bed when my mother came and took me home. She told me the Lavaud family had taken seriously ill, and I had to stay away or I'd be ill too."

His face was drained, reliving that moment. "When the new term began, Philippe was not in school. Nor was Victor. We were informed that he was an orphan now, and he'd been taken to Nice to live with his aunt. I hadn't particularly liked him, but I felt sad that his parents had died of their illness. I'd lost my own father just three months earlier. And then one of the lads in the upper school laughed at me and showed me a newspaper with my brother's photograph on the front page, and he told me that Philippe was on trial for murdering Victor's parents. That he was going to the guillotine where they would chop off his head, just as he'd chopped off the heads of the Lavaud family. I couldn't sleep for a fortnight."

The cruelty of children.

"They were stabbed," I said gently. "Along with two maids in the kitchen."

"Yes, as I learned." After a moment he added, "Will you go to the police, now?"

"I don't know. Not tonight." I found the photograph I had been given in Rouen and held it out to him. I had brought it with me on purpose.

Paul Moreau took it reluctantly, as if afraid to look at it. Then, with a shrug, he turned it so that he could see it clearly.

"I wouldn't have known him," he said slowly. "I wouldn't have recognized him if he spoke to me on the street. You are certain this is Philippe?" He peered at it. "It's been, what, eighteen years? Still. And why is he wearing an American uniform?"

"There wasn't a French uniform that fit him. He'd been wounded, you see."

Puzzled, he stared at the photograph a little longer, then passed it back to me.

"I don't understand."

"His was in a very sad state." I told him what I knew.

"It wasn't life threatening? His wounds? Ironic." He grimaced as he looked down at his leg. "They've set it twice, you know. The bone refuses to knit."

I rose from my chair by the fire, thinking about the long drive back to Paris in the cold. "Are you managing? They should have sent you to a clinic that deals with such things."

"I wanted to come home. My war is finished. I might as well begin to think about myself as an ex-soldier. God knows, there's enough to do around here. It will keep the demons at bay." He got to his feet.

It wasn't a grand house by any means, just what one might call in England a manor house. But if the rest of it was as well proportioned as this room, with its blue-and-silver wallpaper and elegant molding, including a white plaster circlet of roses in the center of the ceiling, matching the garlands that ran out from it, it had been handsome in its day and might be again. But where would come the staff that had once kept it polished, and comfortable, and well maintained?

What I'd heard this night was what I'd feared since I witnessed that outburst of German there in Base Hospital Three, where all this began. It was why I couldn't let the matter go. But now that I had all the answers, what was I to do about it?

I was very glad that it was Simon here with me, and not Captain Barkley or Major Vernon. I could depend on Simon not to act rashly and report what he'd heard as soon as we reached Paris. Despite what I'd said about a murderer going free, I needed a night to think, to take in what I'd been told here and decide what to do.

Captain Moreau seemed to draw himself up, as if expecting a blow and preparing himself to deal with it. "Is that why you have come, with British officers? Is it the court martial charges, rather than the murders, that will take precedence if he is caught? I need to know. I'm the one who will bear the brunt of whatever he's done. I need to be ready to face what is coming. I don't know how much more I can deal with."

I didn't like what I saw in his face. I was glad Simon was here with me.

"Swear to me! I told you in good faith what I knew. *Swear to me that you won't turn him in.*"

"I don't know," I said again, my uncertainty in my voice.

And then I realized what he was saying, what was behind his words. Wounded and in pain, coming home to an empty house with nothing but memories haunting its shadows, he was telling me that he would rather end his life than lose this last refuge.

We stood there, his gaze holding mine, his own will there in his eyes. Without warning, the expression changed, as if he was weighing up his chances.

What worried me then was what I could see very clearly in his face. That Paul Moreau could kill too.

The moment passed. Perhaps he realized that he was no match for Simon, not with that leg. Perhaps when it came right down to it, he couldn't bring himself to stop us from leaving with what we knew.

The danger passed. He stepped back, nearly stumbling on his bad foot, catching himself just in time with a hand on the back of his chair. He swore under his breath, his expression one of defeat and shame at his own weakness.

"Look at me. I could barely kill a spider crawling up the wall." And he turned toward the fire to hide what he was really thinking. That he wouldn't always be a cripple.

I walked out of the room. He didn't follow us as we went down the passage and closed the door to the house behind us.

Chapter Fifteen

"WHAT DID YOU think of Paul Moreau?" I asked Simon when we were well away, past the first of the villages between Petite-Beauvais and the main road into the city.

Simon was silent for a time. "I'm not sure," he said finally. "He's paid for Philippe's crimes ever since he was ten. Now that he knows Philippe is in Paris, he might well decide it's time for a reckoning."

"I shouldn't have told him. But then how else could I make him understand why we had come to speak to him? Jerome Karadeg would mean nothing to him. Nor would what happened to Marie-Luc. Or even to Captain Barkley."

"Now that you know what Philippe's capable of, what will you do? Go to the Army?"

"Or the police." I gave it some thought. "Even Paul didn't know who the murderer was, in that house. Why were the police so certain it was Philippe?"

I was about to find out.

We arrived at the clinic to find Inspector Duplessis impatiently waiting in the library, late as it was. He was not in a very good humor. Simon had walked with me to the door, given what had happened in the courtyard the night before.

Our only warning came as we stepped into Reception. The

orderly, greeting me, jerked his head in the direction of the rooms behind him, and said, "Someone called. He insisted on waiting."

"Who is he?" I asked, but with a sinking feeling, I thought I knew.

He leaned forward, his voice dropping to a whisper. "If I were in London, now, I'd say he was a copper."

Turning to Simon, I said, "The motorcar. You need to take it back."

"Half an hour more won't matter."

He followed me to the library, and Inspector Duplessis rose as I came in. The policeman's gaze took in Simon, then turned to me.

"Does Matron approve of such late hours? Is it part of your recovery?"

I smiled. "Actually, I spent the day in the country. It's considered to be good for one's health."

To my surprise, he smiled in return. Then it vanished as he said, "I have searched the files for the inquiry you spoke of."

"Have you indeed?" We sat down, Simon just to one side of me and the Inspector across a small table. "And what did you learn?" I tried to keep my voice casual, afraid I might betray what I'd heard in Paul Moreau's sitting room.

"That Philippe Moreau was taken into custody for the murders. But not straightaway. The police had collected preliminary statements from the outdoor staff, and the rest of the house staff who had the afternoon off. Apparently no one had seen or heard anything. They had asked the Lavaud child what he knew, and he told them he'd quarreled with the younger Moreau child, and he thought perhaps Paul Moreau had killed everyone."

"Paul?" I repeated. It was unexpected.

"Yes. He'd been taken to one of the cottages as soon as he returned from riding. It was a kindness. His mother was sent for. Mercifully she was in Paris, and she arrived within a few hours. After speaking to both of her sons, she told the police that Philippe had confessed to her."

"He *what*?" I sat there, shocked. Paul Moreau hadn't told us that.

"She was weeping. They believed her. And allowed her to take her younger son away."

"But why? Why would the older child have done such an awful thing? Why would she not stay there with him?"

"She told the police he had a pocketknife given him by his father. And Monsieur Lavaud had taken it from him. We had already learned that Monsieur Lavaud had quarreled earlier in the day with his own son, about returning to the school for next term. Philippe was upset about that as well. He and the Lavaud child were friends. He went down to the room where the hunting rifles were kept, but they were locked in cases. He took a knife instead. When one of the maids tried to stop him, he killed her, as well as the other maid in the pantry. And after that he killed the family."

A twelve-year-old boy? It was possible, yes, because the attack would have been unexpected.

"They were found in different rooms. The dead. He had stalked them."

I sat there, finding it hard to believe what I'd heard. Whatever she had felt about the boy brought into the household by her husband, how could Madame Moreau have abandoned him to the police with such callousness? And then she had left him to his fate. But even if she was telling the truth, had she also realized that she had a chance, finally, to rid herself of someone she hated? After all, gloating, she sent the cutting to the fräulein.

"You seem surprised," the Inspector said.

"I never knew these details. I didn't know Madame Moreau had spoken to her son."

"Yes, it struck me as rather pitiless as well. Still, I expect that's why the authorities were willing to believe her. It would seem she had come forward at great sacrifice to herself, to tell them the truth."

I shivered. What on earth had gone through Philippe Moreau's mind when faced with the knowledge that his own mother had turned him in? Granted, it was an horrific crime. But surely she would have stood by him, throughout the inquiry and the trial, if only to see that he was treated well and represented by a competent lawyer? Instead he'd been abandoned to the mercy of strangers.

"This also means," Simon commented, "that there is no certainty that the boy had done what he was accused of. If there was no further investigation of the facts."

"Yes, I've thought of that as well. There were additional suspects, several more likely than the others, but once the boy had confessed, there was little point in pursuing those avenues. After all, he'd been found with blood on his hands. The problem is, even I can think of no reason why Madame Moreau would tell such lies about her own child, if it were not true. Perhaps it is time that the matter was looked into more thoroughly."

"It won't be easy, after eighteen years, to get at the truth. Madame Moreau is dead, for one thing."

He turned to me again. "There is the nun, who appears to be at the center of this matter. I must ask you now, Mademoiselle, if you know this man's whereabouts?"

Put on the spot in such a fashion, I was very glad I could answer truthfully, "I'm sorry, Inspector. I don't have any idea where he may be."

To my astonishment, he believed me. I hadn't expected him to give up so easily.

"It's too bad," he said, nodding. "I had hoped we might settle this matter tonight."

I said, unable to stop myself, "From everything I've learned about the family, Madame Moreau hated her adopted son."

His eyes narrowed as he took that in. "Did she indeed? I wonder why."

I suddenly realized what he was thinking. That to protect the younger child, she had given the police the older boy.

"I can't tell you whether Paul Moreau was guilty of the crime or not. But I don't think it mattered to his mother. I don't know that the truth mattered to her either."

"Indeed."

A few minutes later, he thanked us and took his leave.

I listened to his footsteps receding down the passage. Then I said to Simon, "Paul Moreau will be very unhappy about this turn of events."

"It can't be helped. I can't believe that he ever knew what his mother had done."

"No." I sighed. "She must have been an awful woman."

"Why didn't Juliane Theissen come to his defense? If she was his mother—or even his sister? Despite what he was said to have done."

"That's a good question. Perhaps she couldn't. She had to earn her living. But I can't help but wonder if she stayed away because she wanted to help Philippe get away without being suspected. She must have felt strongly, all the same, to come back to Petite-Beauvais and live within a stone's throw of the Moreau family home."

"It could well be her way of reminding them of what had happened. Still, the governess had given up the boy herself, once. Either willingly or under pressure." He walked across the room to stare down at the dying embers of the fire. "One could almost feel sorry for Philippe Moreau."

"Yes. I know. Do you think Inspector Duplessis will reopen the inquiry?"

Simon turned back to me. "It will depend on whether or not he finds sufficient cause to pursue the matter. Or if he thinks he can find Moreau. If he's even still in Paris. Meanwhile, you've done enough, Bess."

"There's the court martial."

"I know. Pass the word through someone here. Barkley or the Intelligence officer. Let them take it forward."

Before I could answer him, the library door opened, and the orderly poked his head around it. "Matron is starting her last rounds," he said in a whisper. "Thought you should know."

"Yes, thank you." As he closed the door behind him, I smiled at Simon. "I wish you didn't have to go back to England."

"You have no idea how much I regret it," he said grimly. "But Colonel MacInnes took me on for your mother's sake, and I can't make trouble for him. Besides, she'll probably be at the dock in Folkestone or Dover, waiting for me to land."

"It would be just like her," I agreed, and walked with him to the door.

"Don't go wandering about on your own, Bess. Promise me that. If it's Philippe Moreau who tried to stab you, he won't give up so easily. For that matter, I wouldn't put it past his brother to do what he could to keep you from stirring up the past."

"I'd thought about that too," I said. "Captain Barkley will be up and about soon enough. I'll try to be sensible until then."

I walked with him through Reception and out into the courtyard. The wind was cold tonight, and I wrapped my arms around myself to stay warm as he cranked the motorcar.

And then Simon came back to where I was standing, put a hand on my shoulder, and said, "I'll be glad when this war is over, and you're safely back in Somerset."

He refused to leave until I had gone back inside. But I stood in the doorway and watched the motorcar disappear from sight, and Simon with it.

It was close to dawn when I awoke, alarmed.

Then I realized that it was Madame Ezay, shaking my shoulder.

"Mademoiselle, you must come. There's someone from the hospital downstairs. You're needed."

I shook my head to throw off the last vestiges of my dream. I'd been at home in Somerset, helping my mother and Iris put up the last of the damson plums, the kitchen filled with the rich smell from the pans on the cooker while the scalded jars sitting in tubs of hot water gave off additional heat.

The past faded as I sat up. "Who is it? What do they want? Did they say?"

"They wish to speak to you. It's a very serious matter, they said."

I gave a fleeting thought to Simon's warning about not wandering about on my own.

"What time is it?" I asked. My window was still dark.

"Going on six," Madame said. "I'll leave you to dress."

She had turned up the lamp, and I had no trouble finding my clothes. I'd discovered when I came up last night that my mended apron and uniform, carefully pressed, were hanging in the cupboard, but I didn't bother with them, catching up what I'd worn the day before. The fire had burned down to embers, and the room was cold. So were my shoes and my garments.

It took only a few minutes, and then I was putting my hair beneath my cap, wishing for a cup of real tea, with real sugar and milk.

The stairs were dark, only the night lamp on each landing guiding my feet. When I reached Reception, I saw that it was Sister Claire who had come for me.

"What is it? What's wrong?" I asked, crossing to the door. She already had her hand on the knob, eager to be on her way. "Wait. What is it?"

"I have a taxi waiting. We must go."

"No, tell me now."

"It's Sister Marie-Luc. She has had a reaction to some of her medicines. She's half out of her mind. Mother Superior thinks you might help her."

"But she sent me away—" I began.

"I'm sure she regrets it already. Please, come."

Madame Ezay had followed me down the stairs. I turned to her and said, "I'm going with Sister Claire. But I want you to know where I will be. St. Anne's Hospital. In the event anyone comes looking for me. I should be back by breakfast."

Something in my tone of voice, perhaps the tension I was feeling about this summons, alarmed her. "I will fetch my coat and come with you."

"There is no time," Sister Claire began, but Madame Ezay was already gone. She was back in only a moment or two, nodding to me as she followed us out the open door.

The night was quiet. The sound of the taxi's motor echoed off the walls of the houses as we drove down narrow streets, twisting and turning, heading for our destination. Sister Claire was silent, and Madame Ezay stirred uneasily from time to time, as if regretting her decision to accompany me.

I was glad of her presence, knowing that otherwise I'd have had to make this journey back to the clinic alone when I'd finished at the hospital.

We were admitted when we arrived, and it was clear that something was wrong.

I could hear voices from Marie-Luc's room before I reached it. Asking Madame Ezay to wait outside, where there was a bench for visitors, I went in.

Marie-Luc was sitting up in bed while two of the nuns were trying to calm her down. I could see that it had been a long night.

"Marie-Luc? Is everything all right?" I asked, uncertain how to approach her.

"Thank God." She freed one hand and reached out for me. "You must go at once to the café. They won't let me. I need to speak to Madame Karadeg as soon as possible. You must tell her to come."

Her words were spilling over each other, and I could see that she was frantic.

I took the hand she was holding out to me, and with a smile for the two nuns, I stood at the side of the bed. And then one of them brought a chair for me to sit in.

"Now tell me what's wrong. I can't go haring off to the café—it isn't even open yet, I'm sure. And Madame Karadeg will demand to know what it is you want. Breakfast is one of their busiest times. She will ask if it can wait." I was trying to be as practical and reassuring as possible, without knowing what I was supposed to be reassuring about.

Marie-Luc, distraught, clung to my hand as to a lifeline, her fingers crushing mine with her intensity.

"Tell them to go."

I looked over my shoulder at Sister Claire and the others. "Please, could you leave us? I'll call if I need anything."

They reluctantly filed out of the small room, and it seemed to open up without them and their wide, winged headdresses.

Marie-Luc waited until they had shut the door behind them, and then she said, "I had a visitation in the night."

"A what?"

"A visitation. Jerome. He came to me in the night. I could see him as clearly as I see you. And he said that he had never hurt me, that he was wounded by the accusations that he'd tried to kill me. That it hadn't been him."

"You've said as much all along," I reminded her.

"Yes, yes. But he said he'd been there, and he'd seen who it was. I was so frightened at first, and then I realized that it wasn't a dream, that he'd come back to tell me, to set my mind at ease, to let me know that he didn't blame me for what the police had done."

She was crying now. I thought it was partly her slow recovery from the infection and partly whatever the doctors had given her for pain that had created her visitation. She had been trying very hard to convince the police that they were wrong about Jerome, and she had felt such terrible guilt over his suicide. Or was it murder? I still wasn't sure what the police believed. I couldn't tell her that. It would only add to her own burden of guilt.

As I found a handkerchief and passed it to her, I opened my mouth to say that it had all been a dream, when I realized that she didn't want to hear the truth. Her vision had, somehow, absolved her from her remorse, letting her believe that she had been understood and forgiven.

Her face was wet with her tears, her eyes almost as red from exhaustion as from weeping.

"What is it you want me to do?" I asked simply.

"They tell me I can't leave. But you must bring Madame here. She blames me as well, and I want her to know that Jerome is at peace, that he knows it was not my fault."

"Then I'll sit with you for a while until the café opens. It's cold outside, Marie-Luc, I don't want to stand in a doorway for an hour or more." But I knew the Karadegs were probably already in the kitchen, preparing for the first customers.

"No, you must go," she pressed. "What time is it? It must be close to dawn by now."

I smiled. "Well, it's not. Lie back, try to calm yourself. You shouldn't let yourself get so upset."

But she wouldn't hear of resting until I'd done as she asked.

"All right," I told her. "But on one condition. You've frightened the other nuns. Lie back and be quiet while I'm gone."

"They didn't believe me. They told me it was the morphine they'd given me to help me sleep. But I know better. I know the difference between opium dreams and reality."

I wasn't sure she did, but she herself believed it.

Still, I insisted, and when she was finally quiet enough, I said, "It will take me some time to find a taxi and go there. And to come back. You must promise to be patient, and not wake half the other wards wondering where I am."

"Yes, all right." She let go of my hand reluctantly, as if torn between keeping me there by her side and sending me on my way.

She stopped me as I reached the door. "You do believe me, don't you?"

"Yes, of course I do," I said.

"He couldn't rest. He said it himself. 'I can't rest worrying about you. After all you've done for me.'"

"I will see that the Karadegs understand." And I was out the door before she could call me back again.

Madame Ezay was sitting quietly on the bench. The nuns had gone about their duties.

"I could hear her," she said, crossing herself. "Poor woman."

"I must go to a café on the Left Bank," I said. "There's nothing for it. Will you come with me?"

"I will," she said, standing and walking with me out to the main door. It took a little time to find a taxi, and I was uneasy walking down the dark streets. Madame Ezay reached out and took my arm, as though she felt it too.

At length we were lucky, and I climbed into the Renault with something like relief, giving the driver the direction of the café.

It was already open, busy with its usual clientele. We walked in and took a table near the window that had just been vacated by two workmen who had had what passed for coffee and rolls.

We sat there for some time. Madame Ezay said, "Why won't they wait on us? That other pair, over at that table, have already been served, and they came in after us."

I knew why. The Karadegs wanted no part of me. I smiled, and shook my head. "We aren't rushing off to work. They must know that."

"It's more than how we look," she grumbled. "I could do with a coffee."

But we were among the last to be served. When it was apparent that we weren't leaving, Madame came over herself and asked how she could help us.

We gave our order, and with poor grace, she went off to fetch it. When it came, it was her husband who brought our plates to us and poured the coffee.

"I know you aren't happy to see me here," I said quickly before he could go away. "But Marie-Luc—the nun—wanted me to come to tell you and your wife that she saw your son in a dream last night." I could hardly call it a visitation. "He doesn't hold her responsible—"

His face flushed, and he reached out, sweeping our plates off the table, sending the rolls and shards of china flying in every direction, just missing my coffee cup. I leapt back, expecting the scalding liquid to splash all over me.

"Don't talk to me about my son. Let him rest in peace, damn you. He was hounded like a criminal until he couldn't stand it any longer. She can have her dreams, I want no part of them. There's nothing she can say that will bring him back, and I'll not have her going about telling lies about him when she doesn't know anything about—"

His wife had come up behind him, a cleaver in her hand.

"Get out," she said. "I'll not say it again. Leave the living to mourn for the dead, and don't come to us with foul lies."

I wanted very much to tell her that her son had been murdered, that it wasn't suicide. But perhaps the police had already told her, and it hadn't mattered. Jerome was still dead.

"It was a dream—she wanted you to know how real it was, and how it gave her peace, absolution."

"Real or fancy, dreams or ghosts, we want no part of it."

Madame Ezay was scrambling to her feet. "Mademoiselle? We must go."

I got slowly to my feet. "I'm going," I said and held their gaze as I walked around the table and made my way in Madame's wake to the door.

What I read there in the twisted, heavy Breton features was anger. Mixed with fear.

I could have told Marie-Luc what had happened. Instead I led her to believe that Jerome Karadeg's parents had been grateful for her words of comfort.

She lay back against the pillows exhausted, the frenzy that had possessed her during the night seeping away. There were circles under her eyes, and I thought she had lost weight since I'd first met her, for her cheeks seemed sunken, her hands thinner.

"Are you sure?" she asked. "Did they understand that I did all

I could for him? And that I tried to tell the police what had really happened?"

There was a basin of water on the table beside me, with a clean cloth over the edge. I picked it up, dipped it into the water, wrung it out, and began to wash her face and hands, cooling them and making her more comfortable.

She talked about Jerome for almost another half hour, about the boy she'd first met sitting in the doorway of his parents' café, carving a bird from an old bit of wood, of the man he'd become, and the soldier, mentioned in dispatches multiple times. She said nothing about the broken wreck sent home by the Army and left to his own devices, to survive or to end it all as he saw fit. Her voice began to slur, her eyes grew heavy, and yet she fought sleep. I could see that while Jerome's presence in her mind had been a powerful symbol of relief, she was unsure whether she wanted to experience it again.

I wondered if this young soldier she had tried to save had represented all the other young men she had failed to save, or if he had become the son she would never have, a borrowed child whom she had learned to love. So very different from Madame Moreau, who had willingly sacrificed the child she hated.

And then Marie-Luc was asleep and I could go.

Sister Claire was waiting for me. "We've changed the dosage of her sedatives. Thank you for coming. Will the family she was so concerned about be calling on her later in the morning? Do you think you ought to stay to guide that meeting?"

"They won't be coming," I assured her. "I carried her message to them. It will suffice."

"Thank you," she said again and glanced toward the closed door behind me. "It's for the best." With a nod she walked on. Madame Ezay appeared out of nowhere and fell into step beside me.

Ahead of us a postulant was scrubbing the floor and we gave her a wide berth, staying close to the wall. We'd just passed her with a smile when a woman coming down the other way, her arm in a sling, slipped in a puddle of soapy water. I could see the danger before she started to fall and hurried forward to help her. As she fought for balance, the sticks that braced her swollen arm hit me hard in the side, taking my breath away. We collided with the wall together, and it was a miracle that we didn't go down on the hard stone paving of the floor.

She was profuse in thanking me, and for a moment clung to me as the shock passed, then went on her way.

"Are you all right?" Madame Ezay asked, her hand on my shoulder.

"It's fine. It only hurt for a moment." But I felt it all the way out to the street, where we walked to the third corner before finding a taxi.

It was nearly ten in the morning when we stepped back into the clinic, and I went down to the kitchens for a late breakfast.

I couldn't face the dining room and the chatter of the walking wounded sitting at the little square tables that must have replaced the long table that had belonged to the family. The bustle around me and the clatter and banging as the staff washed up the dishes and the pots and pans, talking among themselves, was soothing. Impersonal.

I had a good deal to think about. And I wished Simon had stayed on, so that I could talk to him about the morning's experience. It had been unsettling.

Afterward I went up to my room and sat there. Tired as I was, I was restless, my side hurting still with a dull ache. Bruised, but no other damage. Even when I lay down on my bed, sleep wouldn't come.

There wasn't much more I could do, I thought. I should have left with Simon. After all, Inspector Duplessis knew about Philippe Moreau now. He could sort it out. If nothing came of his inquiry, Paul Moreau for one would be quite happy. And I had done my duty to those who had suffered at Philippe's hands. I could leave the judging to others.

And what was I to do with the envelope I'd taken from the fräulein's cottage? By right it belonged to Marie-Luc. I must see that she got it before I left Paris.

I heard the rumble of ambulances coming in from the base hospitals, bringing us new convalescents. I collected my coat and went down to offer my help. But there were enough hands this time to do the work. I walked around them and decided—since it was broad daylight—to go on, aimlessly, using the exercise to help me think.

I had no idea where I went or how I got there, deep in thought, feeling safe with the numbers of people on the streets this morning.

There was a café ahead, the outdoor tables under an awning, the chairs stacked to one side, waiting for spring. But there was a man sitting at one of the tables, a lonely figure reading a newspaper, a cup of coffee at his elbow.

I didn't recognize him until I was almost on him, and he looked up as I approached, as if he expected someone to join him, or perhaps liked to know who was near him. I realized almost in the same instant that he had his back to the restaurant wall, and that he was using the newspaper as a shield.

We stared at each other, and he got slowly to his feet.

I closed the distance between us, and then when I was near enough, I reached for a chair and pulled it to his table, effectively blocking him, unless he chose to shove me to one side.

"Hallo," I said in French. "What an unexpected pleasure."

It was Philippe Moreau. Still wearing his American officer's uniform.

CHAPTER SIXTEEN

SINCE I'D ARRIVED in Paris, I had seen him only in the dim light of a taxi as we passed. I could see him clearly now.

He looked like a man recovering from a long illness. His face was drawn, his eyes shadowed, and there were lines of pain around his mouth.

He stood there, his gaze riveted on my face, and said nothing.

"I know you can speak French. And English. And German," I added. "Which language do you prefer?" And all the time I was thinking about what Simon would have to say about this confrontation. It wasn't yet noon—he was still in Paris. But at the embassy, not here.

That remark must have stung, because Philippe Moreau snapped, "Oh, shut up," in French, and then switched to English as he sank back into his chair. "What do you want?"

There was a cold wind blowing over my left shoulder. I would have liked to go inside. The windows were steamed, and it would be warm. But I was afraid that if I moved, he would leave.

"How are you?" I changed my tone of voice. "Have your feet healed?"

"Well enough," he answered grudgingly.

I didn't believe him. They must still hurt when he wore shoes or walked too far on cobbles or the boards that kept much of Paris out of the mud in the back streets.

"The English doctors deserve the credit."

"All right then. Thank you." It didn't sound like gratitude.

"How did you know where to find me?" I asked then. "When you tried to frighten me in the dark."

"I've no idea where you live in Paris."

I let it go. He sat there across from me, saying nothing unless I asked a question. He'd picked up the cigarette lighter that lay on the table. I'd seen that kind before. It was made from a cartridge casing. Toying with it now, turning it about in his fingers, he stared at it for a time, then put it in his pocket.

I let the silence lengthen.

"What do you want from me?" he asked for a second time.

"I don't know." And I meant that. Having found him, I didn't know what I should do. Run screaming for the nearest gendarme? I smiled at the thought.

At length I said, "The truth, I expect."

Surprised, then wary, he looked up at me. "I don't think I know what the truth is anymore."

"Did you kill the Lavaud family?"

He recoiled, as if I'd struck him with the newspaper that lay between us, or thrown the contents of the coffee cup all over him.

What I read in his face then was terrible, and I wished I hadn't mentioned the past.

Quickly changing the subject, I said, "I saw Paul last night."

He looked away.

"He's convalescing from his own wounds. But he'll be all right. Fräulein Theissen died recently. The complications of age. But you must have realized that the end was near. Did you know Sister Marie-Luc? She's a nun."

I might as well have been sitting there reminiscing about family members, cousins we hadn't seen in years. The way people do when they have known each other for a very long time but haven't kept in touch.

He cleared his throat. "Should I?"

"I don't know. Someone tried to kill her. She says it was you."

That brought his attention back to me. "Why?"

"Because she knew about the house near the Bois."

He neither confirmed nor denied it. We sat there in silence again. The café door opened, startling both of us, and a soldier came out with a pretty girl on his arm. They were laughing, a touch of the normal world going on around us. I felt a sweeping sadness.

"What are you going to do?" he asked.

"The police know that you're in Paris. They'll be looking for you."

"It doesn't matter. The war is nearly finished," he replied, his face haggard, his voice so tired that I knew without being told that he was no longer able to run. "Are you sitting here, waiting for them to come? Is that it? A marker, so they'll know where to look?"

"No. I didn't expect to find you here. There's only me." I realized it was not the smartest thing to say. But I didn't like being thought of as a marker for the police. He'd been betrayed by the woman he'd known as his mother. I couldn't add to that by letting him think I'd come here to betray him too. I gestured to the street at my back. "You are free to stand up and walk away. But this Inspector, his name is Duplessis, is a very sharp policeman. He'll find you in the end."

"Thanks for the warning." His voice was bitter.

And then, as if to test my words, he rose, looking up and down the street, preparing to walk away.

I had only seconds now. I said, "Did you spy on your own country?" And then, realizing that he might well consider another country to be his own, I repeated, "Did you spy on France?"

His face was twisted in anger now.

"Go to hell!" he shouted at me in English. And then he was walking away, limping heavily—whether for my benefit or because walking was still painful, I couldn't tell.

Passersby were staring. It must have looked like a lover's spat, a nurse and her officer sweetheart having words. I managed a smile, and then turned and purposely walked the other way.

It occurred to me all at once that this was another candidate for the river. Philippe Moreau looked to be at the end of his strength, with no will to run again. More than one hunted man had taken that way out.

I wished with all my heart that I hadn't seen him sitting there this morning. It's easier to hate at a distance.

Over my shoulder I watched him go, and then on the spur of the moment, an indication of my own distress, I looked around, realized where I was—how far I had come from the clinic. I should have gone back there. Instead, almost without conscious decision, I started to walk toward the British embassy. It wasn't noon yet; Simon would still be there. I could still accompany him back to England.

I was only two streets away from the embassy when I saw Colonel MacInnes's motorcar leaving Paris. It was too far away to hail. I stood there, willing Simon to look out the back window and see me.

But he didn't. Even if he had, I was only a distant figure. Bess Crawford had no reason to be in this part of Paris. He wouldn't have looked for me here.

Eventually I found my way back to the hotel. Footsore and tired, I went down to the kitchen to beg a cup of tea.

It was as weak as could be, as if the leaves had been used several times, and they were bitter. But it was hot and there was even a little honey to put into it.

I sat there cradling the cup in my cold hands, my feet stretched out toward the kitchen fire.

I didn't hear Major Anderson come in. The first indication that he was there was his greeting.

"Bess? What are you doing hiding down here in the kitchen?"

I turned quickly and managed a smile. "Hallo," I said. "Not hiding, really. It was warmer by the fire. I'd been out walking, and I forgot my gloves."

He smiled. "I'd been looking for you. I've learned the name of the man who was court-martialed. I thought you'd want to know."

"Yes. Yes, of course. Thank you."

"A sergeant by the name of Allard. The charge was desertion. He'd gone home to tend his farm. It was time to plow and there was no one else. My brother-in-law felt someone had turned a blind eye, and Allard had simply rejoined his regiment. Not the first such case, I'll be bound."

"How interesting," I said, although Paul Moreau had told us much the same story. "Thank you, Major. I find it hard to blame such a man. I'm glad he wasn't shot."

"There was a very different case two years ago. In 1916. Claude hadn't anything to do with the court martial, but it was the talk of the Army. A Lieutenant Theissen, that was. Claude didn't know much about the man or the trial, but Theissen overpowered his guards and got away. He had a knife hidden in his boot, threatened to cut their throats. The Army tried to hush that up, but the story got out. He released two German officers incarcerated in the same building. Rumor was, the three of them made it to German lines and were never seen again." He smiled. "That's a better story to tell your father one day."

I sat there, caught completely by surprise.

Shrugging, he said, "That's all I could discover."

I managed to collect my wits and ask, with unfeigned interest, "What was his first name? Do you know?"

"Claude didn't say. Well, he wasn't on that court."

"I'm thunderstruck. And to think it actually happened." It was the best I could do.

"Not a name you'd know."

"No. And a good thing." I got to my feet and set my cup in the dry sink. "Well, my curiosity is satisfied."

He followed me up the back stair to the ground floor. "Bess. Did you expect it to be Moreau?"

"I didn't know," I answered truthfully. "I was afraid it might be. Just as well it wasn't."

"Yes."

I thanked him again and accompanied him back to the wards, looked in on Captain Barkley, who was sleeping, and went on up the stairs. This time I locked the door to my room and took out the tub of soldiers. I retrieved the envelope and went to the window, standing there for a moment with it in my hand.

What had Fräulein Theissen been thinking when she put these bits of her life away, hiding them from casual prying eyes?

When Paul Moreau had come to the cottage the night that Captain Barkley and I were there, was he looking for them? Or for a bed, as he claimed, when the house beyond the church was closed, cold, and empty?

Had Father Robert ever looked for them, driven by curiosity or a need to know the truth?

I was beginning to think that the best thing I could do would be to burn the lot. It was a measure of my uncertainty and frustration. Certainly there was no need to keep the cutting. Marie-Luc knew about the murders. She too must have known how much they had hurt Fräulein Theissen. Paul already knew more than he could live with. And so did Philippe Moreau.

Inspector Duplessis didn't need it—he had access to the original file.

But somehow I couldn't bring myself to throw any of the contents on the fire.

Instead I took the papers to the chair near the hearth and went through them again, this time reading a few more of the letters.

From former pupils, they were touching. She must have been a fine governess, because invariably the letters thanked her for the care and upbringing she had given her charges. Most were from young women, although there were a number from young men as well. A few, dated after the summer of 1914, even mentioned the fact that she was French in their eyes, even though she was from Alsace. One spoke of her father, who had been killed in the fighting a generation ago, adding that he had lost his own father in this war.

I felt guilty reading these very personal tributes to a woman who had spent her life educating other people's children.

I almost didn't read the last several, but I felt guilty about that too, as if I owed it to Fräulein Theissen to care. She must have done so, to save them for so many years.

Tucked in with one of them was a message without an envelope, written in a child's hand, like a number I'd already opened. There was no salutation, and at first I thought it had been included with the previous letter, two children sharing an envelope. But as I started to read I realized it was far different from the ones that had gone before, and, either by accident or design, slipped in where it wouldn't be easily discovered.

You must not come to me. You must not say anything. She told me they were going to arrest Paul for what happened. She asked me to confess and save him. He is only nine. I gave my promise. For Papa's sake. Please. I love you. Good-bye.

There was no signature.

I sat there, tears in my eyes.

This was the last part of the story. And Philippe Moreau had said nothing all these years.

A vicious, selfish woman had got her revenge in spades. She had used one boy's love for his supposed brother to condemn him. And lied to both sons as well as the police.

I realized suddenly that I must see that Inspector Duplessis had this, before he found Philippe Moreau.

I remembered what Philippe had said, that the war was nearly over, let it go.

I understood now. If he told what he knew, he believed, he would be betraying his brother.

But if the brothers hadn't killed the Lavauds, who had?

And who had attacked Marie-Luc, if it hadn't been Jerome Karadeg or Philippe Moreau?

There was the man who had threatened me in the courtyard, shuffling away on still-tender feet.

Philippe? Or someone who wanted me to believe he was?

I remembered the black lacquer box that I'd never found in the cottage. Had someone else found it, only to discover it didn't hold what it was thought to have inside?

I desperately needed to talk to someone. Captain Barkley? Major Vernon?

If only Simon had had one more day in Paris.

I put my hands over my eyes, trying to think clearly, leaning back in the chair.

There was a twinge in my side, and I sat up straight again to ease it, remembering the patient slipping on the wet floor, and the boards from her broken arm jabbing me where I'd been wounded.

And something fell into place in my mind.

I nearly leapt out of my chair, standing in the middle of the room, furiously trying to remember. I had been so concerned about people that I hadn't paid any heed to something I understood, had done since I had begun my training as a nurse.

Marie-Luc, cut across her chest. Captain Barkley cut across his arm and chest. The thin little trickle of blood beneath the bandages at my side.

Why had all of us been slashed in the same place? Why not stabbed in the chest or the stomach, the blade aimed at our hearts if not our throats?

We had all been so sure it was Philippe Moreau who'd attacked us. But was it? If he'd killed before, it was likely that he'd kill again. And it would come easy to him. And yet he hadn't.

Or—hadn't been able to.

But there was nothing wrong with his arms.

Paul Moreau had an arm in a sling. But why should he want to kill Marie-Luc?

I put the envelope back where I had kept it all this time and picked up my coat. I was going back to the hospital to speak to Marie-Luc. I needed to know what she knew about Philippe.

Taxis were scarce again, but I found one at last, and when we reached the hospital I asked my driver to wait.

He grumbled, but he agreed. I got out and hurried inside, going directly to Marie-Luc's room.

Mercifully, she was awake, though groggy and pale, lying there like someone who had run a long race and lost. She looked up as I came in, and I smiled in greeting, wondering how to begin without stirring up memories of Jerome Karadeg.

To my surprise, she seemed pleased to see me.

We chatted for several minutes, about the weather, about what the doctor had told her about her side as he was doing his rounds, about the war, about Sister Claire. And then I had no choice but to come right out and ask.

"Tell me," I said casually, one nurse to another, "about working in Belgium with the wounded. It must have been rather difficult, with the Germans occupying most of the country."

"It was." She launched into an account of trying to keep enough supplies on hand, fearful that this was all they would ever get, then told me how she felt about nursing several wounded Germans who had been brought in for treatment. I guessed that Philippe was not one of them, because she talked quite calmly about them now.

"You told me once that you'd encountered Philippe Moreau in Belgium?" I asked then. "Wearing a German uniform. Was he one of your patients?" She'd told me before that he was standing on a street corner, but this was the best entrée into the subject that I could think of.

Her face tightened. "Thank God. That traitor? He was not."

"I wonder if he was ever wounded while fighting for the Germans. It wouldn't have done for him to fall into Allied hands."

"I knew how it would hurt Fräulein Theissen if she knew. I never had the heart to tell her. I was traveling through occupied territory, trying not to get myself noticed. He was standing there, laughing with a group of German officers. That was bad enough. A few minutes later, he came past in a motorcar, and he stopped one of the men walking ahead of me. I'd seen the man before, as I crossed the frontier. He began to question the man in fluent French. I heard the man call him Hauptmann Theissen. I recognized him then from pictures she had of him. She called him her best and brightest. I always wondered if she loved him best. I looked away, but he had seen me looking at him. He let the man go and then stopped me, wanting to see my papers. Thank God, they were in order. He had her eyes, and I knew then I was right. Because of that, I couldn't look him in the face. And that made him suspicious. They kept me for two days. I was afraid to go back to Belgium after that. I found another hospital near Verdun that needed nurses. That's how I recognized him on the street here in Paris. Or thought I had."

It was reason enough for Philippe Moreau to want her dead.

But how had he found her? For that matter, how had he found me?

I lost the thread of what she was saying. I was trying hard to think. And then I realized she'd asked a question.

"I'm sorry?" I said.

"I asked if you were tired. You must be. You were here most of the night."

"Yes, I'm afraid I am, a little. I think I missed my lunch as well. Perhaps I ought to go have a lie-down. You're a nurse. Why do you think you were stabbed in the chest, and not the heart? Or the throat? If the intent was to kill you?"

She frowned. "It was strange. The doctor told me I was lucky that whoever it was had been clumsy."

"An odd thing to say," I agreed. "I wonder what he meant?"

Marie-Luc ran a hand through her short hair. "It struck me at the time that he hadn't put a hand over my mouth, to stop me from screaming." She closed her eyes for a moment, grimacing as she re-lived that terrible moment. When she opened them, there were tears. "When the blood ran down my body, I thought I would surely die. I thought he had done just what he'd meant to do, cut a major artery. I say my prayers every day that I lived."

We said good-bye soon after that, and I left.

All the way back to the hotel, I tried to put together everything I knew. And everyone I'd met since I'd come to Paris.

And slowly I began to reach an unexpected conclusion. It didn't make sense, but I could think of no other way to account for all that had happened.

I had walked, to give myself a chance to think. Now I hailed an-other taxi, eager to get back to the clinic and pay a visit to Captain Barkley.

He was sitting on the edge of his bed with a tray on his lap, toying with his food. When I came into the ward, he looked up, saw me, and grinned. "I thought you'd forgot me," he said, but there was relief in the comment too. After all, he'd promised my father he'd watch out for me, and instead he was confined to a bed with wounds of his own.

I said contritely, "I've been tired. I'm sorry to neglect you. But there are prettier Sisters attending to your every need. I didn't think you'd miss me."

"You haven't been doing anything foolish, have you? I asked Major Vernon to keep an eye out for you. He said there was little to report."

Thank God for the Major's reticence to say too much about Petite-Beauvais.

"He's very nice. What do you know about him?"

"I've never served with him, but word gets around. You know how it is. Bright and a good man to have at your back."

"I'm sure he is. And Captain Broussard? He of the available motorcar. Do you know him well too?"

"Not really, but the man who was in Paris before me—the one I was seeing off when I ran into you at the Gare—told me that if ever I needed transportation, Broussard was the chap to speak to. He's kept his motorcar in Paris, but he seldom has time to run it."

"Did you tell him why you were borrowing it? And for whom?"

"Well, of course. It was his motorcar, after all. He deserved to know how it was being used. I even asked him directions to Petite-Beauvais. Remember, I brought him here and introduced you to him."

"Yes. How did he lose his arm?"

"At Verdun, I expect. It was a blood— it was a disaster. That's how we got ourselves involved with the Somme offensive. Trying to take the pressure off Verdun before the French line collapsed under the German assault."

"What do you know about his background?"

"Very little. He's from Nice, had his motorcar down there, and as soon as he was out of hospital, he went down and brought it back. Nearly went off the road several times, trying to manage it with one arm. Imagine shifting on some of those mountain roads. As soon as the war is finished, he's going to have it refitted for him."

Nice. The south of France, where the Lavauds' son had gone to live with his aunt.

"Do his parents still live there?"

"I think they're dead. You'll have to ask Anderson or someone. They might know." He frowned. "Why this sudden interest in Broussard?"

I shrugged. "He's been very kind about lending out his motorcar."

"I can tell you, he probably won't allow you to drive it. You'll have to wait until I'm well enough to escort you."

"Of course. Is he an only child?" At the Captain's raised eyebrows, I added, "If he had sisters, he might feel differently about women driving."

"No idea. He came to see me, you know. Last evening. I was still in a great deal of pain, and I wasn't good company."

Came to see the results of his handiwork? Unwilling to wait to read of our deaths in a newspaper?

I said, "How kind of him."

"Yes, he's one of the few Frenchmen I've liked."

I rose. "You seem to be feeling much better. I'm glad."

"I've been after the doctor to let me out of here. But he says another day. He has to be watchful for infection. A bit of my shirt was driven into the arm wound."

I said good-bye, promised to look in again later, and went up to the Nursery.

A man with one arm, I was thinking as I climbed the stairs, would have a problem with balance. He couldn't use the force of his other shoulder to counterbalance a knife thrust into someone's body. What's more, he couldn't allow anyone to notice that he had only one arm. And so he'd come in from the side, where the power of his good shoulder could drive the weapon home.

He hadn't been able to put one hand over Marie-Luc's mouth because he was stabbing her . . .

I stood in the middle of the room and tested my theory, nearly falling as I held one arm tightly against my side and thrust with the other. Too high, and he was off balance. To the side, he still had control. That's why he'd caught the Captain and me just coming out the restaurant door. The facade behind us held us in place, well positioned for his attack. He couldn't have accomplished it out in the open. Not two people.

All well and good. But how to prove any of it?

I paced the floor, thinking.

There was one possibility. It was dangerous, but it could work.

I went down the stairs in search of Madame Ezay. And then I went to speak to Captain Barkley.

It occurred to me to speak to the doctors first.

They agreed that a gentle outing would not harm the Captain.

"I promise to bring him back safely," I said, smiling. "But he's restless, and it might cheer him up."

"The food will be no better than it is here," Matron told me.

"Perhaps he won't notice," I said, and she smiled in return.

After that I went to speak to the Captain. He was in the worst of moods, and as I chatted with him, I realized that he was worried about something.

"What is it?" I asked. "Is something wrong?"

"Nothing," he said, turning away. "Everything. Being pinned to this bed is enough to drive any man mad."

"Then I have a proposal. I'm inviting you to dine with me tonight."

"I haven't been allowed to walk as far as the dining room."

"At a restaurant. I hear there's one near here that Captain Broussard favors. Do you know it? Will you escort me?"

His mouth twisted. "Only if you smuggle me out of here."

"I'll do just that. Is the food any good, do you think? Or is there a pretty girl working there?" I teased. "Is the captain in love?"

Captain Barkley laughed. "Both. She's the daughter of the owner, and since her mother's death from influenza, she greets diners and seats them. As for the food, the owner has a farm near Lyon. And the chef can work miracles. So I'm told."

"Then I must go there. I'm so tired of carrots and onions and turnips."

He studied me, suspicious. "Are you up to something?"

"I'm feeling much better. I think Matron and the doctors are planning to discharge me. I expect it's a celebration."

He was only half convinced, but I rattled on, and in the end he agreed to take me to La Porte d'Or. The Golden Door.

I had only to speak to Madame Ezay now. And after she had accompanied me to the hospital to see Marie-Luc, I was rather afraid she might have second thoughts about what I was going to ask of her.

Instead she greeted my suggestion with a quick embrace. "I have lived a very dull life until now. I am more than curious about this business. Will you tell me why you are doing this?"

I explained as best I could, and she nodded as she listened. "I don't think there will be any danger for you," I finished. "But you never know."

"I shall need something more *à la mode* than this," she said, looking down at the rusty black of her uniform. "But I will manage. My sister will help me. She lives not too far away. Tonight?"

"Yes, please."

"I must speak to those in the kitchen. I am to help prepare the meal."

And what if the staff said no? I couldn't cause trouble for her.

"If they give you any trouble, tell me. It can be another night." But I wasn't convinced of that. I was feeling a sense of urgency. Duplessis might be making an arrest at any moment.

That urgency wasn't helped by an encounter with Matron as I was going up the stairs.

"Sister Crawford? A word."

"Yes, Matron?" I turned and went back down to follow her to her small office, feeling like a schoolgirl caught in the act. She wouldn't appreciate what I had been up to, and I could very easily be given my marching orders sooner than I'd planned.

"You are fully recovered, if you can venture out as often as you do. Yes," she went on as I was about to speak, "I have had a word with the orderlies on the desk. To their credit, they were reluctant to answer me. I think it's time you return to duty as soon as possible."

"Yes, Matron," I said, praying as I did that it wouldn't be tonight. Or tomorrow.

"There is a convoy of patients coming in tomorrow evening. I wish you to be ready to accompany the ambulance back to Rouen. You will find your orders waiting for you there, and transport to your next post."

"Thank you, Matron," I said.

And then she stunned me by asking, "What is it that you've been up to, Sister Crawford? Policemen coming here, your leaving and returning at odd hours . . . If you are involved in anything rash, I should be told."

"Unfortunately, I became involved after the stabbing of a French nun. As she knew no one else in Paris, I was sent for when she was ill. Sadly the man who was to be charged for this crime drowned himself in the Seine. The police were not able to question him, and there is some doubt still that he was indeed the man they were after."

Matron was no fool. "Did this have anything to do with the attack on Captain Barkley? You were uncertain when I spoke to you before."

"The man who attacked Sister Marie-Luc was dead by the time the Captain was stabbed."

"I see. We don't encourage our staff to involve themselves in the affairs of civilians. As a rule, I strongly agree with that policy. But if the nun was alone and ill, I can appreciate your wishing to care for her."

"She had left her convent to nurse the wounded. She has worked in Belgium and Verdun and Boulogne."

"Ah. That's clear then. Thank you, Sister Crawford. Be prepared to leave tomorrow night."

I was dismissed. Outside the door I allowed myself to breathe again. Matron, whoever might be serving in that position, had the power to send me back to England for punishment if I broke the very strict rules of the Queen Alexandra's. It was one reason we were held in high esteem. The other was our training and our discipline.

I was hurrying back to the stairs when the outer door was flung back so hard that it slammed against the wall.

A man came storming into Reception, stopped short when he saw me, and said in a rage that was barely controlled, "What have you done with my son?"

I hardly recognized Monsieur Karadeg without his apron, and wearing a coat and hat.

"I—I don't know what you mean," I stammered, staring at him. My first thought was that his mind had been turned by grief.

He reached for me, took my shoulders in both hands, and shook me violently. The orderly at the desk had leapt to his feet as soon as Monsieur Karadeg had come through the door, and he lunged now at the man, pulling him away from me.

"We'll have none of that here," the burly orderly told him. "State your business, calmly, like a gentleman, or I'll have you out that door before you can blink your eyes. Now state your name and your business, if you please."

"Karadeg," he said, breathing hard. "I want to know what this woman has done with my son."

"Sister? Do you wish to deal with him in this state?"

I said gently, "Monsieur, your son is dead. Can we summon a taxi for you? You would be better off at home, with your wife."

"He's not dead, the fool! He went to see the nun, and he hasn't come back."

I blinked. "What?" And all the while, my mind was running through the facts. The visitation. The suicide victim who had been murdered . . . "But you yourself identified his *body*," I added, before he could answer me.

"Damn it, that wasn't Jerome. We told the police it was, to stop them from searching for him. We took him to Brittany and left him there with his grandmother. But he's quite mad—"

"He's not mad, he's shell-shocked," I countered automatically, but he went on as if I hadn't spoken.

"—and he came back to tell Marie-Luc that he hadn't hurt her. And now he's vanished."

As he stopped to catch his breath, I repeated, "Jerome Karadeg isn't dead? Is that what you're telling me?" I leaned against the corner of the orderly's desk, still feeling the shaking I'd just been given, my mind reeling as well. If this man was alive, and wandering about Paris, knife in hand—but why stab me? Or the Captain?

It seemed to turn everything I'd thought earlier upside down.

"I don't know where he is," I said. "I give you my word, Monsieur. I thought—it seemed to me that the visit to Marie-Luc was a manifestation of her own guilt. That she was finding a way to come to terms with her failure to convince the police in time to save your son. I thought—I don't know what I thought."

"*Where is he?*"

"I don't know. I have never met your son. He could come to that door and ask for me, and I would have no idea who he was. I give you my word."

Fright was slowly replacing the anger that drove him. A heavy, unwilling fear that something had happened to Jerome after all, that he might, finally, have gone to the river in truth.

"I wish I knew. I wish I could offer you some comfort. Send a telegram to your mother. He may have done what he felt he must do, and gone back to Brittany."

It was his only hope, and he could see that, and still he was afraid it would not find his son.

He glared at me and at the orderly, standing between us looking like a man who wished himself anywhere but here. "You won't tell the police. Give me your word."

"Gladly," I said. "But how did you find me?"

"I followed you from the hospital today. I have been waiting in the street for my son to come out of this place. I couldn't wait any longer."

But he wasn't satisfied that I was telling the truth. He reached under his coat and pulled on a chain, bringing out the crucifix he wore. "Put your hand on this and swear."

The orderly stepped between us. "Now we'll have none of that," he began.

"No, it's all right, I'll swear if that's what he wants." And I did.

Monsieur Karadeg looked down at the crucifix, kissed it, then carefully restored it to wherever it had come from.

"I will be back," he said. "If you are lying, I'll come back, and that one won't stop me." He jerked his head toward the orderly. And then he was gone, leaving the door standing wide.

The orderly hurried after him, shutting it quickly. Then he turned to me and said, "Are you all right, Sister?"

"Yes." I was still staring at the door, and I brought my gaze back to his worried face. "His son is suffering from shell shock. It's been very difficult for his family."

The orderly almost sneered. "That's it, then?" And under his breath he added, "Bloody coward."

"No," I said firmly. "He did his duty. And he was wounded, just like the men in there, honorably and courageously." I pointed angrily toward the wards.

But I heard him say as I turned and started up the stairs, "Not like that lot."

Prejudice dies hard, and even soldiers who had fought beside the men who came back shell-shocked felt much the same way. I wasn't going to change his mind.

But the question was, must I now change my evening arrangements?

CHAPTER SEVENTEEN

I DID A good bit of soul-searching over the next few hours. Had the news about Jerome changed anything? Not if I proved what I'd begun to suspect. But would the arrangements I'd made work as I'd planned? Or would the reaction I was hoping for never happen? It was always difficult to predict how another person would behave in a crisis, however carefully a trap was prepared and carried off. I realized then that I hadn't prepared for the possibility that my suspicions were wrong. Above all, would Madame Ezay bear the brunt of trouble that wasn't of her making? The last thing I wanted was for her to be dismissed from the clinic because of me.

In the end, I had no alternative but to go forward. I dressed with care, leaving my apron behind and wearing a pretty pin one of the other Sisters had loaned me in place of the little watch I usually wore on my left shoulder. Another had given me a silk scarf that would match my coat very nicely. They were Captain Barkley's nurses, and very pleased that he'd be allowed to dine out for a change.

It was against regulations, but I thought no one would mind. What's more, I had my reasons for wanting this dinner to appear to be a special occasion and allay any misgivings our arrival at the restaurant might arouse.

Jerome Karadeg was still very much on my mind. I truly hoped he'd been sensible and returned to Brittany, but there was nothing I could do tonight to help his father find him.

At exactly seven o'clock I went down the stairs to find Captain Barkley, leaning on a cane, waiting for me.

"I don't need this," he assured me straightaway, "but Matron wasn't having it if I didn't take it."

"No one argues with Matron," I agreed, and took his uninjured arm. "Let's find a taxi, shall we?"

"You look different tonight," he said, noticing me for the first time.

"Well. I'm convalescing too, not on duty. I didn't wear my apron or cap."

"Your hair is very pretty," he said, and I smiled at the compliment.

We were fortunate enough to find a cab in a very short distance, and I gave the driver the direction of The Golden Door.

We drove to the Champs-Élysées and found the restaurant easily enough, not many streets over from Napoleon's Arc de Triomphe. With all the buildings dark, I could hardly see it in the distance, a darker shadow among shadows.

La Porte d'Or was quite a fashionable restaurant. In fact, it took its name from a door that would have done justice to Kublai Khan's great palace. In the low flickering light of the oriental lamp hanging beside it, it appeared to *be* gold, not just painted, and there were swirls of clouds carved in the wood that seemed to be moving as the flame danced. I suddenly wondered if they would allow a nurse inside.

But I was admitted by the smiling doorman, and we were passed on to an elegantly dressed young woman with an intelligent and attractive face, who greeted us with pleasure but not effusiveness, and in turn passed us on to the maître d'hôtel. We were taken to be seated right away. I thought perhaps the Captain had slipped a few francs into the man's palm. On our way we passed a staircase and left our coats at a little door. Our table had a full sweeping view of the room.

I readjusted the number of francs that must have changed hands. Captain Barkley was the son of an American who had made his fortune in railroads, and he knew what was required of a guest wanting the best.

We settled ourselves, and I looked around the room. It was quite a spectacle, with the war still on, and women wearing lovely gowns and glittering jewelry, however military the cut might be. No feathers—they would have had to be imported through the gantlet of U-boats, and there was no room on the ships that did get through for anything but direst necessities. But lots of braid took their place, and there was color everywhere, as well as elegant fabrics. I felt decidedly drab. Most of the younger men were in uniform. The older ones who were not in the Army or Navy wore evening dress. The waiters moved with quiet precision, and there was no loud conversation, only the sounds of fine cutlery and crystal, like bells.

It was worth the price of the dinner, I thought, to see the gold brocade drapes at the windows, and the Louis Quinze chairs upholstered in a dark green. The war seemed very distant, and one could pretend nothing had changed since 1914.

But as I looked about, I saw no one who looked like my quarry—in fact no one with his arm pinned to his sleeve except for a Colonel three tables from us and a young Lieutenant just coming into the dining room. What if tonight, of all nights, Captain Broussard had had a previous engagement that had taken him elsewhere?

My stomach was suddenly full of butterflies.

We were given a menu, and I looked at it in amazement. It was printed on heavy paper, written in an elegant script, a gold ribbon holding the pages together, the tassel swinging free. But the dishes were wartime meals, in spite of the outward appearance of normality.

I was about to order when the maître d' ushered another pair into the room and seated them not far from us.

Captain Broussard and a Lieutenant I didn't know. A moment

later, the woman who had greeted us came to their table and presented the Captain with a bottle of wine for his dinner. He rose politely, flushing a little, to accept the gift. It obviously pleased him.

"I think it's his birthday," Captain Barkley was saying. "I was here once before when someone received a bottle, and that's what I was told."

"Very nice. He seems to like her much more than a little bit."

"So it's rumored."

The waiter politely said, "Mademoiselle?" and I chose a soup, a main course of fish, and a gâteau for dessert, without giving the menu more than a glance, wondering if I would be able to eat any of it, much less finish it.

Our waiter had gone away, and the wine steward was filling our glasses with something that the Captain had chosen when out of the corner of my eye I saw Madame Ezay come into the room.

Even if the Captain had met her at the clinic, I was sure he wouldn't have known her. She was wearing a gown that was prewar but quite elegant, a dark blue with silver half-moons set in the bodice and a long sweeping skirt of the same shade. Her hair was done up and a band around her forehead boasted three ostrich feathers in a gold clip at the side. I wondered where on earth Madame had found them. So must have a dozen other female diners, who followed her entrance with interest.

Her makeup was impeccable. She could have passed for a duchess.

She went to the table chosen for her and sat down with a flourish. I wouldn't have been surprised if she'd produced a feathered fan at that moment. She seemed to look around the room as if hoping to find friends dining there as well.

She spotted Captain Broussard, and after a moment, with the slightest movement, turned toward me. I inclined my head, and she looked away.

"Who is she?" the Captain asked.

"I met her on the train coming to Paris. Her husband's in

something hush-hush. I expect he's busy this evening." It was the first thing I could think of.

"She looks vaguely familiar," he went on, frowning as he tried to remember.

"Possibly at one of your evening soirees?"

"Yes, that's likely."

I tried to think of some way to shift the subject. "What were you really doing, going to these salons? Hardly the place for deserters to congregate, I should think."

"You'd be surprised."

At that moment, Madame Ezay got to her feet and walked calmly across the room toward the table where Captain Broussard was deep in conversation with his companion.

I swallowed wrong and nearly choked, then got myself under control in time to see him rise politely, napkin in hand, when she paused at his table. She extended her hand with the air of a princess of the blood and said something to him.

And as I watched, he turned pale, and then almost at once a deep red. It was a parody of the flush of pleasure I'd seen earlier. I began to rise out of my chair, fearing he was about to strike her. I could see his hand on the napkin clench into a fist so tight his knuckles were white, the nails digging into his palm. Apparently oblivious, she was still smiling, still talking to him.

And then he must have remembered where he was. He said something to her, something that left the young Lieutenant staring, and threw his napkin at the table. It knocked over his wineglass. The wine spilled like dark red blood across the white linen of the table-cloth, and the Lieutenant got to his feet in a hurry, as it looked to be running across to his side of the table.

In the same instant, Captain Broussard shoved Madame aside with such force that she staggered, keeping her balance only by a miracle, one hand clutching at the back of a chair behind her. The man occupying the chair next to it rose as well.

And Captain Broussard was striding angrily toward the door, pushing past the woman greeting a man and a woman just coming into the restaurant. He flung the outer door wide and disappeared.

Waiters were rushing to the table he'd vacated, one with something in his hand to soak up the wine, another coming to the aid of Madame Ezay, who put her hand to her forehead, as if about to faint, just as he reached her.

Everything was happening at once. Captain Barkley was standing now, preparing to cross to the other table, and I was grateful when the waiter, with Madame Ezay leaning heavily against him, led her toward the rear of the restaurant.

Following the Captain, I heard him say to the Lieutenant, "What happened?"

"I don't know, sir," he said, standing too. Out of the corner of my eye, I could see that other waiters and the woman from the front door were busy trying to settle the rest of the diners once more. "A case of mistaken identity—I wasn't very sure—but she called him Victor. Victor Laveau or Lavaud, something like that, and asked after his aunt. She appeared to know him."

But Captain Barkley was no longer listening. He grasped my hand, saying over his shoulder, "This is your doing. I should have guessed," as he led me toward the outer door.

We were in time to find the French officer outside, waiting for his motorcar to be brought around. He wheeled when Captain Barkley spoke to him, then his gaze fell on me.

He reached out with his good arm, grasping at my shoulder, then fumbling for my throat. The pin I had borrowed went into the palm of his hand, and he leapt back, swearing, as if I'd stung him.

"Stop," Captain Barkley said sharply, shoving him away.

"She put that woman up to it. I told her—*I told her* to let it go, to leave Philippe alone. It was none of her affair. If it hadn't been for that damned nun, none of this would have happened," Captain Broussard shouted, reaching for me again. "I would gladly strangle you if I had two good hands."

Captain Barkley hit him then, knocking him to the ground just as someone brought up his motorcar.

People on the street were stopping to stare, but Captain Broussard scrambled to his feet and swung at the American. I heard a whistle, and then a policeman was running toward us.

I stepped back, giving a fleeting thought to Madame Ezay as Captain Barkley slammed his assailant against the restaurant wall.

The policeman was there by that time, threatening to take both men into custody and throw away the key, or words to that effect.

I stepped forward. "This man," I said quickly, pointing to the still-furious Frenchman, "is a wanted man. Inspector Duplessis will want to know that you've found him. He just attacked a woman inside the restaurant and then threatened to kill me. His name is Victor Lavaud. He's wanted for other murders."

At that moment, the woman from the restaurant appeared, bringing my coat and scarf and the Captain's greatcoat. She took in the confrontation literally on her doorstep, and her face was cold with disapproval. Not even Captain Broussard would have found her attractive then.

I realized all at once that I was shivering with the cold, and took my belongings from her gratefully.

I also realized that she was effectively asking us not to return to our table.

I held out his coat to the Captain while the policeman was asking Captain Broussard questions about what I'd said. Broussard was denying it all vehemently, and shoved the policeman, who had put a hand on the officer's empty sleeve. It had been a conciliatory gesture, but Broussard was having none of it. He swung at the policeman, and at that point it was all over.

I was grateful that Madame Ezay was not included as we were marched to the closest police station.

By the time Inspector Duplessis had been found and summoned, I was longing for the dinner that I hadn't had.

He came striding into the small room where Captain Barkley and I had been put, looking as if his own dinner had been interrupted.

"Mademoiselle," he said. "Captain. What is this all about?"

The Captain and I had had more than an hour together, shut in that little room, and I don't think he quite forgave me for what I had done. And yet it was he who had brought Broussard into the picture. I hadn't guessed, in that meeting with the French officer at the café, that he had known at once who Philippe Moreau was. No wonder he was so willing to let Captain Barkley borrow his precious motorcar and do his hunting for him.

I said, "Inspector. You looked into the inquiry into the murders of the Lavaud family. Well, the man you have in custody for striking an officer of the law is their son. I think you'll find he killed all those people. His name was changed—I expect because it must have been a sensational case in its day, his aunt wanted to shield him from what had happened. At any rate, he also stabbed the nun at St. Anne's hospital, and Captain Barkley here. If you examine his possessions, you'll no doubt find he has a knife."

"If I remember correctly, young Philippe Moreau was to be tried for that crime."

"I am in possession of a letter he wrote at the time, telling the family's governess that he'd been persuaded by his mother to confess, because the police were about to charge his younger brother with the crimes. Paul Moreau was only ten, you see. But the two brothers weren't allowed to speak to each other. Paul was kept in the gardener's cottage, while Philippe was in the house. Neither of them had had anything to do with the murders. It was Madame Moreau who turned her elder son in, to be rid of him."

His face was hard as he remembered. "Yes. Quite," he said. "But this doesn't prove that Broussard is the killer. What would have been his motive?"

I had no idea what his motive must have been. I said, "Statements at the time indicated that he was sulking in the kennels. Was he angry enough to kill anyone in his way? He threatened to kill me tonight. He even tried. You'll find a scratch on his hand where he encountered the pin I'm wearing. Captain Barkley was a witness."

He looked to the Captain, who nodded.

"This bears investigating. Now, start at the beginning."

I did, explaining that someone had come up to him in the restaurant and called him by the name of Lavaud. "There's a witness to that—the officer he was dining with. After that, he went rather wild, as the restaurant staff can attest. It could so easily have been passed off as a case of mistaken identity. He could have been polite about it, and it would have ended there. She was an older woman, it quite upset her when he reacted as he did. But why would he behave like that, unless it *was* true?"

He went away then, to speak to Captain Broussard.

"Who was that woman at the restaurant?" Captain Barkley asked me when the Inspector was out of hearing. He still didn't know who she was. "It wasn't the nun."

"No, she's still in hospital. And it really won't make much difference whether the police manage to find that restaurant guest or not. The Lieutenant was a witness to the exchange."

"Do you think he believes you? The Inspector?"

"I don't know. But given that scene at the restaurant, he must investigate. What other conclusion can he draw?" I paused. "If the woman had come to our table and called you by another name, you'd have spoken politely to her, assured her that you were not the person she had thought you were, and she would have been a little embarrassed as she went back to her own table. No harm done."

He couldn't argue with that.

After a time he asked, "Why was Broussard so upset?"

"I don't know," I said again. "But I'm very glad he was." Privately, I thought this confrontation was the last straw for a man who had been under a great deal of strain for some time.

* * *

It was close to dawn when Inspector Duplessis let us go. Sometime in the night I had folded my coat into a square and put my head down on it, falling into a restless sleep. The room was not the most salubrious. It smelled of those strong French cigarettes with their Turkish tobacco, and other things I didn't want to think about, primary among them stale sweat. The captain's head had sunk to his chest, his long legs were stretched out in front of him, and he had fallen asleep in the way men in the trenches had learned to do over four years of war.

The Inspector came into our room looking as haggard as I felt, but he said without greeting, "It appears that for the past eight years, Captain Broussard has been paying a goodly sum to someone named Theissen. Blackmail."

We must have looked as blank as we felt.

"This woman claimed to have a paper signed by the groom at the family's home stating that the Lavaud child was not at the kennels the entire time. She died recently, and it seems that Broussard thought the nun, Sister Marie-Luc, had found the paper and was intending to continue the blackmail. Apparently she had stayed with the woman during her last illness and had searched the house for a certain black lacquer box. He himself had searched for it when he saw the notice of the older woman's death. He had reason to believe that you had found it instead."

There had been no black lacquer box. I had searched—for Marie-Luc. Had there also been no paper signed by the family's groom? Was this the revenge that Juliane Theissen had sought for the suffering she and Philippe had endured? But how had she guessed that the child had killed?

The answer came to me after a moment. Broussard—Charles Lavaud—had paid her to keep silent. The wonder was that he hadn't killed her instead. Somehow she must have convinced him that the groom's letter would be turned over to the police if he tried. And an aging governess living in a backwater village far from Paris was less of a threat than renewed police interest in the Lavaud murders.

Cutting to the chase, I said, "Is it true, then? Has he confessed?"

Captain Barkley said, still refusing to accept all of this, "But his name is Broussard."

"It was his aunt's surname. Lavaud's mother's maiden name, you understand. She had it changed because of the notoriety surrounding the murders. He was still a child at the time. It wasn't difficult. He was christened Victor Henri Broussard Lavaud."

"What will you do about this matter?" I asked.

"Investigate it thoroughly. In the meantime, I have spoken to the Army. Since the crimes in question took place before 1914, we have jurisdiction. He will remain in our custody."

Which surely meant that the police—and this man in particular— were not satisfied with Captain Broussard's explanations.

"You have looked for Jerome Karadeg in connection with the attack on the nun. Is that still outstanding?"

"Sister Marie-Luc claimed from the start that it was not Karadeg who attacked her. I now believe that she was right."

I told him my theory about the attacker having only one arm.

"Very astute, Mademoiselle. I will consider the possibility. Very well. You are free to leave. With my apologies. But the matter required sorting out."

I was sure that it had. Inspector Duplessis was the sort of man who took nothing at face value.

We walked out into a misty dawn. Captain Barkley and I found a taxi soon after. He yawned as he sat back in his seat, and I thought his wound was hurting more than he cared to admit. He had been sitting in a very uncomfortable position for a very long time. And there had been the struggle outside The Golden Door. Matron would certainly not have approved of that.

But what had become of his cane? Was it still at the restaurant? I realized I hadn't seen it since.

He said, when we were halfway to the clinic, "Why did Juliane Theissen let Marie-Luc think that Philippe Moreau was a monster?"

"To protect him? She dared not tell the truth."

"Not because her blackmail would have to stop?"

I shook my head wearily. "God knows. She must have spent a good deal of time and money looking for Broussard."

"I'm not convinced of that. Perhaps she never found the groom. Perhaps she found that all she had to do was tell Broussard that she had the paper. Somewhere along the line she must have come across him. As a governess, she might have met him in any number of ways—even through her own charges when they went off to school. Through the families that employed her. Someone might have written to her saying that they had met a child whose entire family had been killed. Gossip to most people, but gold to her."

"But why did he kill them? I would like to know. To have such an awful thing make sense."

The taxi pulled up in front of the Hôtel de Belle-Île, and we climbed stiffly out.

As we walked up to the door, Captain Barkley said, "There's still the question of Philippe Moreau, and what's become of him."

I said, "Yes."

The problem was, where to find him?

CHAPTER EIGHTEEN

As soon as I'd seen Captain Barkley to his bed, I went in search of Madame Ezay.

I couldn't find her anywhere, and giving up, I went to my room. For all I knew, she had stayed at her sister's house.

Opening my door, I thought longingly of my own bed, just as the creak of the rocking chair wiped all thought of sleep from my mind.

"Who's there?" I demanded of the dark room.

"It is I, Mademoiselle. What has kept you so long? I was so afraid that there would be repercussions from the events at The Golden Door," Madame Ezay answered almost on the heels of my words.

I was so relieved, I could hardly light the lamp. "I've looked everywhere for you," I said, turning to see her in her accustomed black. "That man, the one you spoke to, is in police custody. We've been at the police station as the Inspector checked all the information I gave him. All is well."

"Thank God," she answered fervently. "I shall go to my own bed now."

"I must tell you, you were brilliant," I said, kneeling to put a little more coal on the sinking fire. "I had no idea you could carry it all off so beautifully. An actress could have done no better. And how did you leave the restaurant? I didn't see you after you were taken away, nearly fainting."

"Through the kitchen door. I told them I was so embarrassed, I couldn't face that room full of people again. That door led to an alley, and I came out on the next street."

"Wonderful," I said, embracing her.

"As for the actress," she said, a touch of pride in her face, "I was one, you know. Many years ago, before Monsieur Ezay forbade me to appear again on the stage."

"Were you, indeed?" I asked, staring at her. I had missed that. I had seen only the charwoman who helped wherever she could in this English convalescent clinic.

"There are surprises everywhere you look," she said. "My sister was also on the stage. Only she had kept several of the gowns and some of the makeup." She smiled. "I have not lost all my training."

And she was gone.

Afraid that I would sleep for hours, I took her place in the rocking chair and watched the coals send up little licks of flame that soon grew to warmth. I must have drifted off for half an hour before I woke with a start.

The sun had just broken the horizon, sending long shards of light between the buildings and down the avenues, when I left for the café where I had last seen Philippe Moreau.

For three wretched hours in the cold I sat there at the table he'd used, ignoring Australian soldiers eager to make my acquaintance, the disapproving stares of a number of women, and what seemed to be at least half the French Army.

Finally I got up and walked on. I'd hoped it might work, that he would watch that café to see if I came again—especially since the police hadn't followed him that day.

But he was too wary a fish to be caught so easily.

I was perhaps a quarter of a mile from the café when someone came up behind me and took my arm. I wheeled, expecting to find another Aussie on leave, and looked straight into the face of the man I wanted to see. He was still wearing his American uniform.

"Keep walking. Why did you sit there waiting? Was it for me?"

"Yes," I said. "There has been a recent development that will interest you." And I told him about Captain Broussard.

"By God," he said, "are you quite sure?"

"Fairly sure. Yes, quite sure."

"I never thought—but it makes sense, you know. Now that I'm no longer a child. I couldn't imagine—at the time, events seemed so catastrophic that nothing else mattered. But he was angry that day. Did you know that I'd been invited to stay a few days with the family? And Paul had come as well. Only two years between us, and he was a good sport. I think the family was pleased to have him."

"What makes sense?" I demanded, looking up into his face. We were walking at a snail's pace because his feet were still so tender.

"Victor was told that morning that he wouldn't be returning to the school we'd been attending. His father had had a row with the headmaster, and he'd been withdrawn."

I stopped in the middle of the sidewalk, staring now, searching his face for signs that he was lying to me. Several people nearly collided with us, walking around us and glaring at us. "You don't kill five people because you aren't going back to a school you like. And as it was, he was sent to his aunt in Nice. He'd gained nothing."

"He was twelve, he hadn't thought it through. Paul and I were at the school. A number of his other friends as well. That's why he was sulking. Why Paul took out one of the horses. Why I retreated to my room."

"Did Paul know this?"

"I don't think so. But I'd overheard the argument. It was hard not to overhear. It took place in the room next to mine. He and his parents and his grandmother were going at it hammer and tongs."

"But his clothes must have been bloody. They would have to be."

"He wore some of mine to kill them," he said grimly. "He must have done. I found them in my room after the police sent me there while they contacted my mother."

"Then they must have found them there. It would have sealed your guilt."

"I thought Paul must have killed them. God help me, Mama told me that he had. And so I buried the clothes under the mattress in one of the unused rooms."

Where they must have been found. If this was true, the newspapers, everyone, had got it wrong when they said he'd been wearing clothing with blood on it.

I was torn between sympathy for this man and the knowledge that he had betrayed his own country. Could anyone blame him? After what he'd been accused of doing?

I said, bluntly, "I hope you are telling me the truth. Inspector Duplessis is questioning Captain Broussard right now. If you are lying, I will know it."

"I'm not."

"Do you know why your mother wanted you to be charged?"

He shook his head at that. "I'd always known she favored Paul. She would have done anything to protect him. I wasn't surprised when she asked me to save him. I thought it a brave thing to do. I thought my father would have been proud of me. I thought it might make her love me. More fool I."

"Then why did you spy on your own country?" It had to be answered. Philippe Moreau—Lieutenant Theissen—wasn't out of the woods yet.

He was the one who stopped short then. Taking my arm in a tight grip, he pulled me into a service alley between a restaurant and a hotel. I was suddenly frightened, trying to think what I could use as a weapon.

"What the hell are you trying to do?" he said savagely, pinning me against the wall.

"The evidence is there," I said. "And Captain Barkley has the proof, Major Anderson as well. So you might as well let me go."

"I don't want to hurt you, damn it."

"You're going about it in the wrong way, then. *Let me go.*"

To my surprise he did, stepping back, his face in his hands, as if he was uncertain what to do. He dropped them after a moment. "I got out while I could. I put on a dead man's uniform, such as it was, and made for my own lines. Germany is collapsing, you have no idea what it's like there. I didn't want to get caught in a German uniform."

And then, before I could stop him, he was gone.

I ran after him, but he'd vanished. With his feet still healing he couldn't have got far, and so I went into the restaurant and then into the lobby of the hotel, searching for him.

The only thing I could think of was that he'd gone up the hotel stairs. Or into a lavatory, where I couldn't follow him.

One of the hotel staff came up to me and asked if he could be of assistance.

"There was an American officer who came just now," I said. "He has a terrible limp. I think he's a friend of my fiancé. I wanted to let him know I was in Paris too."

"I saw no one like that, Mademoiselle. I'm sorry."

"But I'm sure he came here. I was behind him on the street, I thought I saw him step through the door."

He had been friendly. Now he was suspicious. "If Mademoiselle will give me a name, I will have this man paged."

I couldn't give him a name.

I shook my head. "My fiancé will be so disappointed. I must have been mistaken." And with a smile, I turned and walked out of the hotel.

I was scheduled to join the convoy as soon as the ambulances came from Rouen with their wounded. That didn't leave much time.

I could turn Philippe Moreau over to the police. But they had got it wrong twice, with the boy Philippe and later, with Jerome.

As for the Army—there was still the court martial charge, not to mention spying, which would mean death by firing squad. The Army was never wrong . . .

Suddenly I remembered Jerome Karadeg and Marie-Luc. I must not leave Paris without letting her know that Jerome was alive. Wherever he might have gone after leaving St. Anne's. It would lift the weight off her heart.

I found a taxi, and was soon walking into her room. They were preparing to move her back to the ward, and I saw her stand shakily as the nuns helped her out of bed.

"This is good news," I said, more cheerfully than I felt. "You'll be discharged soon. I've come to tell you that this evening I'll be returning to my own duties. I'm glad I'll be leaving you feeling much better."

She nodded as they brought the wheeled chair up behind her and were there to lower her gently into it. "I feel like myself for the first time. I've asked to be taken to the chapel before I'm carried on to the ward. I've much to thank God for."

"There is more," I said quietly, as the nuns went ahead and I pushed her chair. "I spoke with Monsieur Karadeg this morning. When you saw Jerome, it wasn't a gift from God. He'd slipped into the hospital to speak to you, only you were so heavily sedated you didn't realize it. His parents claimed a body taken from the river. It wasn't their son. They wanted the police to believe he was dead, and then they took him to Brittany with the body of that stranger to be buried in their son's place."

She was still fragile. "Are you very sure?" she asked, closing her eyes, as if afraid to read my answer in my face. "Don't lie to me, in the name of God."

"I haven't lied to you." I thought she was going to weep then, but she dashed away the tears, and calling to Sister Claire, she asked again to be taken to the chapel. "I will say a prayer for him. And for the man pulled from the river."

I said, as we moved down the passage, "There's something more. The police have found the killer of the Lavaud family. It was their own son."

Frowning, she said, "Are you sure of that?"

"It seems very likely to Inspector Duplessis. You remember him."

"No, I can't believe it. They must be wrong."

I walked as far as the chapel with her, but I couldn't convince her of Philippe Moreau's innocence.

Making my way back through the busy corridors, I thought to myself that it would take more than a confession from Captain Broussard to persuade her. For she had seen Philippe Moreau in Belgium, with German officers. She was prepared to believe anything against him.

At the clinic, I packed my belongings, readying them for the evening, then went downstairs for my lunch. I'd missed breakfast completely. On my way, I stopped to return the pin and the scarf that I had worn last night.

I found Major Anderson in the dining room, just sitting down to his own meal.

"Have you heard?" he asked almost at once. "Captain Broussard has been arrested. It's unbelievable news. There was a to-do at a restaurant last night, and the police took him into custody."

"What is the charge?" I asked, unfolding my napkin and putting it across my lap.

"That's just it. No one seems to know."

"How did you hear about this?"

"One of his friends sent a message. Broussard's motorcar was still standing outside the door of the restaurant this morning. He went inside and found one of the waiters, who told him that there had been an altercation, and the police had come."

"It sounds quite serious," I said, wishing for butter for the tough slice of toast just set down by my plate.

My mind was still on what to do about Philippe Moreau, and I was listening now with half my attention until the Major said, "I must go to the bank in a bit. I'm running out of francs. Can I change money for you?"

"What? Thank you, but no, Major, I'll be leaving this evening, according to Matron."

"Lucky you," he said, smiling ruefully. "I shall miss you, you know. And you've never finished that book."

"I hope someone else will."

He left, and I was alone with my thoughts, shutting out the voices around me, the clink of cutlery and china, the footsteps of the staff.

The bank.

What had become of the sums that Fräulein Theissen had collected from Captain Broussard?

From the look of the cottage, she had been comfortable enough in her retirement, but it had been a simple life. Commensurate with the income she must have made over the years as the governess to families with young children. What had she done with the money she had been paid for her silence?

There was nothing in the envelope I'd taken. No bank book, no will with directions to deal with her estate. Had she not wanted to keep it? Had she only wanted to punish Captain Broussard?

I couldn't believe that. She had had a reason to stoop to blackmail, surely. If she couldn't prove her case against the real killer, she could at least make him aware, every day of his life, that someone else had such power over him that she could ruin him in an instant.

And where ought the money to go?

To the child she had brought with her from Alsace and given up to a better life.

But where was this money? Had she sent it on to Philippe Moreau? Kept it safely for him if he should ever be cleared? Given it to him on his last visit?

Who would know—who would Juliane Theissen believe she could trust?

Marie-Luc?

But she had taught the nun that Philippe was all that was said about him, in order to protect him. To let the world think that she believed it too.

A bank? But how would Philippe know where to find it, much less to claim it?

The priest, Father Robert. Who probably knew more about Philippe than anyone else alive, now that Fräulein Theissen was dead, and Madame Moreau. Who would be honor bound to keep the secrets of the confessional at any price.

A priest who had been so anxious every time we spoke to him. Was he fearful that we might be hunting for that money?

Of course, it had to be him!

Leaving my meal unfinished, I got up, forced myself to walk sedately from the dining room, and then took the stairs at speed. Catching up my coat and my gloves and a woolen hat I'd been given by a villager at home who had knitted it "for the dear Sister Crawford," I left the clinic and almost stepped in front of a taxi I wanted to stop.

Giving the address of The Golden Door, I sat back, silently urging him to hurry. Would it be there? Had someone already dealt with it for the Captain?

But no, when we turned the nearest corner, I could see the motorcar still parked in front of the restaurant like a deserted ship. I shoved my cap in my coat pocket and pulled the woolen one over my hair. There were enough pseudo-uniforms in the city that no one would take notice of my coat.

I stopped the taxi driver, paid him, and thanked him, then watched him out of sight before I went down the street to the motorcar.

The restaurant was closed until five in the afternoon. So proclaimed a discreet sign in a window.

I turned the crank and got into the motorcar without looking to see who might be watching. As if I had every right to be there. And then I was off toward the Champs with apparent calm, turning into a side street as soon as I could.

There was sufficient petrol. I found a place where I could leave the motorcar safely, then went looking for Philippe Moreau. I sat in the cold wind for an hour in my accustomed place at the café, telling myself that he wouldn't come. He would avoid me now after our confrontation in the alley.

But there he was, suddenly, across the street. He hadn't been there—then a lorry had crawled by—and he was standing in the doorway of a shop. Watching me.

I left my table and the cup of coffee that had enabled me to sit there for so long, and set out across the street. A taxi narrowly missed me, blowing its horn, the driver shouting at me out his window, but I kept my eyes on the man in uniform, for fear he was going to bolt.

"You must come with me," I said urgently. "I have a motorcar. This way."

"Come where?"

"I'll explain on the way."

It took ten minutes of persuasion, but in the end he followed me to the motorcar, walking four paces behind, still wary of a trick. Then, as I turned the crank, he said, "Where are we going?"

"There's something you ought to know. I'm taking you to Petite-Beauvais."

"No. I don't want to go back there."

"If you don't, you'll regret it for the rest of your life," I said, impatient now to be on our way before some passing French officer recognized this motorcar and stopped to ask questions.

I thought he was going to refuse. But in the end, he said, "Move over. I'll drive."

"I can drive, you know," I said, affronted.

"It will attract less attention if I do," he retorted, and I knew he was right.

We traveled out of Paris in silence, wary of policemen and officers and the possibility of being seen and reported. But on the open road, I told him what Fräulein Theissen had done.

"If I'm to be shot as a spy, why are you telling me this?" he demanded.

"Because she wanted you to have it. It might pay for your lawyers."

"I don't need any lawyers."

"Then it will pay for a nice tombstone."

We said nothing for a number of miles.

"Why do you trust me?" he asked then. "This road is all but deserted. I could kill you now, toss your body in that ditch just ahead of us, and who would know?"

I had also brought with me the little pistol that Simon had once given me.

"I was there when you were found. I was there when you spoke in German at the base hospital. I know you were court-martialed. I know too that you were seen in a German uniform on a street in Belgium. But the money ought to be yours. I'm leaving tonight. I won't be back in Paris. The French Army will find you eventually. What happens to you then will probably depend on how magnanimous they feel."

"Then turn me in. There must be a reward."

Stung, I said, "I don't want a reward. We probably saved your life at the aid station that night. The base hospital nursed you back to health. I have done my duty. I found you in Paris, against all the odds. I have helped to show that you weren't a monster, as Marie-Luc thought. I expect you have nowhere else to turn, or you wouldn't have met me again."

"It's true," he said, and pulled to the side of the road.

Alarmed, I felt in my pocket for my pistol. I was a good shot. I wouldn't miss at this range. For an instant I wondered if perhaps he would prefer to be dead.

"All right. Do you want the truth? I'll give it you. I escaped to Alsace, with some help from Juliane. When the war started, I didn't want to be drafted into the German Army. I came back to France, and using my name from before I was adopted by the Moreau family, I enlisted as Karl Theissen. Somehow the French Army discovered I was an escaped murderer. They told me I could go back to Paris and stand trial. Or I could spy for them in Germany. We faked the court martial, to give me a reason for fleeing to the Germans. I took some secrets with me to buy my way into their confidence and helped two German officers escape. It was touch and go—which side would shoot me first. But in the end the Germans were desperate for good officers, I was Alsatian, and I spoke fluent German. More than half their sergeants had been killed, and there were no replacements. Still, they nearly broke through to Paris this past winter. That was touch and go as well. I did what I was ordered to do, and I found ways to send information back. Truces to find the wounded and recover the dead. Signals. You wouldn't believe how inventive I was, because I knew they'd betray me to the Germans if I failed." He took a deep breath. "The war is finished, all but finding a way to end it. I was afraid I'd be abandoned. I didn't want to be sent to Berlin with the rest of the Germans. But I knew if I told the French where I was, there was a good chance they'd hand me over to the police to stand trial for the Lavaud murders. I've got no home, you see. I don't belong in Alsace, if it stays German. I won't belong there if it comes out that I spied for France. I don't belong in France. I don't—I can't—trust anyone. Even you. And yet I couldn't stand the loneliness any longer."

I listened in growing horror. Was he lying to me? Or was he telling the truth?

"How did you live? With no money, no friends, no help?"

He smiled, but it didn't touch his eyes. "I begged on street corners in old clothes I found in a dustbin. It was the only way. It barely kept me alive, but I was grateful to those who dropped a few sous or a few francs into my cap."

Dear God.

If only I could find Simon, or the Colonel. If only I could decide if this was the truth or if he was a master at manipulating it.

"Drive on," I said finally. "I must be back in London by this evening, or Matron will send out a search party."

He looked at me for a moment longer, and then let in the clutch and drove on.

We found Father Robert at his devotionals, and I waited quietly in the back of the little church for him to finish. At last he came up the aisle to where I was standing, and he said, "I wish I knew why you persecute me this way."

"I don't," I said. "I've come to ask a favor of you. Did you keep secrets for Fräulein Theissen?"

"I can't answer that."

"Then here is someone who may be able to ask—and receive an answer." I opened the church door, and Philippe Moreau stepped inside.

The two men stared at each other.

"You've aged, Father," Philippe said.

"I am not sure I know you."

"You should. When I was a child you protected me once from my mother's wrath."

"When you had taken Paul riding, and he was thrown. I have never seen any woman so angry," Father Robert said slowly, searching the face of the tall man in front of him.

"I didn't know then. I didn't understand. But she must have thought I'd deliberately tried to kill him."

"Yes. I knew better. So did your father. You loved your brother."

"I thought he *was* my brother. Until much, much later."

"Why are you wearing an American uniform? I don't understand."

"A long story. I won't be wearing it much longer."

"You have your mother's eyes," the priest said after a moment. "I should have seen that straightaway. Forgive me, my son. Come with me to the rectory."

"I can't. I don't want to be seen. I was not here for Juliane's burial. While I waited in the church porch, I went out to look for her grave. There's no stone."

"It has been ordered. It will come." He asked us to excuse him for a moment and left us standing in the cold church.

Philippe looked around him, remembering. *Too much?* I wondered.

He said, "I used to imagine, sitting here, what was in store for me. Even though I was the eldest, I knew the house and land belonged to Paul. That was made clear to me early on. That he must have them, but I would be taken care of. My father would take me for long walks and talk to me about that. That I would always be safe. I believed him."

I said nothing, looking up at the beams in the shadows of the vaulting above our heads.

After a time, the priest came back, and in his hands he held a black lacquer box. "I was to give this to no one but you, my son. It has been a grave responsibility. There was a time when I wondered if it was beyond my power to carry out."

Philippe took the box, started to open it, and instead walked a little way toward the altar. With his back to us, he sorted through the contents, reading some bits, setting others aside. I heard him clear his throat once or twice, as if moved.

When he finally came back to us, he said, "I can't keep this money."

"You can," I replied, before Father Robert could speak. "It is a small recompense for your suffering." Possibly not what my mother would have told him, but he was penniless now, and he would need it.

He refused to argue, but he thanked Father Robert for his stewardship, and gave him some money for care of the grave of Juliane Theissen. And then we left.

"You're a fool," I said, "if you don't keep it."

But he was standing there on the church porch, looking toward the house where he'd grown up. Then he turned toward Fräulein

Theissen's cottage and said, "I came once or twice to that cottage. In the dead of night, like a thief. She met me in Paris once. That was all the time we had."

He stood there a moment longer, his expression sad, then roused himself and said, "We must go."

He drove out of Petite-Beauvais without looking back. We didn't speak for a while. Then he said, "What am I to do?"

"How's your Flemish?"

He turned to stare at me, nearly missing a bend in the road and rocking the motorcar as he recovered in time. "I speak German. It's not so very different."

"How would you like to become a Belgian soldier in the British Army?"

He shook his head. "You mustn't laugh at me."

"I'm not. If you want to leave France, I can arrange it. I think."

"No. This is my country. Whatever happens, I must stay. And fight, if I can."

It was the ultimate test. And he'd passed it.

"You need to speak to Captain Barkley," I said, and wouldn't tell him why.

Chapter Nineteen

Captain Barkley, sitting in a chair in the library, was furiously angry.

"I won't do it," he said. "Bess—you don't understand. This was the man I was sent to Paris to find. Matron at the base hospital contacted Army HQ and they decided to send me to Paris because no one would think an American was looking for him."

"She didn't tell me what she'd done," I said, equally angry. "She told me not to be concerned. Otherwise, I'd have left it to the Army. I'd have left *him* to the Army."

"You're not an officer in the Army."

"But I am. I have comparable rank."

"It's not the same."

"Isn't it? Matron would never have known about this man if I hadn't told her. I should have been told. After all, I found him, didn't I? And you used me as well; you pretended to be helping me to keep my father happy, and all the while you were letting me discover what you couldn't find out on your own. It's unconscionable."

"I didn't have much choice, Bess, and you have to believe that. But I won't be a party to this."

"Then I'll ask Major Vernon. He's an Intelligence officer."

"Great God, Bess, will you leave it alone? Why do you believe this man is innocent?"

"This man, as you call me, is sitting right here," Philippe Moreau put in. "I have a say in this matter."

"No, you don't," I told him roundly.

"Listen, Bess. Go back on that convoy tonight. You'll be disciplined if you don't. It isn't worth it. *He* isn't worth it. Don't you see how he's using you?"

That brought Philippe to his feet. "I have used no one. I'm leaving."

"No, you aren't. You're my responsibility now," Captain Barkley said in almost a shout.

"I found him," I put in. "And if you won't listen to me—"

At that moment, the library door opened, and the orderly from the front desk stuck his head in.

"Inspector Duplessis to see Sister Crawford." And before he could withdraw, the door was pushed open wider and the policeman stepped into the room.

If we didn't look like cats who had just eaten an entire cage of canaries, I would have been surprised to hear it.

He looked from one to the other of us. "I have interrupted something?"

Philippe rose and said quickly, "I was just leaving."

Only, the Inspector was blocking the door.

He said, "I've come to say, we have a full confession from Broussard. He will be processed now. I wish to thank you for your assistance, Sister."

I thought perhaps he'd rather eat glass.

"My pleasure," I said, "but I need to know. Will this clear the man who has been considered guilty for all these years? Philippe Moreau?"

"Yes, I have seen to it only this afternoon. He is exonerated."

"Thank you, Inspector."

From the lobby I could hear the call for nurses and staff. The ambulances from Rouen had arrived.

Inspector Duplessis heard it as well. "Do I understand from Matron that you will be returning to your own lines tonight?"

"Yes. I believe so."

He bowed punctiliously and said, "It has been my pleasure, Sister."

And then he was gone.

I said to Philippe, "You heard what he said. You've been exonerated. Publicly."

"But not from the charge of spying," Captain Barkley replied. "That still stands."

"If there are records of the court martial, there will be records of why he was allowed to escape. If you take him to Army headquarters and vouch for him, then it will go a long way to seeing that he's treated fairly. That's all I ask of you, Captain. To see that he's treated fairly. It isn't too much to expect. After all, you've done your duty as you were ordered to do it. You've found the man that Matron was worried about. You've heard for yourself the fact that he's no longer accused of the Lavaud murders. It remains only for the French Army to recognize what they had asked of him, and to let him finish his own war in peace."

I don't know that he would have relented if it hadn't been for the Inspector's arrival. Or perhaps he just needed to put his anger aside and see the truth for himself.

Captain Barkley threw up his hands and said, "Very well. All right. I'll do it. With objections noted."

"Duly noted," I responded.

"You aren't leaving me to the mercy of this man?" Philippe asked in dismay.

"I must. He is a witness to what the Inspector has said just now."

"I must trust to you once more," he responded wryly, and took my hand in his. "*Merci*," he said quietly.

The door opened again. It was the orderly.

"Matron is waiting to say good-bye."

"Thank you. My kit is in my room. Could you bring it down, please?"

When he had gone, I turned back to Philippe Moreau. "Good luck, Lieutenant. It should be yours at last."

And then I crossed the room to Captain Barkley, rose on tiptoe, and kissed him on the cheek. "We always manage to quarrel, somehow. I am so glad to see you again. Stay safe. They'll be waiting for you in Michigan."

He smiled against his will. "I swear to you, Bess Crawford, that you could—and no doubt have—tried the patience of saints and made me question my own duty. At least I'm getting you out of Paris in one piece, which your mother will be grateful for." In his turn, he bent and kissed me. "I earned that."

"Yes, you did."

The orderly was back, my kit bag in his hand.

There were any number of the staff waiting to say good-bye. I got a kiss on the cheek from Major Anderson and Major Vernon, defying Matron's frown, and an embrace from Madame Ezay. And then I walked out the door to the waiting ambulance without looking back.

I had left Lieutenant Moreau to Captain Barkley's conscience, but he was an American, after all, and wouldn't let me down. I hoped Philippe Moreau wouldn't either.

There was an envelope waiting for me when I reached the forward aid station where I was next assigned. It had been sent in the diplomatic pouch to HQ and brought out to me by one of the motorcycle messengers.

I tore it open, thinking it might be from my father.

There were only two words on the sheet.

Promise kept.

And under them was a single signature.

Barkley.